ALL THAT IT TAKES

K.L. Ditmars

Where Can I Go? **Book 1**

All That it Takes

Copyright©2021 by K.L. Ditmars

Requests for information should be addressed to:

**SHOALING
WATERS**
P R E S S

PO Box 45029
Victoria, BC V9A 0C3
Canada

ISBN: (paperback): 978-1-777-4101-0-0

kelly@klditmarswriter.com

This novel is a work of fiction. Names, characters, places and incidents are either products of the author's imagination or used fictitiously. Many of the locations in this book are either real or fictitious representations of actual places. No reference to illegal activities in this work of fiction are in any way attributed or intended. Any similarity to people living or dead is purely coincidental.

* * *

A note on spelling . . . as a Canadian author living in Canada, who has set her story in a Canadian city, I have made a conscious choice to use Canadian spelling. All efforts to notify me when you find an error are greatly appreciated but please double-check Canadian spellings before you hit send on any message.

Dedication

For the Best Mummie in the whole wide world.
I miss you every day.

Where can I go from your Spirit?
Where can I flee from your presence?
If I go up to the heavens, you are there;
If I make my bed in the depths, you are there.
If I rise on the wings of the dawn,
If I settle in the far side of the sea,
Even there Your hand will guide me,
Your right hand will hold me fast.
If I say, "Surely the darkness will hide me,
And the light become night around me,"
Even the darkness will not be dark to you;
The night will shine like the day,
For darkness is as light to you.

King David
Psalm 139: 7-12

". . . all the devil wants of the son of God — to be let alone.
That is all that the criminal wants of the law — to be let alone.
The sin of doing nothing is the deadliest of all the seven sins.
It has been said that for evil men to accomplish their purpose
it is only necessary that good men should do nothing."

Charles F. Aked (1864-1941)
Baptist Minister and Advocate for Social Justice

CHAPTER 1

JULIA BOWEN COULD SEE HER WIDOWHOOD reflected in the scarlet pool where her husband lay. Julia dropped to the floor, afraid the man standing over Hal's body would see her.

That man held a gun.

She put her hand over her mouth, desperate to prevent the scream building inside her from escaping. Muffled voices from the library drew the gunman away. Crawling backwards, she stood only when she was sure she wouldn't attract attention. In the master bedroom her heart was pounding in her chest and she closed the door, careful not to let it click.

Frozen in fear, Julia stood at the foot of the bed. *Not again, not again,* she thought, as images from her past flooded into the present. Events she considered long forgotten kickstarted old survival patterns. *Don't focus on the pain right now, choose an action. Get beyond this moment. Think.*

Then she knew what she had to do. She had to hide, but the gunman and his companions stood between her and the only place in the house she could effectively conceal herself. No. She had to get out.

"Now move." She spoke aloud, getting out of her head and into her body. It wouldn't be long before they came looking for her. She pushed her feet into the runners lying nearby. As she tied the laces, she surveyed the room and her options before spotting the replenished emergency backpacks.

From Hal's backpack, she transferred the pouch containing his extra wallet into the top of hers. Then, with her pack on her back, she zipped up her hoodie and stepped through the French doors onto a small balcony. She closed them behind her so as not to alert the men to her exit route when they searched the bedroom. Moving to the end of the balcony where she could look around the corner of the house, she glanced down. No one lurked in the narrow, grassy passage leading from their driveway to the back yard. Safe for the moment, she dropped the emergency rope ladder over the railing. With the end of the ladder swaying, she stepped over the railing and started the climb down.

Julia was two rungs from the bottom when, just below her, the light in the vacant guest suite came on.

She jumped the last couple of feet.

Grabbing the bottom rung, Julia pulled the ladder out of sight as she stepped into the shadow beside the house. The wooden rungs dug into her ribcage as she pressed them between her and the exterior wall. She held her breath, listening for the sound of the sliding doors that opened from the guest suite to the back yard.

No sound came, and the light went out again. She released her breath, making sure the ladder hung without swaying, then let it go. Running along the fence, out of range of the motion-sensor light, she made it to the far end of the yard.

A gate with a chain and padlock stood between her and the safety of the forest beyond.

Crouching behind the rhododendron next to the gate, she dug out the extra ring of house keys from her pack's hip strap. Her hands shook, and she dropped them in a pile of accumulated plant droppings. Glancing back at the house, she made sure the men weren't looking out a window. A small LED flashlight hung from the pack's shoulder strap, and she clicked it on to search for the keys. She found them. Looking again to the house, making sure she was still unseen, she unclipped the flashlight. Holding it in her mouth, Julia stood up and unlocked the padlock. She pulled it free from the chain, opened the gate and stepped through. To buy herself some time, she drew the chain back around and secured the padlock on the outside of the fence. She turned towards the forest, flashlight now in hand, a beam of light illuminating the trail ahead of her.

The yard light came on a split second before a piece of the gate exploded above her.

Julia took off at a run.

A sense of panic increased her already frantic pace when she heard the men cursing at the chained gate. Her flashlight trained on the path, she fought to gain ground on the steep climb up Mount Newton. At the base of a red serpentine arbutus, she stepped into the bushes.

She followed a familiar game trail that led into a narrow valley, her last downhill section. Grateful for the reprieve from the intense exertion of climbing, she focused on not falling. Branches of wild shrubbery slapped her face as she stumbled over roots. Propelled by momentum and adrenalin, she regained her balance and soon found herself scrambling up the other side of the valley. She reached out and felt cool moss covering a great fallen tree overhanging the ridge. Pulling herself up, she hugged the log's solid comfort and turned off her flashlight. This ridge marked the border of her property and the provincial parkland.

She lay against the log, trying to calm her body and listen. Over her pounding heart, she could hear the men as they ran along the trail. Sound travelled through the dark forest. Their inability to move silently enabled her to pinpoint their location. They had gone past where she left the main trail.

She pushed up from the log and prayed Charlie was in his camp. She was afraid of leading these men to him, but didn't feel she had a choice if she was going to survive the night.

❖

The three men moved in unison, their guns, equipped with silencers, raised and ready to fire. At a fork in the trail, without breaking stride, their point man signalled one of the men to take the upper trail while he and the third one turned downhill. Ten minutes later, the two broke from the forest onto the paved surface of an access road into the provincial park. Stopping, the point man pressed the communication device on his collar. "Kent, any sign?"

A voice crackled in his earpiece, "Nothing."

"We must have missed something. Meet back where we separated." Mac released the button. They turned back.

At the fork, Kent was waiting, infrared goggles raised.

"What next?" Leo asked.

Mac checked his wristwatch. "We go back to the house and finish up."

"Someone's not going to be happy we let her get away," Kent commented.

"No," Mac responded, his voice hard.

Back along the trail, Mac spotted a broken branch and stopped. He bent, moving more branches aside and noticed the narrow game trail leading off the main path. A low-hanging branch from a large Garry oak had obscured it coming from the other direction. He ducked onto the trail; the other two followed. It was narrow, but not difficult to navigate.

Mac motioned for them to stop.

"Is that singing?" whispered Kent.

"I hear it too," Leo confirmed.

Mac made the signal to fan out, and then crouched. Kent and Leo stepped off the trail, merging with the shadows.

The approaching man held a strong flashlight which caused Mac to flip up his goggles. The words to the song he was singing were now clear.

"Amazing Grace, how sweet the sound

That saved a wretch like me.

I once was lost, but now I'm found;

Was blind but now I see."

The man continued to hum as his flashlight's beam came closer. Mac stood as the circle of light reached his position.

The man stopped.

The pool of light traveled up Mac's body until it highlighted his face, then dropped to his chest. Despite the light, Mac could see the man standing in the middle of the path. His rigid stance reminded Mac of his old army sergeant.

"Lost?" the man asked, his gravel voice matching his craggy face.

"Have you seen anyone in these woods tonight?" Mac demanded.

Shining the flashlight back into Mac's face, the man stood his ground. "So, not lost then?"

"Have you seen anyone? I won't ask again."

Leo rose, and a red dot appeared on the man's chest from the laser sight of his gun. Kent also stood up, making his presence known. All three of the gunmen now had a clear view of the man. Somewhere over 70, greying, unshaven sunken cheeks below hard, piercing brown eyes in a weather-wrinkled face. His bearing belied the gaunt physique draped in dark pants, a down vest over a flannel shirt and a blue toque.

"No."

"What are you doing in the forest at night?"

"Walking. You?"

Mac hesitated then lowered his gun. "A little night training. Sorry if we scared you."

"You didn't."

Mac tensed, ready to rise to the bait, but then relaxed. "You've served."

"Army. Forty years in. Out 15."

Mac nodded. "We're done here." He turned and headed back the way he had come. Leo and Kent fell into step behind him.

When they reached the main trail, Mac stopped. He waited about a minute, then dropped his night vision goggles back into place. Back in business, he turned around to follow their new target, Leo and Kent on his trail.

They kept the man in view as he moved deeper into the forest. He dropped out of sight for a while, but they found him in a clearing encompassing a small campsite. Mac signaled the other two to move into a flanking position around the camp. He crouched to observe the man as he started a fire. Mac lifted his goggles once the fire caught. The man sat on a low stump, humming again.

When he added another log, increased light illuminated more of the clearing. Mac surveyed the campsite. There were two woodpiles. A small one was neatly within arm's reach of the fire. The other stood closer to the forest. It was larger and seemed to be a pile of debris wood collected when the man had cleared the area.

The firelight focused on the man's face. He stopped humming and looked up into Mac's vicinity. "Need directions?"

Mac hesitated for a moment, then rose from his position in the undergrowth. "You're good for someone who's been out 15 years," he said as he came into the light.

"Have your brothers step out too."

Kent and Leo did.

"You've had too many desert deployments. Sand is quieter underfoot than drying leaves."

"We wanted to see where you went and make sure you were alone."

"Hmmph." The camper looked around watching the three men's movements.

"Where was your last deployment?" Mac asked.

"Africa."

Mac observed the man as he looked over his left shoulder at Leo kicking the large pile of loose branches and brush. He turned his head right to see Kent bend to inspect a makeshift lean-to under an earthen overhang. He could tell the man didn't like being at the centre of their triangulated position.

Impressed by the man's calm, Mac crouched, bringing the man's attention back on him. "You're sure you haven't seen anyone else in these woods? Or heard something?"

"It was a peaceful night. Until three gun-toting trespassers came crashing through the undergrowth. Must be someone mighty important you're hunting."

"Someone from our unit playing rabbit." Kent and Leo nodded to Mac and held their positions, waiting for his direction. "We won't disturb you any further. Sorry to intrude. I guess we've been outwitted."

"Better luck next time."

The three shadows melted back into the forest. Before moving out of range of the clearing, Mac turned. He could once again hear the man humming while watching his fire send sparks into the night sky.

Charlie gave the men a one-minute lead, then followed them. When he caught up, they were on the trail behind Julia's house. Charlie stepped off at a high vantage point behind the house and stopped. From the inner pocket of his coat, he pulled a small pair of field binoculars he used for birdwatching. Crouching down at a spot that gave him an unobstructed view, he rested his back against a tree. He settled in to watch the scene playing out inside the house, grateful for the lack of window coverings.

Charlie could see the men clearly in the interior as they moved from room to room. One man placed a gun down near a body on the floor just beyond the dining table.

The second man, his back facing the bay window, sat at a desk focusing on a computer screen. Beyond the desk, Charlie could see walls lined with books. It took a few minutes before Charlie spotted the third gunman. He appeared on the second-floor balcony and went to the side where, hand over hand, he lifted up a rope ladder. Charlie realized this must be how Julia had escaped. He looked back at the man on the computer and wondered what they were looking for and why they were making the scene seem like Julia had murdered her husband.

An hour later, Charlie heard an engine start, then saw headlights as it drove away from the house. The lights went off and two gunmen exited from the rear sliding doors. They walked across the grass towards the back gate where they stopped and worked together to best repair damage to an obviously broken slat. Charlie watched and waited. When the men were finished making the gate look as good as possible, they turned towards the forest and disappeared up the trail.

CHAPTER 2

AYDEN SAWYER HAD TWO CHOICES. Respond to the assistant knocking on the office doorjamb or answer the cellphone on the desk. The phone continued to ring.

"I'm heading over to the courthouse to file some documents. We have a walk-in. Do you want to see him?" the assistant asked.

"Does he look like he can pay?"

"Yes, but he also looks . . . "

"What?"

"Like he could be guilty. Of anything."

"Show him back, then leave for the courthouse. Thanks, Jane." Jane left.

Hayden checked the missed call log on the cellphone as a shadow filled the doorway. The visitor stepped into the office and approached the desk where Hayden sat.

"I told you never to come to my office."

Mac did not respond.

"Is it done?"

"The husband is dead."

"The wife?"

"We lost her in the forest."

"Unacceptable.

"It looks like murder. Planted the gun we used and drove their vehicle and ditched it near the ferry terminal."

"Did you find anything connecting him to me?"

"No. His computer held only the usual work files, personal correspondence and photos. No links to you or the network."

"Well, that's something at least."

"There were a lot of photos of the two of them around. I took some pictures with my cell and will send them to you."

"Put the word out to our people on the street and the women's shelter. I expect you to find her before the cops do."

The man nodded and left.

The cellphone rang again. Hayden threw it against the wall.

CHAPTER 3

THE PASSERINE'S DAWN CHORUS pulled Charlie from his fitful sleep. He pushed away the wool blanket and crawled out from under his lean-to. He could feel his heart racing, even though he had just woken. The disturbance to his solitude the previous night had rattled his nerves. He stretched in an attempt to infuse some calm into his sleep-deprived body. Looking up at the lightening sky, he took a moment to listen. The wild creatures were stirring. He could detect no human presence.

In the cool of the early dawn, he pulled on his boots and vest then made his way down to the main trail. He walked for a while in both directions. Finding no sign of the gunmen, he returned to his camp.

Charlie reached down. He grabbed a thick branch from the bottom of the large, haphazard pile of brush. He lifted, revealing a wooden platform which supported the entire woodpile.

"All clear, Julia. It's safe to come out now."

She climbed out of the hole, dragging Charlie's worn sleeping bag with her and stood before him. Blinking up at the treetops and bright sky, she let it drop to the ground and pushed back the hood of the sweatshirt Charlie had loaned her the night before for extra warmth. As if someone had emptied a bottle of black ink, her hair poured over her shoulders in messy tendrils. Charlie lowered the platform, noting the dark circles under Julia's eyes. Her pupils constricted in reaction to the bright sunlight, the grey of her eyes, saucer-like, reflecting the storm within. Bringing her gaze down from the treetops, she focused on his face. She couldn't speak, her legs were shaking and she started to cry.

Charlie led her to a stump next to the fire ring. He put a hand on her shoulder, guiding her to sit, and let it rest there for a moment to calm her. He picked up the sleeping bag and wrapped it around her, then stepped away to rekindle the fire.

"I have to pee." Julia stood abruptly; letting the sleeping bag drop to the ground. Charlie went to his lean-to. He came back with a roll of toilet paper and a small hand trowel. Handing both to her, he said, "You can go anywhere in that direction." He pointed to the left of the lean-to. Charlie watched her push her way past the brush to a spot beyond his vision. He walked to a nearby tree and untied a cord, lowering the food bag that hung out of reach of wildlife.

When Julia returned, Charlie watched as she put the paper and trowel back in the lean-to. She turned towards him, and he stopped fixing his meagre breakfast offering and stood. "Let me show you my fresh water source." He led her along another game trail, this time to the right of the lean-to. A five-minute walk later, they stood beside a small, running brook. "I dug this deeper hole in the middle of the stream so it's easy to dip a pail or water bottle in to fill it. It's safe to drink right from here."

"You've thought of everything," Julia said, looking at the babbling water.

She wasn't focusing on anything and looked like a lost soul. The bright and vivacious woman he knew, killed — as if the gunmen had succeeded in their efforts. He wondered how she was going to get through this, if she had the inner strength it would take. He felt a compassion he hadn't felt in a long while. When she shivered, he spoke, breaking her reverie, "Let's get some oatmeal into you."

Charlie turned, and Julia followed him back to the fire.

They took turns dipping into the pot of oats, Charlie with a fork and Julia with the only spoon. As the meal passed between them, Charlie told her of the gunmen at her house after they left the camp the previous night. How it looked like they were framing her for Hal's murder.

"Why?"

"I don't know."

After taking a drink of tea from the solitary enamel cup, Julia passed it to Charlie. He took a big swallow and gave the cup back to her.

"I'm going to go down to the house to see what, if anything, is going on."

Julia's eyes got bigger and her body tensed.

"You're going to stay put. You'll be fine. The men are gone. I checked around the trails earlier. But while I'm gone, I want you to listen. Listen to the sounds of the forest, become familiar with what is normal and natural. When you don't hear anything, when all seems to go quiet and there's no bird song, the forest is listening to something. Even if you can't hear what, I want you to get back into the hole."

Julia nodded, fear still lingering in her eyes.

"I won't lie. Another visit from those men is a good possibility."

"I'll get back in there now."

"Not necessary, just listen. Do you understand?"

"Yes: listen, and hide if I don't hear anything."

"Good. I expect to be a couple of hours depending on what I find." Charlie got up and looked down at her. "Let the fire go out, I only have it when I cook during the day and sometimes at night." Julia nodded and continued to stare at the fire.

"Julia?"

She didn't look up at him. He knelt in front of her. "I will be back."

Julia looked him in the eyes and nodded. He saw relief in their stormy depths.

She straightened her shoulders. "OK. Charlie?"

"Yeah?"

"Do you think Hal's still alive?"

"I don't know. But we can hope." He didn't think the gunmen would have risked leaving Hal if he was still alive, but he wanted to give her something positive to focus on while he left her alone.

Charlie headed down to the main trail. He turned about 20 feet beyond the edge of the clearing to watch Julia.

Still sitting on the stump, she looked up at the treetops again, listening. *Good girl*, he thought. He too could hear the birds calling across the swaying uppermost branches. The breeze sent a flutter through the leaves. It was peaceful.

Julia slid down using the hard stump as a backrest as she sat on the earth made softer by a covering of pine needles. She pulled the sleeping bag tighter around her shoulders. She sat alone in the woods. Staring at a dying fire.

Satisfied, Charlie turned and walked away.

The fire was a cold pile of ash when Julia picked herself up off the ground. She dropped the sleeping bag from her shoulders, folded it and carried it to the lean-to. Next, she lifted the lid on the dugout. Moving the secure pile of wood camouflaging the entry took very little effort; she realized how deceptively light it was. She dragged her backpack out and returned the lid to its closed position. Back at the fire circle, she sat on the stump with the pack between her legs and she waited, listening.

The birds still sang. Bugs still buzzed.

Julia took the empty water bottle from the net on the outside of the pack and laid it aside to fill later at the stream. She pulled the drawstring cord to open the top end of the bag. Then she saw the pouch containing Hal's wallet. She placed it on the ground beside her.

Next was a change of clothes: khaki pants, a lightweight turtleneck, T-shirt, a rain-proof jacket, down vest, socks, underwear, a toque and gloves. She put them in a pile next to the pouch.

Julia stopped and listened.

Needing to strip off the grungy, white cotton outfit she'd worn home on the plane, torn from her struggle through dense brush the night before, she stood. Overwhelmed with feelings of vulnerability at the prospect of stripping in the open, her knees quivered like saplings in the wind. Two days before, she and Hal had been soaking up the last of the Hawaiian sun before flying home. Now she stood alone in the forest, exposed.

She looked to Charlie's lean-to. Too low to facilitate the changing of her clothes. Not wanting to leave her pack unattended, she shoved everything back in and stepped towards the dugout. She walked around it, hoping to use it as a shield to change behind, but it wasn't high enough. She would have to climb back into the dirt hole, its roof reminiscent of the car trunk a stalker had once thrown her into, bound and gagged.

She detached the small flashlight hanging on her pack and clicked it on. She gripped it in her teeth as she used one hand to lift the platform and the other to hold her pack. With the platform raised, the earthen steps were illuminated by the morning sun. She stepped down, afraid she might start hyperventilating. She lowered the platform above her and forced herself down into the hole. Reaching up, Julia clicked on the battery-operated lantern Charlie had placed on a shelf carved out of the earth. Roots from nearby trees wove their way through the dugout's walls. Her hands shook as she pulled out her change of clothes.

She tossed her dirty clothes on the evergreen-covered alcove burrowed into the back of the dugout where she had lain the night before, her old nightmares merging with the present and robbing her of sleep. Once changed, she turned off the lantern, picked up her pack and climbed out. She dropped the platform into place, the resounding thump freezing her in her tracks. She listened. She could still hear the birds. She sat once again on the stump by the dying fire and turned her attention to the contents of the backpack.

As she took each item out, she remembered working with Hal to assemble them a couple of months ago. He had been anxious, which was unusual for him. She was the one who jumped at shadows. When did he become so paranoid? Had her usual apprehension transferred to him? She wracked her brain to try to make sense of it all. Hal had always been meticulous in his organization, but he also had a relaxed flexibility. He never believed there was only one way to do something: if something didn't work, he adapted. He had adapted and she had followed his lead, confident in her life partner. Now she was the one who had to figure out how to adapt. Julia had learned that flexibility from him. A history of running from danger had given her survival skills most women, or men for that matter, did not possess.

The pile of items grew. A separate bag with her birth control pills gave her pause. She looked at the round discs through the bag, turning it over in her hand. It became obscured through her tears. She blinked and a few streamed down her cheeks. A month ago, they had decided to try to have a baby; their Maui vacation had seemed an ideal time to start.

"Well, I guess I won't be needing those." Speaking aloud startled her and she realized tears were running down her face. What if she was pregnant? The grief came harder, unstoppable, and she succumbed to weeping.

In an effort to regain her composure, she lifted her head, wiped the tears away and put the pills on the log next to her.

She stopped and listened. The songbirds were content and filling the air with their music.

She looked at the pile of clothes and bagged items beside her and panicked. What if someone came? She wouldn't have time to put everything back quickly. She frantically started stuffing everything into the pack. There was nothing else she needed right now. She hesitated, holding Hal's pouch in her hand, and listened.

Fear of capture sent her pulse racing again.

Birds still sang, bugs still buzzed. She tucked Hal's pouch in on top and pulled the drawstring tight.

She pulled the pack around, allowing the top storage flap to lie across her lap. From it, she pulled out her own pouch with wallet and opened the zipper.

The first thing she took out was a baggie containing two photos laminated back to back. One of Hal she had taken on their vacation last year. He was standing on the dock of a friend's lake house, fishing rod in hand, smiling at her like a big kid. Julia brushed her fingers across Hal's face, her eyes refilled with tears. She kissed his image through the plastic. Flipping it over, the second photo was of the two of them, taken at a backyard party at their old house. They were sitting on one of the wicker lounge chairs; she was between Hal's legs and leaning back against his chest. His arms were around her and they were both smiling at the camera. The photo became blurry and she slid it gently back into the baggie and resealed it.

Julia refocused on the pouch and found a roll each of quarters, loonies and toonies. Dropping the rolls of coins back into the pack, she pulled the elastic from the bundle of bills and began to count.

There was a total of 2,000 dollars.

Folding the bills and placing them back in her waist pouch, she said, "Thank you Hal. I'm sorry I ever teased you for your tendency to be overprepared."

Julia reached for the other pouch on the ground next to her foot. She pulled out Hal's wallet and another package a few inches thick.

"Hello," she said, untying the string that wound around the brown paper package. Julia peered into the envelope and inhaled sharply. "Hal? What on earth?" She pulled out a large stack of $100 bills. Counting it out on her knee, it totaled $50,000.

Julia sat, unmoving. She felt bereft all over again. Whatever Hal was involved in, he had felt the need to stash this kind of cash in case of an emergency. It was clear to her that it wasn't an earthquake he was anticipating. The stashed money, the overpreparedness, these things made Julia wonder if Hal believed they might have needed to run for some reason. If they had, why wouldn't they run to the police? It didn't make sense to Julia. What should she do? Go to the authorities? Tell them what she knew to be the truth about last night? What would Hal do if their roles were reversed? He obviously knew something she didn't. And he didn't feel he could tell her. Betrayal replaced bereavement.

As she sat and wondered, betrayal was subsequently replaced by fear. Knowing Hal as she did, there was someone or something causing him to take these actions. Someone who sent men in the night to kill them. Someone who felt he could order the death of another human and get away with it. Someone like that would have power, financial resources and connections. Maybe even connections in law enforcement. Julia remembered her early days in learning to paddle white-water canoes. Her instructor once told her: when in doubt, do nothing, take your paddle out of the water. She decided to take her paddle out of the water. She would do nothing. For now. She would wait and see what played out in the coming days.

A raven's deep, gurgling croak brought Julia out of her contemplation. She re-wrapped the brown paper and shoved it to the bottom of her pack. She fastened her own pouch around her waist and pulled the clean T-shirt down over it. Pulling the drawstring on the top of the pack, she closed it up before hiding it back in the dugout for safety. She picked up the empty water bottle and headed to the stream.

Charlie stood behind the police barrier that kept the handful of neighbours several hundred metres down the street from Julia and Hal's place. Their house bordered the forest, the last one of only four on the quiet country lane. The police barrier stood just beyond the closest neighbour to Hal and Julia. Each house was separated from the others by a thick stand of trees.

At the foot of Hal and Julia's driveway, a man stood off to the side holding the leash of Aengus, Julia's Irish Wolfhound. He was speaking with a constable and stooped to soothe the dog by rubbing his chest. When the constable walked back towards the house, the man led Aengus to the rear of his SUV and opened the doors. After some gentle encouragement and a handful of treats, the wolfhound jumped in. The man got in, drove towards the barrier and nodded to the constable as he was let through. A uniformed officer lifted the barricade back into place.

Charlie realized the loss of Aengus was going to be a double blow for Julia.

He turned his attention to the small crowd that had gathered. He scanned it, looking for the gunmen from the night before. None fit their description. The people there were locals. Some were still wearing housecoats; others were in untied runners. The professionals stood dressed smartly; jingling car keys, travel mugs in hand, waiting until the last possible moment before leaving for work. He stood on the edge of the crowd, watching and waiting.

The medical examiner's van sat next to three police vehicles outside Julia's house. Charlie had been there only 20 minutes when two men accompanying a gurney laden with a body bag exited. A hush fell over the bystanders lining the road as they watched the van approach. The constable standing near the barrier moved it aside. All watched as it exited the quiet, tree-lined lane and turned onto the main road.

The crowd returned to its whispered chatter. Speculation made its way through the onlookers like gossip through a church.

"Who's dead?" asked one lady with wild, platinum, punk-rock style hair standing on end and a bright orange bubble coat. Finally voicing what they were all wondering. "We only saw one body bag come out of the house. Was it Hal or Julia?"

The officer at the barrier responded, "I can't say, so move along folks. Back to your homes. Expect a police officer to come to your door later. Please." He motioned for everyone to leave.

Most did, but a few remained, allowing Charlie to stay and not be conspicuous. He turned when a car from a local newspaper pulled up. A slim woman, her long auburn curls barely contained in a ponytail, got out. She carried a notebook, her press credentials hanging from a lanyard around her neck. It was obvious the officer recognized her; he moved towards her and spoke in a low voice. Turning his head to listen, Charlie could hear their conversation:

"Hey, Bess."

"Hi, Sean. Rough start to the day?"

"Yeah."

"What can you tell me?"

"Come on, you know I can't. I'll get in trouble."

"Ah, come on, you know me. You can trust me."

The constable looked around, then at her. "This has to be off the record."

"Sure."

"Male victim. Dead under suspicious circumstances. Any more than that you'll have to wait for the press release."

"Thanks Sean," she said. "Can I call you later for an update?"

"Sure. Gotta go, Bess." He turned away when another constable signaled to him.

Charlie watched as Bess stood for a minute jotting down notes. Lifting her eyes from her pad, she watched the scene outside the house.

Charlie decided it was time to leave. The reporter headed in his direction. He hesitated.

"Excuse me. I'm Bess Delaney and I work for the *Colonist Herald.*"

"I recognize your name from the paper. You're a good writer."

"Thank you. You are?"

"Charles Sebastian."

"Can I ask you a few questions?"

"Sure."

"Did you know the victim?"

"Yes."

"How well?"

"Not well. I encountered both of them on occasion walking their dog in the mountain forest behind the house."

"Do you live on this street?"

"Nearby."

"What were your impressions of the couple? Happy?"

"From what I could tell on such brief encounters, yes."

"Thank you for your time and willingness to talk to me."

Charlie nodded, and the reporter turned to interview another bystander. Not wanting to draw further attention to himself, Charlie walked away.

At the bottom of the lane, he headed up a path that the locals used to enter the mountain's trail system. He walked into the trees and looped back via the forest trail until he came up behind Julia's house. He looked for signs of the three men from the night before, but noticed nothing.

He stepped off the trail at his high vantage point. He pulled his binoculars from the inner pocket of his coat. Crouching with his back once again against the tree, he watched the same stage, this time with different players.

The officers, clad in white coveralls, were photographing evidence in the crime scene. Littered across the floor, yellow tent cards marked each piece with a number. He watched for a while as their tasks changed from photographing to collecting. He hoped they would move outside and discover the broken gate, but they didn't. He decided he wouldn't learn anything more. He rose. It was time to head back to his camp.

When Charlie entered the campsite, Julia was nowhere in sight. He went to the woodpile and lifted. "Julia? It's me."

Julia climbed out and stood next to him. "Well?"

"Come sit down." He led her to the stump and crouched in front of her. He knew there was no easy way to break the news, so he got to the point.

"I'm sorry. Hal's dead."

He felt helpless at her weeping. He waited and prayed. When she could catch her breath, she let out a long, hiccupping sigh. Seeing that her emotion was easing, he relaxed.

"I was hoping against hope that he might have made it somehow, but . . . Charlie, what do I do?"

"What do you want to do?"

"I don't know." Julia didn't say any more. She slipped off the stump onto the ground and hugged her knees to her chest.

He watched the silent woman sitting by the cold fire ring. He noticed for the first time she had changed clothes.

"Where did you get the clothes?"

"My backpack."

"That was convenient."

She looked at him, fire in her eyes. "That sounds like an accusation."

"It's not."

"It's a go-bag in case of an emergency."

"What kind of emergency?"

She hesitated. "Like an earthquake."

Something told Charlie there was more Julia wasn't saying, but he let it go.

"Hal and I were the prepare-for-anything couple. He always said it wasn't 'if', but 'when'. We had an emergency stash in the house, a box in the vehicle, and a grab-and-go-bag in the bedroom. Each pack contained a change of clothes and some basics to get us through the first 72 hours." Julia's defensive tone turned to heartbreak. "When the gunmen broke into the house . . . "

Charlie watched as Julia wept into her hands. "You did good. Hal would be proud." She used her sleeve to wipe her eyes.

"I'm going to leave you here for a while. Do you think you can handle it?"

"For how long?"

"An hour, maybe a bit more?"

He could see her fear, but he wanted to do another reconnaissance before he decided what to do next. He didn't share his thoughts with her, not wanting to add to her fears. She was somewhat calm at present and he hoped she would stay that way.

"Stick close to the camp. Same drill: listen and hide." He didn't give her an option, just got up and left.

CHAPTER 4

C HARLIE LOOPED AROUND THE FOREST TRAILS, searching for signs of the returning gunmen. He saw only a couple of locals walking their dogs. Satisfied for now, he retraced his steps to the back of the house. He watched for a while, but there was nothing new to see. He checked his watch then headed to a nearby pub.

Shifting onto a stool at the bar, he nodded to Stan, the afternoon bartender.

"Usual, Charlie?" Charlie nodded. Stan pulled a pint of a local brewery's amber ale.

Charlie saw the noon news had come on and Julia's house came into view behind the reporter. "Turn up the TV, will you Stan?" Charlie asked. A man Charlie recognized from the crowd that morning stood beside the reporter. Stan turned up the volume.

"I am on the scene where a man was found dead this morning under suspicious circumstances. We have been here for the last couple of hours. It appears that a domestic incident escalated to a fatal shooting. I am here with one of the neighbours. Can you tell us about the victim and his wife?"

The reporter turned the microphone towards the man, whose mop of brown curly hair was in disarray due to nervously scratching his head. He obviously wasn't used to being on camera.

"The couple living there were new to the area. They built the house and moved in less than a year ago. A pretty normal couple, didn't appear to have any problems, seemed happy. But you never know what goes on behind closed doors, I guess."

The reporter turned the microphone back to himself. "I'll continue to bring you coverage of this tragic story as we learn more. Back to you in the studio."

Charlie tuned out the rest of the broadcast, glad he'd left before the TV cameras arrived at Julia's house. As the amber liquid in his glass decreased, he tried to think of all the options. What should he do? What should Julia do? None of the choices were for him to abandon her in the forest. When there were only a few bubbles of foam left in the bottom of the glass on the bar in front of him, he made his decision. They would have to leave the camp. He would not leave her to fend for herself. He was haunted by another time on foreign soil where he could not intervene in the horrors around him. This time he would act. He would do all in his power to protect someone. He felt an electricity run through his body. *Was it fear*, he wondered? No, it was purpose. He had a purpose again.

His decision disconcerted him. He had finally made peace with his solitary life. The mountain forest had been healing. God had met him there. He was no longer alone with his nightmares and fears. He knew he could carry this newfound peace forward in whatever was to come. He wouldn't stand aside. Not this time.

"Hey Stan, can I get a couple of your burgers to go and some of those yam fries?"

"Want another while you wait?"

Charlie looked at the empty glass. He answered no. He wanted a clear head.

Julia woke with a start; she was still on the ground, her back against the stump. It was too quiet. She had fallen asleep. Cursing her foolishness, she grabbed her pack and water bottle in a panic and stumbled to the dugout. She hopped into the deep hole, dragging her pack behind her, lowered the lid within a couple inches of touching the ground and watched. She didn't see anyone, but was too afraid to wait longer in case any movement would alert an intruder to her hiding place. She let the lid drop to the earth, blocking out the sunlight.

She clicked on the lantern.

Now familiar with the layout, she sat and picked up her earlier discarded clothes to distract herself, rolled them up and stuffed them into her pack. She had been too afraid to turn on the light for long when Charlie had first hidden her in the underground hideaway. She had merely used the lantern to light her way to the bough-covered bench and curled into a ball before turning it out.

To keep her mind on the present, and not the trauma of her past brought back by the dark hole in the ground, she made a conscious effort to take in her surroundings. The smell of earth and cedar from the boughs were the strongest. But there was also a subtle hint of wood smoke and human presence. She examined some of the items on the shelf next to the lantern and found a couple of dog-eared paperbacks, a worn New Testament and a couple of cans of beans next to a can opener.

She began to realize that the gentle man she met in the woods was hiding from something. But what? Who digs a hiding place in the ground in the middle of the forest? Was there something else in these woods she needed to fear? Was that something else Charlie? Who did he dig this hole for, if not for himself? Maybe he was another stalker, or worse, a serial killer. In her mind, she jumped from one life-threatening situation into another. How much could she really trust Charlie? Did she make a mistake in running to him?

She heard something. She strained to listen, then realized it was Charlie singing the same hymn from the night before. Then the lid lifted, and he was silhouetted in the entrance. For a brief moment, she had a sense of panic, her mind flashed back to another time when her stalker had locked her in the trunk of his car. Julia retreated further in the dugout, her back against the earthen wall of the sleeping alcove.

"All clear. You can come out, Julia."

Charlie's voice brought her back to the present. He had saved her last night, she told herself. He held the lid for her as she climbed out. He let the woodpile down softly and walked over to the fire circle. He zipped open his windbreaker and pulled out a paper bag. "I brought a couple of burgers."

"I'm starving, thank you." Sitting on the stump, she wasted no more time talking and started into the burger and fries. When half of the burger was gone, she stopped and took a moment to digest. She needed some answers to her questions regarding Charlie's character and intentions before she felt she could take any new steps.

"How long have you had this camp, Charlie?"

Charlie looked at her and then back at his burger. "Five years and eight months," he said, picking a few yam fries from the bag.

Julia studied him. With the heat of the day, he had removed his warm toque. His long sleeves were rolled to the elbows. Freckles were sprinkled among copper hair on his forearms. "No one has attempted to kick you out?"

"No one has discovered me. Not exactly on the beaten track." He looked up at her, his ruddy and wrinkled cheeks showed years of exposure to the elements.

"Why the dugout?"

"I made the dugout early on, big enough to hold me and my stuff if need be." He took another bite.

"What would the need be? You're off the beaten path, as you said." She didn't like how he evaded her questions, but she understood from her own experiences. She knew she was pushing him beyond the boundaries that had been the framework of their acquaintance, but in her current circumstances she wanted some reassurance. She needed to know him more to completely trust him.

Charlie continued to chew.

Julia wondered if Charlie was on the run from someone, or thing. She knew what that meant and the signs of brooding tension that come with it. Charlie didn't show those signs, but there was something behind his choice to live apart.

"What drives you to seek isolation, Charlie?"

Julia saw the shutters start to lower in the look Charlie gave her. He still didn't say anything.

"Charlie, I know this isn't any of my business, how you live your life or why. I'm sorry to pry, but I overheard most of your discussions last night with the gunmen. I learned more about you during that brief encounter than I have since we first met on the trail eight months ago."

Julia watched Charlie as he swallowed and smiled. "You surprised me that day. It wouldn't have happened if you'd had Aengus with you."

"Aengus, oh my. Charlie, Nick was supposed to bring Aengus back this morning. What happened to him? Did you see?"

"I saw a man with Aengus. He was at the house for a while, but then left with him. He drove a red Toyota 4Runner."

"Yes, that's Nick's vehicle. At least he'll be safe." Her throat tightened, making coherent speech impossible. She sat on the stump and from her inner depths a murmured keening arose. As darkness envelops a forest at night, Julia felt a shadow of heartbreak hover over her for the second time that day. She rocked herself, trying to contain her emotion, the half-eaten burger shaking in her hand. The minutes passed. Charlie's presence through her grief brought her comfort. When the wave passed, he was still sitting on the ground next to her, unmoving, waiting. A new conflict arose: how could she feel comfort from a stranger who lived in the woods? Pushing her grief over Hal, and now Aengus aside, she renewed her questioning.

"Charlie?"

"Yes."

"You allowed me the freedom to visit you here. Why?"

"You didn't demand anything of me. You were easy to have here; you didn't talk needlessly and were content to listen to the forest. I began to believe that not all mankind . . . " Charlie didn't finish and put the last of his burger in his mouth, crumpling the foil wrapper in his fist.

"Not all mankind?"

Julia watched Charlie shake his head, not answering. He stood up.

"Where in Africa were you last deployed, Charlie?"

Charlie looked down at her; she saw the non-verbal wall go up between them. After a long pause, the hand holding the crushed wrapper relaxed. He answered in one murmured word.

"Rwanda."

He put the wrapper in his pocket and took a couple more fries from the bag. Julia watched as he walked to his lean-to. He pulled out his pack and started grabbing a few belongings and stuffing them into it. Julia quickly finished off her meal, realizing she had pushed Charlie as far as she could for now.

She remembered hearing about the genocide and Canada's participation in the tragic peacekeeping mission. She didn't know what to say, so she didn't say anything. As she crumpled the empty wrappers into a wad, she rose as Charlie approached and slid his pack to the ground next to the stone fire ring.

"We can't stay here."

He didn't wait for her to respond and Julia had to decide: follow Charlie or stay put in the forest and take her chances alone? He returned to his lean-to and started to dismantle it. Julia went to the dugout, opened it and pulled out her pack, parking it next to his, her decision made. She was glad she didn't have to spend another night in a hole in the ground.

"What can I do?"

"Toss the stones from the fire circle into the dugout, then use the trowel in my pack to scatter the ashes in the bush."

Charlie continued to break down the lean-to's frame. He added the main poles to the pile of rocks inside the dugout. Over the bare spot that once held the fire, he artfully arranged the cedar boughs to conceal any evidence.

When they were both done, Charlie pulled his pack on. Julia followed suit. She waited as Charlie stood for a moment and surveyed the site. He turned to her.

"Let's go."

She hesitated. Based on the little she knew of Charlie, could she follow him or try to make it on her own?

He didn't look back.

She adjusted her backpack and stepped into line behind Charlie on a trail that took them deeper into the forest.

❖

Charlie's mental processes kicked into overdrive. He worked through all contingencies that might arise in the coming days. His main objective: what could he do to ensure a positive outcome?

One concern was casting a shadow over his mental planning. He was about to bring someone he barely knew into his private space. Yes, he was content with Julia at his camp, with its boundaries that were open to the sky. But contemplating her occupation in the close quarters of his home increased his anxiety. *Lord, I need you*, he thought as he continued down the trail towards his truck. In this moment, determination drove him to do more than just share his rations with someone whose life was in danger. *Never again.*

The trail came out onto a gravel road. Off to one side sat his old pickup truck. "It's not locked," Charlie said, throwing his pack into the back behind the cab.

Julia climbed in.

"I have a place in Deep Cove. You'll be safe there."

"You saved my life last night, but now I'm a burdensome disruption to yours."

Charlie thought for a moment. She was right, he felt the disruption to his quiet, secluded life, but she didn't feel like a burden. He cleared his throat. "I'm glad you felt you could trust me enough to come to me last night. I don't know what lies ahead. But I do know I can keep you safe until you figure out what you should do."

Julia's eyes filled with tears and she whispered, "Thank you."

"You're not alone, Julia."

She nodded. Charlie turned the ignition and remained silent for the duration of the drive. He turned into the familiar lane that looked like a back alley bordered by trees. It opened up onto a small gravel parking lot overlooking a two-pier marina.

"Is your place in Deep Cove a boat?"

"Yep." He turned to Julia beside him. "We're going to run into people. I will introduce you as my niece." He looked at her. "Tuck your hair up under your toque for now. There's an extra pair of sunglasses in the glove box."

"I don't think we should use my real name," Julia said. She gathered her hair into a high twist, pulling the toque down over it.

"Could you respond to Hallie?"

Her hands holding the sunglasses stopped mid-air. "How did you come up with that on the spot?"

"I've been thinking about it since leaving the camp. It's kind of a play on your husband's name and I thought you might remember to answer to it," he explained.

"What about a last name?"

"As we're related, you could use mine."

She looked at Charlie with a blank stare. "We've always been on a first-name basis."

"Sebastian."

"Hallie Sebastian. I can get used to that." She donned the sunglasses and closed the glove box.

They left the truck and turned down to the marina's main dock. Charlie entered the numerical code to unlock the secure entry gate. He looked around the little marina nestled in a sheltered area at the bottom of the large cove. Seeing no threats, he glanced out over the water. The marina was situated in a beautiful and peaceful cove. A seagull called overhead. Charlie saw one of his neighbours walk towards them with his dog at his heels.

"Hey, Charlie," the man greeted them.

"Hi, Jack. I'd like you to meet my niece, Hallie."

Charlie watched the parking lot while Julia reached out and shook hands with the man, then bent low to greet the Sheltie. "And hello to you too."

"This is Sugar."

"Well, aren't you a sweetie?" Sugar hesitantly smelled the hand Julia held out to her.

"We are Charlie's portside neighbours."

"Hallie is visiting for a while from back east," Charlie said, sorting through the keys on his keyring.

"My wife, Teresa, will be happy to have another female on the dock."

"I look forward to meeting her."

"I'm going to get Hallie moved in. Talk to you later, Jack."

"Nice meeting you, Hallie."

"You too, Jack."

Julia grew quiet as she watched Jack leave the dock and take Sugar up through the parking lot. Charlie figured Sugar would be a reminder to her of Aengus while she was with him on the boat. To distract her, he said, "I'm in slip 7."

Reaching his boat, he bent to a steel box. He spoke to a somber Julia, who once again watched Jack and Sugar. She turned when he spoke.

"This is where I turn on the water and power for the boat. I'm hooked into the marina's services and usually turn it off when I'm ashore." As Charlie stood, he pointed to a sleek, white sailboat next to them. "That's where Jack and Teresa live with Sugar."

Charlie stepped from the dock onto the surface of his sailboat's topside deck. He never failed to appreciate the warm wood contrasted against the white of the hull. A gray stripe above the water line reflected back in the water. He glanced at the blue cover on the main sail, seeing it was still lashed securely. He stepped down and unlocked the companionway leading to the cabin below, pulled open the wood doors and pushed back the top. He turned to check that Julia followed him on board. She was still standing on the dock.

"Permission to come aboard?"

"Granted," he said, smiling at her adherence to the time-honoured protocol.

He watched as Julia grabbed the rails, pulling herself aboard. Charlie climbed down the wooden ladder, and Julia followed. He slid off his pack and took hers, placing them on the cushioned bench lining the starboard side of the hull. Across from this bench was a dining area resembling half a booth in a '50s diner. The walls were a warm teak. Overhead cupboards lined the top of both sides of the interior.

"You've lived in the forest for months when you had this?" Julia whispered and looked at Charlie. "Why?"

"I had this crazy notion of absolute solitude when I bought the boat. Little did I realize how much of a community there is living aboard in a marina. When I want to get away from people, I either set sail or head to the woods."

"I'm glad you chose the woods this time."

Charlie nodded and took a deep breath; he wasn't used to sharing this tight space. "You want the penny tour?"

"Yes."

He nodded, turned towards the ladder they had descended and pointed to the right. "This is the galley, or kitchen." Charlie lifted away a small section of the counter to one side of a bar-sized sink. "Pantry."

Julia leaned over to look inside. "Oh my, how deep is that?"

"It goes all the way down to the keel. I have stacking sections that make it easier to retrieve things. As it is just me, I tend not to use the bottom half. Next is the two-burner stove. And beside it the fridge, which has top loading and side access."

"Not much space compared to a regular size."

"I buy fresh every couple of days, or I eat out. I keep milk, eggs and some basic condiments in here, and ice cream in the freezer when I'm living aboard." He put the lid in place. "This is the engine control panel," he indicated wall of electronics beside the ladder. "This door is access to the aft cabin, or sea berth. I generally use it for storage." He closed the door and turned to the centre of the boat.

"Now we have the dining table which also doubles as a workspace. This is the mid-section of the boat."

Charlie watched as Julia kept a hand on the galley counter for stability, as she wasn't used to the boat movement yet. She inspected the shelves above the padded bench.

"You have a few books. Who is Lincoln Warren? There are eight of his books, I see. All hardback." Julia looked at Charlie. "Wouldn't paperbacks be more space-efficient for living on a boat."

"He's a friend."

"May I?"

Charlie shrugged.

Julia picked up one and opened the cover.

"It's autographed." She flipped another page. "Charlie, this dedication is to you."

He took the book from Julia's hand and put it back. "Let's continue." Charlie wasn't in the mood to discuss it further. "This is the navigation station, and basically the electronic control centre of the entire boat." He turned around and faced the opposite side of the hull.

"Next, we have the sleeping berth." He put his hand on the wooden frame and pulled two panels together which then closed off the bunk. "A Pullman bunk; these shut for privacy."

"Handy, considering you have a house guest."

"You take the Pullman. I'll sleep in the sea berth."

"You haven't had much sleep; you should take your own bed."

"I haven't had to spend most of the night and half a day in a hole in the ground either. I don't sleep much, I'm content out here."

"Thanks."

"Now, below the bunk is storage, and these cupboards too for hanging items," he said, touching the hull opposite the bunk. "Here we have the head, or in land-lubbers' terms, the toilet and shower." He opened the small door that led to the boat's bow and let Julia pass him to have a closer look. "A few rules. Nothing, and I mean nothing, but human waste goes in the toilet. Any paper goes in the wastebasket. Understood?"

"Only poop and pee. Got it."

Charlie was somewhat shocked; it must have shown on his face, as Julia laughed.

"Crude," he laughed back, glad for the break in tension. "So, Miss Potty-Mouth, I'm going to get a few groceries. Meanwhile," he pulled open a drawer under the bunk, "if you don't mind changing the sheets on the bed, here are clean ones." He pulled open the hanging cupboard door and tipped outward a wicker basket. "Dirty linen goes in here. Any questions?"

"Nope," she said, shuffling through the drawer. Charlie turned to the ladder and climbed up onto the deck.

CHAPTER 5

HAYDEN SAWYER LOOKED AT THE CALENDAR and tapped a pen on the desktop. It was one thirty. The receptionist was out on lunch and had left the door open to enable Sawyer to listen for the next client's arrival. The bell above the main door rang. Sawyer went out to meet him.

"Good, you're on time." Sawyer led the way back to the office and pulled a small photograph from a desk drawer, handing it to a street kid named Bird. "I need you to keep an eye out for this woman."

The lanky teen with a bluebird tattoo on his neck took the photo and studied it. "Hmm, want me to scoop her up like the others?"

"Yes."

"Sure," he said, pocketing the photo.

"Now, let's talk about your court appearance tomorrow morning."

CHAPTER 6

J ULIA COULDN'T FIND THE WAY OUT. There was movement, and the first thing that came to mind was being in the trunk of a car. In darkness, she put her hands out, and encountered solid walls on all sides. She kept feeling for an escape route, panic overwhelming her. She smelled coffee. Someone was nearby. Then she heard a hushed voice. She stopped and listened.

Julia opened her eyes, the dream faded and reality dawned, but that voice she heard still lingered. She recognized it. Charlie was speaking in hushed whispers. Fear filled her, trapped in the wooden, coffin-like bunk. She listened, straining to hear what he was saying. Was he on a cellphone? She wasn't aware he even had one. Or was there someone in the boat with them?

She heard the sound of pages turning, and then she made out a phrase.

"Heavenly Father, I thank you for my life. All is in your hands and I leave it there."

Julia relaxed when she realized Charlie was alone, and he was praying. She hesitated before she opened the panels of the bunk, not sure if she should interrupt him. When she heard liquid pouring, she slid down and found Charlie standing at the sink, his coffee cup in hand. Reading glasses lay next to an open Bible and a folded newspaper on the table.

He looked at his watch and then at her. "Good morning."

"Good morning. What time is it?" She adjusted the plaid shirt and sweatpants Charlie had given her the previous night. They hung loosely on her frame.

"Almost noon."

"Noon?"

"You needed it. Coffee, water, juice?"

"Water first please, then juice." She sat on the dining bench and slid around to the back, leaving Charlie's place empty for him to join her. "How long have you been up?" She wanted to look at the newspaper, but was unsure of moving the Bible. It seemed too personal an item to touch.

He poured her the water and juice before setting both in front of her. "A while. I had a chance to go for a walk then get the paper." He closed the Bible and tucked it into the shelf above the table. "There's a small article, but it doesn't give us any more than what we already know." Charlie handed her the section from the paper where he had it folded open.

The newspaper held towards her made her think of Hal. He would always separate the sections, handing her the arts and lifestyle sections, which didn't interest him. The sports and business sections were his primary focus. But, in recent months, he had taken to scouring the entire newspaper — for what she did not know. He frequently commented on what he perceived as shoddy police work on any story he came across. She figured it was a carryover of her experience with the stalker and how the police didn't act as he wanted them to. A few weeks before his murder, they'd had a lengthy discussion about crime in the city.

She realized she was still staring at the paper. She took it and started to read. One paragraph down she read the worst, but kept on to the bitter end. "Oh my, they do think I did it." She drained her glass of water.

"Do you want to go to the police?"

She blurted out, "No."

If they couldn't stop a stalker until he turned violent, or recognize a frame-job, then they couldn't be trusted to believe her side of the story.

Julia could feel Charlie watching her for any further comment or reaction. Numbness invaded her senses like a fog, and she was unable to engage in any logical thinking about what was happening. She knew Charlie was speaking to her, but was unable to respond, unable to lift her eyes from the paper in front of her. The newspaper slipped away from her gaze as Charlie pulled it from her grip. She raised her head.

"Julia, we have to trust the police investigation will go beyond first-glance evidence."

"I want to wait."

She looked at the two glasses in front of her. She picked up the juice. Charlie didn't ask her why she wanted to wait, and she appreciated it.

"Breakfast or lunch?" Charlie asked.

Swallowing anything solid did not appeal to Julia. "I'm not hungry," she said, redirecting her focus to the bits of pulp floating in her half-drunk glass of orange juice.

"You need to eat. Food is fuel."

Julia didn't think Charlie was going to give her a pass on this, so she conceded to toast. Charlie dropped two slices into the toaster oven. "Jam, peanut butter?"

"Just butter."

"Peanut butter has protein."

"Fine. Peanut butter."

Julia watched Charlie. She didn't protest when he cut up an apple and put it on her plate. When the toast popped up, she jumped. She pulled the paper back towards her and tried to reread the article, but only stared at the photo accompanying the text. She accepted the plate Charlie placed in front of her as he slid back into his seat at the table. She spun the paper towards him and pointed to the photo. It was a picture of her and Hal with Aengus as a puppy.

"We took this photo shortly after we got Aengus. At least I know Aengus is safe. Nick will look after him." Numbness left as a fresh wave of grief threatened to overwhelm her. It was now over 24 hours since fleeing into the woods. One night since losing the two lives that mattered most to her in the world. She took a distracted bite and managed to chew then swallow. Taste did not enter into the experience.

"We need to make a plan," Charlie said.

"Charlie, I . . . can't." Her voice was ragged, she cleared her throat. "You didn't sign up for this." What if something were to happen to Charlie? She couldn't forgive herself. Her fingers fanned the edges of the paper.

"Julia."

She raised her head to look at him.

"It has been my experience that I usually get more than I sign up for."

Julia saw the determination in his gaze.

"I don't feel helpless and useless in this situation. I can do something. Let me help you."

"How can you help me besides hiding me on your boat?"

"Hiding you is step one. You can't stay on my boat without coming out of the cabin. We have to hide you in plain sight. Introducing you as my niece explains your presence here. But you need to be out and about, or it will raise questions. We need to change your appearance. How do you feel about a haircut?"

"What?"

"I have barber scissors and hair dye."

"Hair dye? Why do you have hair dye?"

"I picked it up with the groceries yesterday. How do you feel about a short style?"

"Whoa! Why did you buy hair dye?"

"Your picture is in the paper." Charlie waited, silent and still.

"But you bought the dye yesterday. This is today's paper," she said, tapping it.

"Being hypervigilant, overprepared is . . . " Charlie didn't finish.

"Is what?" Her voice now rose with her frustration in things moving too fast out of her control. Julia waited, but Charlie didn't answer. She watched him get up from the table, putting distance between them.

"Finish your breakfast."

"I'm sorry Charlie, I shouldn't have spoken to you like that. I freaked out. I owe you my life, I . . ."

He cut her off. "No, you don't. You got yourself out of that house and to somewhere safe. Now is the perfect time to freak out."

It was all she could do to stop herself from bursting into tears.

"But you're going to have to do better than that weak tirade if you want to say something that deserves an apology. Swear at least."

He was trying to make a joke, she realized, and she smiled. "OK, I'll work on that."

"If you're going to hide here, it would be a good idea to change your appearance."

Julia didn't answer. Why was she so resistant to changing her appearance? She'd done it before out of necessity. What was the difference this time? Then she realized: Hal had been the difference. He had given her a security she'd never felt before meeting him. But he was gone. Once again, she had to go on the offensive and think like the logical soldier she could hear in Charlie's voice. Think like Hal, who she now realized had been preparing for something. But what?

She looked at Charlie. He had changed. No longer the quiet man in the forest, he had become a warrior in these new circumstances. A fact she only found out last night, listening to his conversation with the gunmen from a hole in the ground.

Julia reached across the table and pulled her abandoned plate towards her. She picked up pieces of the apple and ate in silence. She chewed until only crumbs from her toast remained, then stood and handed him her plate. "Let's do it."

He washed it and finished up by hanging the dishcloth over the edge of the sink. "It will be easier if your hair is wet. Ever heard of a navy shower?" Julia shook her head in the negative. "Water on, get wet, water off. Soap up, water on to rinse, water off and you're done."

"Got it."

"Towels are in the bottom left-hand drawer under the bunk."

Julia had been too exhausted the previous night to think about washing. Despite the shower's brevity, having water wash away the grime restored a sense of calm and hope to her soul. She appeared 15 minutes later. To her surprise, Charlie had showered and changed too. His hair was still wet. She gave him a questioning look.

"There are public showers in the laundry shed on shore." He picked up a small tin and shook it. "Three dollars for a hot, five-minute shower. Once we change your appearance, you can use it too. It will help limit the damp in the boat."

Charlie pulled out a small folding step stool and positioned it next to the dinette. He picked up the scissors from the table and looked at her. "Ready?"

She sat facing away from him as he draped her in a large, green garbage bag. He began to cut long sections of her hair, dropping them into a separate plastic bag beside him on the bench.

"So how is it you have barber scissors and you know how to use them?"

"I got a bad haircut while deployed in the Middle East once," Charlie chuckled. "I decided to learn to use a razor and scissors to help out my bros."

Needing the distraction, she asked, "Will you tell me about it?"

He kept cutting. "It was in Damascus. Our unit had employed local Syrians as guards. Their English and my Arabic were rudimentary at best. I needed a haircut and asked one of the guards, with few words and a lot of charades, where a good barber was. Of course, he had a 'friend'. I should have anticipated the outcome."

Julia could hear the smile in his voice. Charlie kept snipping as he talked. "He took me to a small shop on the ground floor of an apartment building. He spoke to his friend in Arabic. I tried to further explain by motioning around my ears." Charlie demonstrated to Julia. "I thought I was doing universal sign language for short hair."

"When the barber handed me a mirror, what stared back at me was me as a kid. Do you remember when small boys all had the same cut, as if their mom had put a bowl on their heads and cut around the bottom?"

"The bowl cut." She lifted her hand to her head. Julia could feel the lightness created by Charlie's scissor action. All the length was now gone. Before she could investigate whether he was giving her a bowl cut, Charlie pressed her head forward. This gave him better access and she could hear the quick snipping. "It was the same cut that my five-year-old nephew had at the time. My security guard didn't understand my shock and surprise. He thought it looked fantastic," Charlie chuckled. "My superior wasn't too impressed after hounding me for weeks to get it done. My only regret was I didn't get a photo of it. I ended up borrowing an electric beard trimmer from a buddy and shaving my head."

"Why didn't you get him to fix it?"

"Fear of something worse, I guess. Believe me, bald was an improvement."

Charlie lay the comb and scissors on the table. "Ready to see your new do?"

"I'm almost afraid to after that story." Julia reached up to the short strands at the nape of her neck. He brushed off the last of the loose hair from her collar. "Go check it out in the head."

She pulled off the makeshift cape. "As no bowls were involved, it should be OK."

What she saw in the mirror shocked her; she was all cheekbones and eyes. She turned her head and looked first at one side and then the other. Charlie had left a few wispy ends in the back for a bit more of a feminine look. Apart from these, Julia had an inch of hair left on the entire surface of her head. She leaned towards the mirror, then stood back and fought tears. Hal had loved her hair, and she had been rather attached to her long locks as well. She wet her fingers under the tap and tried to adjust different segments around her face for a bit more style, but gave up. Without some product, it would sit as it dried.

Pulling at the wispy bits, she stepped out of the head. She dropped her hand and looked at Charlie. "It's really short."

"My speciality."

"I don't think we're going to need the dye, do you?"

"No. This is enough of a change," he said, sweeping up the last of the hair from the floor. "When it starts to grow out, a colour change might work." He put it from the dustpan into the plastic bag and put it in the garbage bin under the sink. "Are you OK?"

"Yes," she nodded. "It is a bit of a drastic change, but I'm sure I'll get used to it. Thanks, Charlie."

"You're welcome."

"What's next?"

"You need to lie low, stay close to the boat and marina for the next while to establish your identity as my niece." He poured her a cup of coffee, handed her the mug then topped up his own.

"How long do you think?"

"At least until your picture is no longer in the media. If there isn't anything new in the case, they usually move on to the next story." Charlie looked at her and the close confines of the boat. "A week or two. Let's sit down and figure out what you are going to need, and I'll do some shopping." Charlie pulled out a notepad and pencil from a box on the table. "You'll need some warmer clothes. It's surprising how cool it can get living on the water, even in the dog days of summer."

Julia looked at Charlie across the small table. "Who would have thought all those months ago when I surprised you on the trail that you'd end up being my saviour? You looked like a homeless lost soul."

"Definitely not homeless and I like to think of myself as a found soul," he smiled.

Julia wondered at this statement, but before she could pursue it, Charlie got down to the business of making a list. Once completed, he put it in his breast pocket.

"Wait a sec," Julia said and went to her pack in the bunk. "Here is some money. That list isn't going to be cheap."

Charlie took it from her and counted 300 dollars. "How did you get this?"

"Part of the go-bag must-haves. Cash in case electronic bank machines are down. I have some money that should help me until I can access my funds."

"Not going to happen. It would alert the authorities to your location. Not to mention those who killed Hal. Best to keep yourself on a low budget." Charlie kept one bill and gave the rest back to her. "I'll cover anything over 20 bucks, and we'll discuss finances later. While I'm gone, you need to come up with a backstory to explain who you are. I'll be back in a few hours. I should be able to get most of this at the drugstore. The warmer clothes, well, I'll look around."

"I can't seem to stop saying thank you, Charlie."

He nodded.

"Thanks for taking the money."

He nodded again and left the boat, closing the hatch behind him.

Julia sat listening to the water lapping against the side of the boat. Soothed by the gentle rocking motion, she relaxed. She heard people walking along the dock and sat up, tension filling her body. She looked for somewhere to hide. The voices faded as the people passed by. She relaxed. Grabbing the two now-empty coffee cups, she went to the sink, still half-full from Charlie's earlier dish washing. Without Charlie, she didn't know what she would have done. She would have most likely been a corpse in the woods.

Galley clean, Julia looked around for something else to do in the tight quarters. "This is going to be a long couple of weeks." She made the bed, then sat at the table with a pen and paper, writing the first idea for a backstory that came to mind. When she was satisfied, she looked up. The bookshelf caught her eye. She reached for the first book by Lincoln Warren and opened to chapter one.

❖

Charlie left the drugstore and scanned the parking lot for signs of anyone taking an interest in his movements. Circling the perimeter of his truck, he checked the interiors of the vehicles parked next to him. Setting his travel mug on the roof, he unlocked the door and put his bags behind the driver's seat. For the past five years, this had been his morning routine: essential shopping, coffee shop then library. It had taken four of those five years to not check the parking lot and every vehicle for a threat.

The hypervigilance was back. Part of him was glad, he could use it. But another part was afraid he'd slide backwards and never come out of it. However, now he knew he had a helper, so he prayed. "Come, Holy Spirit. I need your guidance and balance between my skill and dependence on you."

He relocked the truck and moved the toothpick between his teeth from one side of his mouth to the other. He grabbed his mug from the roof and turned in the direction of the library a few blocks away. As he approached, he noticed an older couple sitting on a bench outside it. A mother struggled to get two rambunctious boys into car seats three parking spaces over. A small dog sat whining as it waited, tied to a wheelchair parking space sign. He detected no sign of a threat.

Inside the library, Charlie sat at a computer terminal with his back to the windows, where he could watch who entered. He signed into his email account. When he was sure no one could read what he was typing, he sent a message to his friend in the local Police Department. He kept it casual. Said he'd been walking and saw the police outside a house in his neighbourhood. Asked him if he knew anything. He hit send, hoping his old army buddy would get chatty about work.

Once he'd signed out, he left to find a warm coat for Julia.

No one was following him, and no one was watching. He had checked.

Pushing the hangers along the last rack of coats, Charlie got to the end and looked around the thrift store. There were a couple of moms pushing strollers through the aisles; no threat there. He tapped his thumb on the bar of the rack and thought of another option. He knew the local outdoor clothing store would have new fall stock in. First, he paid for two long-sleeved shirts and a sweater, then left.

Entering the City Trading Post, Charlie made his way to the rear stairs that would take him up to the clothing department. He found what he wanted in minutes, paid and left. Back in the truck, he pulled a felt-tip pen from the glove box, crossed out the full price and wrote, "Sale: $19.99."

Charlie arrived back at the marina. He turned off the ignition and sat for a moment, looking at his boat floating in the slip. He hadn't felt this energized in years. He felt useful. Then the realization hit him — his increased sense of purpose rode the coattails of Julia's tragedy. Looking back on his time in the military, his service depended on the trauma and tragedy of others. During his career he had been called to circumstances out of his control, confident that his training and natural ability would be enough. They had trained him well: being vigilant and prepared for any conceivable eventuality made him a good soldier.

Until Rwanda. No training or experience prepared him and his fellow peacekeepers for that. *This isn't Rwanda*, he reminded himself. But Rwanda was always there, no matter where he was or what he did. His soul was forever tied to the souls killed during the genocide.

He pulled the keys from the ignition and checked his mirrors, then the surrounding area of the parking lot and marina. He opened the door and retrieved the bags from behind his seat.

He could hear voices coming from inside, so he quietly put the bags down next to the cabin door and strained to hear the conversation. He realized Julia was listening to a talk radio station. Charlie felt a familiar shadow descend over his soul. He picked up the bags, slid open the hatch and climbed down the ladder.

The voices on the radio changed. The boat started to fade away. His shaking hands fumbled the bags, releasing them in his desire to change the station. Desperately, he reached for the dial and quickly found a soft jazz channel.

The boat refocused.

Julia came out of the head.

"No talk radio." Charlie could hear the anger in his voice and mentally counted to 10, then softened his tone. "Music only on the boat."

"OK."

He saw the confusion on her face and the remnants of tears. She looked at her hands, trying to fight them. He regretted his tone. Glad she didn't press him for an explanation, he turned to the scattered bags and lifted them to the table. He handed the ones containing the clothes to Julia. "See if these fit," he said, hoping they would be a distraction for both of them.

He watched as Julia tried on the sweaters first and seemed satisfied. Next, she lifted the coat out of its bag and put it on. It was an all-weather, waterproof one, with a zip-out lining. "This is brand-new," she said, pulling at the price tag hanging from the end of the sleeve.

"They didn't have anything suitable at the second-hand," he shrugged. "I found this on sale," he lied, busying himself by using one of the empty bags to replace the kitchen garbage. When he put the garbage near the ladder, he turned and saw the look on Julia's face. Holding the price tag, she looked at it, then him. He could see her doubt. He used the stare he'd developed in his drill sergeant days. Back then, it served to end many a private's attempt at questioning his orders. It still worked. Glad she kept her skepticism to herself, he watched her remove the coat. She cut the tags off with scissors she found in the bucket on the shelf next to the books. She lay the coat on the bunk and turned to him.

"Thank you. I really appreciate it."

"You're welcome," he nodded, glad the cost of the coat was no longer an issue. "Did you do your homework?"

"Homework? Oh, you mean my backstory. Yes, uncle, I have."

He remained standing with his arms crossed as she sat on the side bench, curling her feet under her.

"I have decided that I am newly-divorced. Daddy liked the ex, so I decided to visit my uncle on the West Coast to get away for a while. It's been difficult for my dad since mom died last year, and he and Dylan bonded over their twice-weekly golf game. When I moved in with him after the break-up, I reminded him too much of mom and being around me made it harder. I'm here trying to make a new life." Julia looked at Charlie. "So what do you think, Uncle Charlie? Does it work for you?"

Charlie looked at Julia, rather stunned at the detail in her manufactured backstory. "Close to the truth. I had a niece, but she passed away five summers ago. She would be about your age. Her dad, my brother Nathan, didn't take it very well, and became good friends with her fiancé." Charlie nodded. "It works for me. My neighbours don't know much about my life. Our conversations revolve around weather and boat repairs."

"Right." Charlie picked up his keys. "Let's give your new look a spin. I'll introduce you to the harbour master and show you around the marina. First up, garbage." He picked up the kitchen garbage by the ladder and handed it to her.

The next few weeks found Charlie and Julia establishing a routine, him going to the library, she for walks. Both waiting for news through Charlie's police contact.

Charlie was back on Julia's street, down the road from the forest trail. To distract Julia from her current limited existence, he had decided to collect her mail. The close quarters on the boat were starting to get to them both. Lost in his thoughts, Charlie crossed the road and approached the community mailbox at the end of the street. He was reaching into his pocket for Julia's keys when he noticed a parked Suburban halfway down the block. It was facing the opposite direction. The side mirror was angled in such a way as to reveal the driver.

The driver watched him. The hairs on the back of Charlie's neck bristled and he went on high alert.

Realizing the man was staking out the mailboxes, Charlie let go of the keys. He withdrew his hand from his pocket as he continued walking past the bank of mailboxes towards the Suburban.

He started whistling to appear casual and nodded to the driver in silent greeting. He made his way to the public trailhead and left the road. He circled around and gained a vantage point where he could observe the vehicle.

Five hours later, Charlie's patience was rewarded. A Jeep approached and parked on the opposite side of the road. The driver exited and made his way to the Suburban. Charlie recognized the driver of the Jeep as one of the gunmen who entered his camp the night Julia came to him. The two men chatted for a few minutes, then the Suburban left. Charlie recognized the stakeout shift change and figured they must be getting desperate to find Julia if they were resorting to this.

CHAPTER SEVEN

T HE PIER PARTY CLOSED UP WITH THE DARKENING SKY. Neighbours, making their way to their own berths, shouted goodnights from slip to slip. As Charlie closed the hatch behind them, Julia made a fresh pot of tea.

"Charlie, what does the name of your boat mean?"

"Nissi is a reference from the Old Testament to God being a refuge."

Julia poured the tea into Charlie's favourite tin mug and passed it to him. He accepted it and sat sideways at the table, his back against the hull, his feet dangling over the end of the seat. She sat across from him, steam rising from the mug she cradled on her lap while it cooled.

"Remember I told you I bought the boat with isolation in mind?" She nodded. "In the past, solitude has been a refuge for me."

"But you said buying the boat didn't turn out the way you thought."

"No, so I kept searching for it. At sea and in the forest."

The rich timbre of Charlie's voice resonated in her soul. She wanted to hear more.

"I noticed you have a well-worn Bible."

"Yes." He dropped his palm on the open Bible on the table beside him. "I grew up Catholic, but lapsed after I joined the military. When I was serving as a Peacekeeper, I . . . "

Julia watched his Adam's apple move as he swallowed some tea.

"It was hard."

The furrowed brow and distant look in Charlie's eyes told Julia he held an internal debate about opening up about Rwanda.

"There was a Chaplain assigned to our mission. While we sat inside our compound at night, listening to the horror outside the walls, he and I chatted. A lot." Julia watched as he seemed to drift off into memory, a sadness passing across his face. She waited, sipping from her mug, keeping her movements slow so as not to distract him.

"After Rwanda, I stuck it out in the military for another five years. Those five years were tough. I was constantly on edge, emotionally numb and disconnected from everyone. They assigned me as a driver to various generals. I had moments of panic while driving. The mass graves on the sides of the roads in Rwanda followed me back to Canada. Looking back, I . . . I wasn't . . . fit. Not to serve. Not in a deployment capacity. I tried talking to my superiors. In those days, PTSD wasn't part of the conversation; they expected you to man up. They allowed no weakness. I got out."

"After I got home, things only grew worse. I was spiralling downward in depression and an increasing sense of being out of control. I contemplated suicide; many of my bros went that way."

Charlie sat staring into his mug, lost to her. When he didn't speak for a while, Julia asked, "Why didn't you?"

He shrugged.

"My religious upbringing, I guess. Good old Catholic guilt. Fear of a hell worse than the one I was experiencing, if that was possible. Despite years of counselling, I continued to struggle. Every counsellor and priest asked me what I wanted. 'I want to be left alone' was my only answer. I thought being alone would be my sanctuary, but the faces of the dead never left me. It took years on the mountain and at sea, but I learned a valuable lesson, a message that the Chaplain in Rwanda had tried to teach me. We are not alone. He showed me Christ, more than any other priest or sacrament ever did."

When Charlie didn't elaborate, Julia prompted him, wanting to understand. "How?"

"He had no office, except in the back of a truck with the men. On patrols, he experienced what we did. Not all Chaplains did that, but he did. Once I asked him why, he explained he wanted us to know God was always with us. He felt his collar was that reminder. After I resigned and came back here, the West Coast reminded me of the forests and hills of Rwanda. They were closing in on me. I saw an ad for a sailing course. That led me to crew on sailing ships for a time. It wasn't easy living in close quarters on sailboats, but the 24/7 nature of manning the boat helped me keep the dead at bay. When I returned from offshore, I bought this sailboat. But I still didn't get the solitude I hoped for." Charlie absently fanned the pages of the Bible under his hand again. "I went to the forest." He grew quiet for a few moments.

"Did something happen in the forest?"

"I eventually understood that a refuge isn't a place, no matter how secluded it is. As much as I wanted to be alone, separate from other people, I couldn't find within myself what I needed to heal. When I woke from nightmares filled with mutilated bodies, I focused on that Chaplain and his desire to be a living example of God's constant presence in our lives. That repetitive refocusing of my thoughts helped me turn a corner, find an awareness that I wasn't alone. In the forest, still experiencing the horrors of Rwanda, I looked for that presence of God. And that Chaplain was right. God showed up."

"I don't follow. How did God show up?"

"It is the spirit in a person, the breath of the Almighty, that gives them understanding when it is time. That's from the Book of Job in the Old Testament." Charlie tapped the cover of the Bible. "My experience isn't something I can explain. You have to go through it yourself. All I can say is this: when I stopped running and let God in, I felt like I could breathe again. He became my refuge. Not a place. Him. The dead are still with me, but Christ is here now too. In my mind when we walk among the dead together, I feel his heartbreak at what happened. It may sound strange, but I feel we comfort each other. When we decide to open our heart to God, he opens his to us and shares what he feels too."

Julia wasn't sure she really understood how someone could feel something invisible. But she envied Charlie's peace. It was a peace she longed for.

After a few moments of quiet, Charlie peered at Julia. "Not what you expected to hear from this once broken-down soldier, is it?"

"No, it isn't. I've never heard anyone talk about God like that. Like it's a relationship."

"It is very much a relationship. Maybe I can explain it like this. That Chaplain was like a matchmaker. He made the introductions. Then the dating period was me starting to get to know who God was. But a time came when God proposed, and I had to make a decision to be all in or not."

"And you are all in?"

"Yes. I am."

Julia thought of Hal and the kind of relationship they'd had. He was all in and so was she. They'd survived so much together. They were a team. She wanted that again. Could she have that with God like Charlie did?

CHAPTER 8

Julia was running blindly through the forest, her heart was pounding, branches were pulling at her clothes. She pushed through the brush and the footfalls of the man chasing her faded as she neared Charlie's camp. But Charlie wasn't alone, she could hear music. It was a fast-paced Irish reel. Her heart hammered to the beat of the music. It grew louder as she got closer to the break in the forest.

She woke with a jolt and sat up in bed. Her heart was still pounding. She touched the familiar wood of the Pullman bunk, which welcomed her back to reality and the protection of Charlie's boat. She was safe. She was just about to push open the sliding doors when she realized the background fiddle music of her dream was also part of the waking world. Was it the radio? She slid out of the bunk and stepped into the salon. Charlie was drinking his coffee and thumbing the corner of his dog-eared Bible.

The radio wasn't on. The sound was coming from somewhere nearby.

"Am I hearing things, or is someone playing a fiddle?" she asked, pouring herself a cup of coffee and sitting on the bench stretching her feet out.

"That's Remi. He's from Cape Breton. Lives five slips down," Charlie said, not raising his gaze from the book in his hands.

"He's good."

"Now he is. Some of us almost threw him in the drink a few times," Charlie chuckled. "I remember a particular summer I stayed away sailing for two months."

"He didn't arrive a fiddler?"

"Nope. He felt he was losing his Cape Breton identity and needed something that connected him to the East Coast." They remained in companionable silence, listening to Remi while enjoying their morning coffee.

When Remi finished, Julia was the first to break the quiet. "I want to go back to my house."

"You do?"

"I want to see if I can find anything to help us figure out why."

"It might be safe now." Charlie scratched his whiskered cheek. "How about we go early in the morning and enter round back through the forest."

Julia looked at Charlie and smiled. "That was too easy. I thought I'd have to talk you into it. What makes you so confident it will be safe?"

"Well, it has been a couple months. There's nothing major in the news and my buddy at the police service says they're at a stall in the investigation. If we go before dawn, I think we'd be OK. Are you willing to get up early and travel in the dark through the forest?"

"You bet."

The next morning, true to his word, Charlie woke Julia up at 3:30 A.M. They left the boat. Charlie drove to the service road and followed it into the forest. When he put the pickup into park and turned off the ignition, he also killed the lights, plunging them into darkness.

"When you get out, press the door closed until it clicks. We'll keep conversation to a hushed whisper." Charlie looked at her, his face illuminated by the flashlight he had turned on. "Follow me."

"Right," Julia whispered, taking the extra flashlight Charlie handed her. They both exited the vehicle, clicking the doors shut.

Julia followed Charlie through the forest trails. She squatted next to him beneath a big Garry oak. It served as a vantage point that looked over her old back yard and into the windows at the back of the house. There was no sign of light or life.

"Wanna take a look?" he asked, handing her a pair of small field binoculars.

She took the glasses and trained them on the darkened windows.

"I don't see anything moving. Not enough light to see too much detail," she whispered.

"It's a good thing your back yard isn't visible by the neighbours on either side. If it was, we might have trouble if we're still here when the sun comes up.

Hopefully, we won't be." Before they moved, Charlie asked, "Are you sure you want to go in?" When Julia nodded, Charlie stood up to lead the way.

They cut down through the forest and entered the gate still broken from that horrible night. The lawn had grown. Standing at the French doors, Julia dug out the keys from her pocket. She turned to Charlie when she inserted it. His head turned away, so she looked in the same direction.

"What is it?"

"We've left a trail through the grass. I don't like the obvious signs of our presence." He looked back at Julia, whose hand was still on the key in the lock. "Not much we can do about it now."

"Do you think they changed the locks?" she said, hesitating before turning the key.

"I don't know. I'm more worried about an alarm," Charlie whispered, looking back towards the trees.

"Right." She pulled the key from the slot and looked unsurely at Charlie. For a brief moment her hand shook, but she knew what she had to do. What she came here to do. She reinserted the key and turned the lock. Before she pushed open the door, she looked at Charlie. "If the alarm goes off, we have about 15 minutes before the security company arrives. I tripped it by mistake once. I forgot to disarm it one morning when I went into the back yard with Aengus. I rushed and thought I'd canceled it, but I missed the check-in call. The security guard arrived and rang the doorbell about 15 minutes later. I was impressed at the response time."

"Do you know what you are looking for and can you do it in 15 minutes?"

"Yes." Julia took a big breath and held it as if she was diving into the deep end of a pool, then pushed against the door.

Silence. No alarm.

Julia and Charlie looked at each other, mirroring disbelief.

"Idiots. Why didn't they set the alarm? Anyone could break in here and wreck the place," she whispered and stepped in through the door.

Charlie locked them in. When Julia looked at him, he said, "Don't want anyone finding an open door while we're in here now, do we? Burglars could get in and steal something." He smiled for a minute, then sobered.

"What if a silent alarm was installed?"

"Really?"

"We should still work fast. If we split up, we can cover more ground. What do you want me to do?"

"I want to check for something upstairs." She led him to the bottom of the staircase.

"Hal's desk is at one end of the library through there. Gather anything as far as paperwork, and especially his laptop. I imagine they've cleaned everything out as part of their investigation, but it's worth a look. I don't know what we're looking for, so I'd rather collect anything we can carry and sort it out later."

Charlie entered the library while Julia took the stairs two at a time.

She noted the boxes scattered around as if someone were moving in — out in this case. If she didn't come out of hiding soon and deal with her and Hal's financial affairs, the bank would foreclose. Most likely they were already starting the process.

She entered their bedroom and noted the stripped bed and missing personal items. She focused on her task and grabbed the footboard. The frame was on casters. She gave a little lift to get leverage and pulled.

With the bed away from the wall, Julia dropped to her knees. She positioned her flashlight on the floor, pointing it at the knob dial of the safe tucked into the baseboards. The dial flew around in Julia's fingers. She pulled on the handle. The door clicked open. She reached in and pulled out a leather satchel, hugging it to her chest for a moment. She put it between her teeth to hold it before closing the safe and putting the bed back into position. Leaving the bedroom, she busied her hands by pulling off the small backpack and stuffing the satchel inside as she made her way downstairs. She didn't want to look down from the landing; in her mind's eye she still saw Hal lying in the pool of blood.

She met Charlie at the entrance to the library. A car's headlights shone around the edges of the drawn curtains at the library's bay window, then went out.

They clicked off their flashlights.

A car door closed.

Charlie turned to run for the back door, but Julia stopped him. She pulled him back into the library. "No time," she said.

He followed her without question and Julia led them further into the room.

Grateful most of the furniture had been removed and didn't trip them up, she stopped at the far end facing a wall of built-in shelves. Julia reached up. She pulled on a small cornice piece on one of the shelves and pressed in with her toe on a section of the baseboard.

Keys rattled in the front door.

With a pop, a panel of the library wall shelving opened outward.

Once they were both in, she pulled the panel closed.

They remained motionless; the faintest sound accentuated the darkness. They could make out the sound of the front door closing, followed by muffled footsteps through the house. They heard no conversation. The footsteps grew louder when someone entered the library.

Julia could hear the man walking around the room. The crackle of his radio made her jump.

"Archie, check in."

"No sign of a break-in. There's a trail through the grass out the back. Someone must have tried to get in the back door and triggered the motion sensors. Nothing appears disturbed from what I can tell," the man said. "False alarm, I guess. I'm going to check all the locks one more time before I lock up."

"Roger that. Pick up some Timmy's."

"Will do. Out."

Still in the dark, Julia and Charlie listened as the security guard moved through the house. They could faintly make out the sound of rattled doors and windows as he went. They heard him enter the library one more time before the front door closed and the lock turned. A car door slammed. An engine started.

Charlie waited until they heard the car pull out of the driveway, then turned on his flashlight.

"I'm glad you locked the door when we came in."

Charlie only grunted in response, then turned his flashlight towards her.

"Aren't you full of surprises. What is this?" he asked, as Julia flipped a light switch. A line of rope lights extended along the floor and ceiling, brightening the narrow space. Charlie glanced over the shelving on what would be the back side of the library shelves. It was full of books and paper files.

"Wow."

Julia smiled and looked at Charlie. "This was Hal's idea. I thought he was crazy." She cleared her throat as it tightened with emotion.

She walked the length of the space and sat on one of two cushioned chairs at the far end. She brushed her hands over the velvet upholstery. The hidden room was rectangle-shaped with warm wood paneling.

"Even though I teased him, I loved it. We designed it after a pub snug we once visited in Oxford. A small fireplace in the corner would have made it perfect." One last time, she looked up at the rare books she and Hal had collected, many of them from vacations together. "These books are rare and cost a small fortune."

Charlie glanced at them, then at Julia. "You and Hal were brilliant."

"I wish Hal were here. It would have thrilled him to . . . " Julia's voice cracked.

She looked away from the line of books to the shelf next to her.

Something caught her eye. She clicked on her flashlight, giving more light to a shelf near Charlie's hip. She moved towards him, and his gaze followed the beam. There on the shelf under some papers was a thin, silver laptop. He looked at her. She looked at him. She handed him her flashlight, reached for the laptop, and pushed the small pile of papers to one side. She went to flip the laptop open, but Charlie stopped her. "Not now, and not here," he said. "Let's wait until we get back to the boat." She slid the backpack from her shoulders. Unzipping the main compartment, she shoved the computer in next to the leather satchel.

Charlie watched as she shouldered the pack. He turned to go, but was stopped short. "Um, how do we get out?"

"Look on the shelf at eye level. See the *Arabian Nights*? Pull down on the spine."

Charlie reached up and as soon as he felt the hard surface, he recognized it was a clever imitation made of wood. He pulled down and the panel behind him clicked open.

"Open Sesame," Julia said with a smile in her voice, turning off the rope lighting.

"Very clever. I would have liked Hal." Charlie stepped out of the hidden chamber.

"Wait," Julia said and turned back in. She switched on the rope lights once again. Charlie followed her and waited as she searched the bookshelves. "Got it," she said, pulling a small volume from the shelf. She dropped her backpack and tucked it inside. Donning the pack once again, she looked up at Charlie. "I would take them all with me because each is wonderful, but this is special, and I can't leave it behind." It was the illuminated manuscript Hal had given her the day he proposed.

"Alright." Charlie nodded and once again turned to go through the open door. Julia turned off the rope lights a final time and pushed the shelving back into place. The click slammed through her like the closing of a jail door, forever removing her from what she once knew and loved.

Charlie came down through the hatch and looked over at Julia sitting at the table. She was tugging on the growing strands of hair at the base of her neck. The fingers of her other hand were tapping the tabletop as she stared at Hal's laptop screen.

She was still locked out.

"Still at it? Let me have a go."

"But you didn't know Hal, how could you possibly come up with his password?" Julia turned to look at him, the full frustration of the last two days showing on her face and in the tone of her voice.

"Random over calculated." At her doubting look, Charlie said, "Come on. It's got to be worth a shot."

"Fine. Knock yourself out." Julia stood up and waved Charlie to sit down.

He sat. Making a play at warming up, he stretched his fingers, wiggling them in the air. He saw her doubtful gaze as she picked up the Lincoln Warren book she had abandoned to work on the laptop.

A few hours later, Charlie didn't break his concentration when he saw Julia in his peripheral vision close her book and start to prepare supper. When a plate appeared beside him, he looked up for the first time since taking over.

"Thanks."

He didn't look at her again, but ate bites of food between pecking on the keyboard.

Time passed, and his frustration grew.

He slammed the lid closed.

His raised gaze found Julia putting the last clean dish away and hanging the tea towel over the lip of the sink to dry.

"I give up."

"Quitter! You lasted mere hours; I've been going at it for two days."

"For tonight only."

Julia laughed and brought over two mugs of tea. She slid onto the side bench and stretched her feet out in front of her. Charlie pushed the laptop to the other side of the table and stretched out as well, taking a sip of the hot liquid.

Over the top of his mug, he saw Julia's gaze go to the laptop. "Let it rest."

Charlie took a drink and leaned his head back against the bulkhead, closing his eyes. He listened to Julia blow on her tea before taking a tentative sip.

It had taken him a while to sort out his feelings of invasion with her in his space. Now he was content. He took another swallow.

"Charlie, will you tell me about your experience in Rwanda?"

So much for contentment, he thought. His knuckles showed white against the blue enamel of his mug. Charlie could hear the wind pick up outside, slapping the rigging against the mast. *I should tune the rigging again soon,* he thought. He needed to distract himself mentally, and began to go over the procedure in his mind.

Julia blew on her tea again. The sound of her quiet patience shouted at him in the confines of the boat and the rigging was forgotten.

He didn't want to talk about Rwanda. Ever again. He didn't want to subject another person to the images that never left him, waking or sleeping. What words could he possibly use that wouldn't generate those images? He reflected on the friendship they had achieved. Considering how much she had opened up her life to him, why couldn't he reciprocate?

Because reciprocity in this moment would stir the demons he dealt with. Yet, his God fought for him. He wasn't alone with the demons anymore. They no longer controlled his thoughts. He released his tight grip on the cooling mug. He drained his tea, dropped his feet to the floor and swung to face Julia.

"I wore the blue beret." He looked into his empty mug, then up at Julia. "Everyone considered it a sexy posting."

Charlie looked at the ceiling. "We were witnesses to a slaughter with no means to intervene. No means, that's a joke. We had orders not to engage."

Charlie looked back at Julia, his voice rising. "I was a career soldier, trained to engage. Do you have any idea what it takes for a trained soldier, accustomed to combat, to not engage? Especially when all that is happening around you . . . "

Charlie quieted, relaxed his tense shoulders, and looked Julia in the eye. "Do you wonder why I don't ever listen to talk radio?"

Julia shook her head.

"The local Hutu-run radio stations broadcast names and addresses of Tutsi people. They did so to encourage local Hutus to kill them. They congratulated the murderers, day and night. I'll never listen to talk radio again."

CHAPTER 9

J ULIA HELD THE LEATHER POUCH she had retrieved from the bedroom safe. She and Charlie had been so focused on the laptop she had forgotten about it. But frustration with the elusive password had sent her in search of a distraction. Unsnapping the closure, she slowly spilled the contents onto the cushioned bench beside her. A bundle of cash tumbled out first. After a quick count, Julia held another 15,000 dollars in her shaking hands.

"Goodness Hal," she spoke to the emptiness of the boat, wondering why he hadn't let her in on whatever it was he was up to. "Why couldn't you confide in me?" She crumpled the bundle of cash in her fists. If she had been more involved in their finances she might have been alerted to Hal's actions. She smoothed out the bills on the bench. *No use dwelling on "if only" scenarios*, she thought.

Next, she picked up a small padded roll which contained her good jewelry. The yellow diamond drop earrings Hal had given her on their fifth anniversary. There was also a few more pieces she had inherited, and more Hal had given her. Julia put all the shiny, pretty things back in the roll for safekeeping.

The last item was a manila envelope. In it, Hal's last will and testament, a life insurance policy and documents for a bank account in the Cayman Islands. She knew Hal made good money, but she never really paid attention to what he did with it, being content to let him look after their joint finances since they married. She managed her own money separately, which consisted of some inheritance and savings from her previous work. She folded the documents to return them to the envelope, but they hit something at the bottom so she turned it upside down.

A small, ivory, linen envelope fell into her lap. On the outside, in Hal's handwriting, were three words, "My dearest Julia." Her hands were shaking as she unfolded the single piece of notepaper.

"My love,

If you are reading this, it means something terrible has happened and I am no longer with you. I have loved you for so long, but not long enough. I could not have imagined a better wife, partner and lover to share my life. I regret that I will not grow old with you or share the raising of children and joy of grandchildren. You are the love of my life and I thank you for loving me. You made me a better man.

I hope you found the laptop I hid in our secret room. Have you figured out the password? Here's a clue. What do the locals call the place where I proposed?

Please forgive me for not sharing with you the dark secrets that are contained therein. I knew what I'd uncovered would alter the course of our lives. We were living a fairy tale, and I didn't want it to end. Not yet.

I hope what I have gathered is enough to expose what is happening and serve as evidence to bring justice.

Keep it safe and find someone you can trust.

Remember, I will always love you.

Yours forever"

Hal's signature floated on a sea of tears as Julia folded the letter.

"Oh Hal. How could you possibly think I could do whatever this is without you? Please come back to me." She wept into her hands, then went to the laptop sitting on the table. She lifted the lid and wiped her tears on her shirt sleeve. The cursor blinked at her as if it were counting down the seconds until a bomb exploded.

Deliberately, she typed each letter.

b-i-r-d-a-n-d-b-a-b-y

Charlie sat at the bar in his local pub and cracked open a peanut from the basket Stan normally kept filled for his customers. Popping it into his mouth, he looked up at the mounted television to watch a men's curling game.

"Hey bro, how's it going?" A hand clamped down on Charlie's shoulder. He turned at the familiar deep voice, one that carried a faint melody of a Caribbean childhood.

Charlie stood, and the two men clasped hands in a warm greeting. "Good. I saw your latest book in the store. Where's my copy?"

Lincoln Warren laughed. His smile shone like a silver moon in a night sky, reminding Charlie of long nights sitting under the stars in Kigali's Amahoro stadium. Neither man able to sleep, they found relief in telling stories of their childhoods to a soundtrack of machine-gun fire and grenades beyond the gates.

Taking a book out from under what remained of his left arm, Lincoln laid it on the bar. Charlie often wondered whether if he had returned from Rwanda with a visible injury, rather than a post traumatic stress injury, maybe he would have been better supported by the military establishment.

Stan approached, and Lincoln waved him off. "I can't stay. I chanced stopping in to see if you were here and deliver this. I'm meeting a realtor," he pulled out a pocket watch, "in about 15 minutes."

"I recommend a boat."

"My books would sink it."

Remembering the library in Julia's house, Charlie took a pen from his pocket. Grabbing a napkin, he wrote down the address.

"Check out this place. It's been empty a while, so it might be for sale."

"Thanks," Lincoln said, pocketing the napkin. Charlie handed him the pen.

Lincoln slid the book closer and opened the cover.

Charlie held the book open, an easy familiar action between them.

Before Lincoln could write, Charlie asked, "Instead of making it out to me, could you make this one out to Julia?"

"A woman? You holdin' out on me?"

"Just someone who's been going through a tough time."

Lincoln finished the inscription, closed the book and pushed it back to Charlie.

Julia looked up as the companionway doors opened and Charlie climbed down the ladder, groceries in hand.

"I'm in!" She could barely contain her excitement and turned to face Charlie as he sat on the bench.

"Well done." Charlie smiled.

"I found a letter from Hal in the legal papers I got from the house. He gave me the password."

"What's on the laptop?"

"A surprisingly small amount of content. But highly explosive."

"Explain."

"Five folders. One contains a document in which Hal explains his theory about a local human trafficking network." Julia noticed Charlie's head snap up in reaction to her revelation.

"Human trafficking?"

Julia continued, "Three folders contain lists of names and organizations involved in the network. The organizations include government agencies, private individuals and commercial businesses. Those involved in this network of companies and individuals supply and manage the local sex and labour slavery organizations."

"Why would Hal have this information? Was he somehow involved?" He sat forward, his elbows on his knees, attentive.

"I didn't want to believe the possibility, but when I look back on the last several months before Hal's murder," she stopped, thinking back before continuing. "He started getting contracts that compensated beyond anything he'd made before."

"What did Hal do?"

"He was an IT systems designer. He used to work for a large company, but wanted to be his own boss and had gained a good reputation in the industry. He decided to go out on his own about a year before we met. He also did some webpage development on the side; he said it fed his creative edge. We moved here from Vancouver a couple of years ago. We wanted the slower pace of life that a smaller city would give us."

Julia saw the puzzled look on Charlie's face.

"How do you think he got involved in what seems to be human trafficking?"

"I don't believe he was involved. It goes against everything I know about the man I married. The last folder contains diarized notes. He outlined his suspicions based on his meetings with individual companies and how they were being linked through the same server platform. He named names, local, national and international, who funneled trafficking money through their legitimate businesses." She looked at Charlie. "His notes start three years ago. All of these businesses used a communal payment system linked to their websites. He stated that he started keeping records when he realized one of the businesses had an escort website." She closed the lid on the laptop.

"If whoever killed Hal suspected, for whatever reason, he was onto them, that would be more than enough reason to murder him."

"Exactly." She appreciated his acceptance of her explanation. "He must have done or said something that tipped someone off."

"If they suspected him of this type of information gathering, they would certainly fear what he was going to do with it."

"Who are 'they' in this scenario?"

"We may find the answer to that question in here," Charlie tapped the laptop. "Also, we may find what Hal was going to do with this information."

Charlie picked up the laptop. "May I?" Julia nodded giving the go ahead, and he opened it. "Let's see."

Content to let Charlie be consumed by the information on the laptop, Julia put away the groceries and started making supper.

Lost in her own thoughts, she couldn't help going back over the months before Hal's murder, examining his actions anew in the light of this revelation.

When the oven timer dinged, Charlie closed the laptop. "We need to make sure that laptop is secure."

He got up. Pulling the cushion off the side bench, he lifted the lid on the storage box beneath. He pulled out a dry sack and turned back to the table. He put the laptop in and showed Julia how closing it properly would keep the contents safe. "We live on a boat; we can't risk this getting wet. When it's not in use, it goes in here." Julia nodded her agreement. "I have a contact in the police force, but we need a strategy. Let's take some time and think about our next move."

Tension engulfed Julia's whole being. If Charlie was concerned enough to take such measures, then the risk was real.

"Before I contact Mike, we have to get ready for what the fallout might be. Once this information starts to come to light, we can expect someone, somewhere, to take notice. If it's the wrong people, I want to make sure we can handle what comes. Once I take this information to him, my buddy will start asking questions. If the wrong people get wind of it, they'll come looking for his source."

"I'm hesitant about involving the police at this point," Julia said. "Are you sure you can trust your friend? What if they find me? Us? I don't want you or anyone else to die because of me. Hal died because those involved felt threatened. They were suspicious, and that was enough. They don't have this laptop. If Hal wasn't ready to share this, it's reasonable to think what we have isn't enough to actually accomplish anything."

"OK then, it's up to you. Will we wipe out this information and let it go?" Charlie asked.

"Then Hal would have died for nothing," Julia whispered, "and I'm on the run with no hope."

"Without knowing what, are you willing to do all that it takes to see this through?"

"Yes." Julia knew this was more than fleeing a stalker. This involved innocent lives, victims of slavery. "Yes, I am."

"So then we have to dig in and plan for any contingency," Charlie said. "Whatever those contingencies are."

CHAPTER 10

W HEN CHARLIE RETURNED LATE the next afternoon, Julia was sitting at the table reading one of Lincoln's books. Charlie had been gone most of the day. From a shopping bag, he pulled out a box containing a pair of walkie-talkies. She closed the book and put it aside. Charlie could see curiosity light up in her eyes.

"We need to have a way of communicating when we're not together." Charlie opened the box and pulled out both hand-held devices and the charger station. "I got these because, unlike a cellphone, they aren't trackable. They have a 50-kilometre range, so we'll keep them on us when we're separated in the marina or in town. I want to go through a plan I've come up with for going forward."

"Does this mean you've emailed your cop friend?"

Charlie sat down on the bench next to the radio station. "Not yet. Before I do, I want to make sure we've put a plan in place to keep you safe. With these, we can communicate, which is step one of said plan."

"OK."

"If I'm away from the marina for any reason, and I feel you need to get away from the boat, I'll say one word: dugout."

"Dugout. Got it," Julia answered

"If I have to use this code word, you are in danger. Step two. Get off the boat. Away from the marina. So, we're going to put a couple of kayaks in the water and go for a paddle." Charlie looked at her to make sure he had her undivided attention. "I know somewhere you can go to be safe. You need to ditch this walkie-talkie, throw it in the water. I don't want them to communicate with you at all."

"But I won't be able to communicate with you either," Julia burst out.

"That may be a good thing. I'll be alright," Charlie reassured her. "We'll make a schedule. I will come find you in one week. If I am not there, then . . . "

"Where?"

"A summer rental belonging to some friends. I look after it while they're in Arizona in the winter. If I don't show up in a week, you need to go to Plan B."

"What's Plan B?"

"Don't know yet."

"Shall I try to see what is happening around the boat?" Julia asked.

"No, consider the boat a no-go zone, period. You'll have to take what you need with you. Leave nothing behind," Charlie answered. "I'll leave a message with Stan at the pub if I can. He'll be our point of contact."

"OK," Julia said.

"Now, Plan A is to get you off the boat and away."

Charlie stood. He picked up a daypack he had prepared earlier that morning. Julia followed him outside and onto the top deck. "I have a kayak. Do you know how to paddle one?"

"Yes. It's been a while, but I took one out once. I am comfortable on the water, I used to white-water canoe," Julia answered.

"Good. I'm going to borrow a kayak from Jack. We're going to go for a paddle. Dress warm. I want you to practice grabbing essentials and make sure you take the laptop. Put everything in a dry sack inside your go-pack. Be ready when I return. Being ready includes getting the kayak in the water. I'll be max 15 minutes. You might have less time, so don't count on that."

Charlie checked his watch, then left Julia to figure it out.

Charlie and Jack carried a kayak down from the storage shed and lowered it onto the water. Sugar was at their heels, pretending to herd them towards the water. Charlie was all business as he pulled on the skirt and PFD, and stowed his pack in the hull before stepping in. Jack gave him a push to release the end of the kayak from the pebbly shore.

Charlie finished attaching the waterproof skirt to the opening, then dipped his paddle in the water and pushed against the stony shallows, propelling the kayak away from the shore. Sugar barked. He waved before turning the bow of the kayak towards his slip. He paddled in front of the boats in the neighbouring slips, then came around the bow of his own.

Julia was waiting, her pack on the dock next to her. She was wearing the kayak skirt and holding the rope keeping the kayak from floating away.

"How long have you been waiting?"

"About a minute." Julia smiled.

He looked at his watch. "Nine minutes. I'm impressed."

"You forget, I've done this before," Julia said, holding up her pack triumphantly. "Under the threat of death. Incentive is everything."

"Let's get you loaded." Charlie proceeded to help Julia fix the skirt on the kayak. Once she was sorted, Charlie pushed away from the dock.

They both put their paddles in the water and made their way out of the marina. Charlie looked back periodically at Julia following in his wake, establishing a pace that would allow her to keep up with him. It was a beautiful day and the exercise and fresh air helped him reset and calm his nerves.

"Once you get across to this side of the point, I want you to stick close to the shoreline. You can hide in the branches that are overhanging the water. If you go too far out, you'll become a clear and visible target. If you have to hide behind other boats, do it. Do whatever you can to not draw attention to yourself."

Charlie led Julia from Deep Cove around the point and down into Saanich Inlet. He followed the shoreline, rather than entering the more open water of the inlet. When they reached Patricia Bay, Charlie took his paddle out of the water and Julia slid up beside him.

"How are you feeling? Need a break?"

"No, I'm good."

"Willing to be a bit more adventurous? We can cut across the bay. It'll be a bit more open water."

"Sure."

Charlie dipped his paddle back in the water. He could hear Julia's paddle splashing behind him. He felt the wind at his back, aiding his efforts to move away from shore against the incoming tide.

During a paddling break, they sat quietly. The water was lapping against the sides of their kayaks, causing them to tap together. They drifted and the tide turned them to face the shore.

"I can't get over the different perspective you get from the water. The tree line is only broken up by the occasional dock and house. I can imagine what it must have been like 100 years ago, undeveloped and raw."

"I'll take you out and do some real exploring. Develop your paddling muscles."

"I'd like that."

It had been close to an hour since leaving Deep Cove when Charlie propelled the nose of his kayak onto a small, rocky beach. "From here, it's a short hike up to my forest camp." Charlie turned to Julia. "How are you feeling?"

"Tired, but good." Julia stretched her arms and shoulders.

"Do you want to get out and stretch or keep going?"

"Is it much further?"

"We're about halfway."

"I could use a break then."

Charlie extricated himself from the kayak and pulled it up on shore. Still wearing the skirt, he turned to help Julia.

They pulled the kayaks above the tideline and found a picnic table. Charlie pulled out the lunch he had packed for them and handed Julia a peanut butter sandwich. They unzipped their windbreakers and fleece vests and ate in companionable silence, listening to the crows squawking in the trees. Charlie knew things were about to change drastically, he just didn't know how. He prayed he had enough of a plan in place to get Julia through whatever was coming.

He crumpled up the wax paper he had used for their sandwiches and put it back in the bag, pulling out an apple for each of them.

Julia rubbed it against her flannel shirt and bit into the crisp skin. She rose from the picnic table, to walk for a bit and looked up at the trees swaying slightly in the breeze. Watching her, Charlie took out his pocketknife and cut slices off his apple. He had eaten three slices when she spoke.

"You said we're close to your forest camp?"

"Yes."

"Then we're close to my house. I wish Hal and I had discovered this park. It's nice. What's it called?"

"Cole's Bay."

"Aengus would have liked it too." Julia pulled back her arm and launched her apple core into the line of trees. She stepped back to the picnic table and Charlie saw her shiver. She zipped up her coat and sat back down. "Hal and I had talked about learning to kayak. We wanted to explore more of the island, especially from the water. He would have enjoyed today."

Charlie continued to listen, not wanting to interrupt.

"But this isn't a leisurely exploration. Hal isn't here. And I have no Aengus to go home to." Julia looked him. "Not that I'm not enjoying your company. It's just that the reality of my situation is rushing back full force."

Charlie saw Julia's tears on the brink of spilling. "I wish I could say it's going to be alright, but the reality is that it may not be." Charlie watched her wipe away a tear. "I'm sorry, Julia."

"I know. More than you realize."

Charlie could see indecision in her eyes.

"I want to tell you something. About my past."

"I'm listening."

"In my 20s, I had a stalker. He was someone I dated briefly in my teens. I had gone to the police, but they were no help. They couldn't do anything until he actually harmed me. I moved a few times, but he always found me. But I got better at disappearing, and it took him longer. It was after one of these relocations I met Hal. About a year into our relationship, Barton found me again. I was falling in love and gradually relaxed and wasn't as vigilant. To cut a long story short, Barton kidnapped me, but Hal saw it happen and was able to follow me. He called the police and there was a stand off which ended with them shooting and killing him. Barton. Well . . . here I am. That was 11½ years ago."

Charlie was stunned and let the silence after her revelation sit between them like a cup of coffee needing to cool. But he also waited to see if she needed to add anything, and she did.

"That's why the go-bag was so well provisioned. I had been through it before, and Hal knew all the crazy preparations I had taken to disappear in the past. I had put that need to be vigilant and be ready to disappear aside when I married Hal." She wiped a few more tears away.

"Only this time he anticipated disappearing with you."

"Yeah."

"Over the last few months, I wondered how you were able to adapt so well to all that has come at you. Now I understand."

He could see relief in her eyes, as if she'd lifted a burden by sharing her past with him. "I'm so sorry, Julia. You've had it rough, and thought it was all behind you and now this."

"You don't need to apologize." Julia put her hand over his. "Guardian angels don't apologize."

"You've given me purpose again." Charlie withdrew his hand to gather their garbage. "Whatever happens from here on out, I'm glad you came to me."

He put their garbage in his pack and stood. "Break's over."

Julia came around the picnic table and hugged him. He stiffened in surprise. It was the first full contact between them. For a moment, he wondered what it would have been like to have had a daughter. Would she have been like Julia? He returned the embrace, wanting to protect her from the world.

A few heartbeats passed before they released each other and returned to the beach.

CHAPTER 11

JULIA WAS RETURNING FROM A WALK. The usually heard-and-not-seen neighbour, Remi, was topside on his boat and waved, catching her attention. He was stringing coloured lights along the deck railing.

"Hey, Remi. With that beard, you could be Santa."

"Hey, Hallie. That's the plan. You tell Charlie we're still hoping he'll join the contest this year."

"Contest?"

"Christmas rigging light-up," he said, shaking the string of lights he held. "Charlie hasn't participated in the past, but maybe with a little familial influence he will."

"I'll see what I can do."

Hopping down the last rung on the ladder into the cabin, Julia looked at Charlie sitting at the table in the lounge reading the newspaper.

"It's almost Christmas."

"Yep."

"I forgot about what time of year it is."

Charlie remained silent.

"I saw Remi hanging Christmas lights on his boat."

Charlie turned a page. He kept reading.

"When are we going to hang lights on the boat?"

"I don't have any lights to hang on the boat. Nowhere to store them."

"Charlie, look at me."

Charlie straightened up and looked at Julia, who was standing with her hands on her hips, ready for a fight. He took off his reading glasses and put them on his head, crossing his arms across his chest.

"I love Christmas. This is my first Christmas without Hal. I would like to hang lights on the boat."

She held his gaze, waiting for an answer. The protective curtain she had seen so often over the last few months lifted just a little and his arms relaxed.

He put his glasses back on and turned his attention back to the paper. "OK. I'll pick some up tomorrow."

Julia raised her arms and gave a silent cheer, then climbed up the ladder and went down the pier to Remi's slip.

"Hey, Remi."

Remi turned, Christmas lights hanging around his neck. "Challenge accepted."

Julia woke early on Christmas morning. She lay quietly, listening to Charlie get up and make coffee. Unwilling to face the reality of Christmas without Hal, she didn't want to leave the bunk. She tried to think of it as just any other morning and almost succeeded, then Remi started playing *I Saw Three Ships* on his violin.

Julia could picture him from two nights before, proud of his full beard, wearing a Santa-suit sweater. None of the inhabitants of the marina had children, but over the years living in close quarters, they had become a family of sorts. And as a family, they had created their own Christmas tradition. December 23rd was their designated night to celebrate and decide who won the rigging light display. They called it "Christmas Adam." Because Adam came before Eve, Teresa had explained. They sat in folding chairs on the pier, bundled in warm clothes and blankets, drinking wine and listening to Remi play carols. It was a lovely evening, and so different from any other Christmas. Julia had relaxed and celebrated with her new friends.

It was especially memorable because she and Charlie had won the rigging light-up. She was thrilled, but Charlie said it was only because he'd never entered before, and they figured if he won he'd get involved next year. Julia hoped he would continue to be a part of this community tradition. "

But that was two days ago. Defeated, she slid down from the bunk and found Charlie sitting at the table drinking his coffee. She went to the galley and poured herself a cup.

"Merry Christmas, Julia."

"Merry Christmas, Charlie." The words squeezed past the lump in her throat. He rose and opened a cupboard above the table. He pulled out a book-sized package wrapped in gold paper and a red bow. Julia went to the bunk and removed a Christmas stocking from beneath the foot of the mattress. She laid it on the table beside his gift to her, then sat down on the bench across from him.

"Breakfast first." He calmly took another swig.

"What?" Surprise pulled her from her funk.

"It was a rule in my house growing up. We couldn't open presents until we'd had breakfast."

"But . . ."

"My boat, my rules."

Julia picked two mandarins from the fruit bowl. She placed one orange in front of Charlie and started peeling. She looked at him as she slowly separated each section of orange, put them into her mouth and chewed, drawing out the performance.

"Aren't you going to eat your breakfast?" she asked when she swallowed the last piece.

"I think I'll just have coffee this morning."

Julia saw the teasing gleam in Charlie's eye and smiled. *It could be worse*, she thought. *I could be all alone this Christmas.* Her stomach rumbled, unsatisfied. She took his orange and ate it too.

He pushed her gift across the table, and Julia turned the open end of the stocking towards Charlie.

They both chuckled.

Julia slid the peelings to the side. She took the bow from her package, and placed it next to them. She didn't unwrap hers further, content to watch Charlie as he opened the end of the stocking. He pulled out a series of small gifts.

A pile of colourful scraps of paper accumulated on the table beside him. As he unwrapped each one, he put them on the table in a line. The first, the largest, was a half kilo of his favourite ground coffee. Next was a pair of new paddling gloves. The packages got smaller the deeper Charlie dug. What followed was a series of useful items for the boat and for camping. Nothing of too much monetary value, but thoughtful nonetheless.

Charlie tipped up the stocking and one final item dropped to the table. He unwrapped a small wind-up toy the shape of a white sailboat. He wound it up and let it sail across the table.

He looked at Julia with a happy expression. "Best Christmas in a long time, thank you." He then pointed at the unopened gift before her and she tore open the paper.

"Oh, Charlie. Is it the latest?"

"Yep."

Julia turned to the title page and found the note addressed to her from Lincoln Warren. Her eyes misted over. "This is wonderful," she said, smoothing her hand over the cover and then looking up at him. "I'll treasure it always."

CHAPTER 12

Thursday, 25 Jan, 2014, 1:39 P.M.
Chuck,
Why don't you get a phone? CALL. ME. ASAP.
Mike

....

At 1:45 P.M., Charlie signed out of the library's public access computer. Fifteen minutes later, he was standing with the cordless phone in Stan's pub.

"Hey Mikey?"

Charlie pulled the receiver away from his ear as Mike's voice exploded from it. He rested his back against the bar, surveying the other patrons.

"Where did you get your information?"

"Rumors."

"Not good enough, bro," Mike said. "Meet me in the parking lot at the shopping centre at Royal Oak in 30 minutes."

The call terminated and Charlie pushed away from the bar. Just as he had feared, he felt a cloud of doom approaching. Now that things were in motion, he prayed his plans would be enough to see this new mission through.

Charlie had been waiting for five minutes. He checked his mirrors for the 100th time, looking for a threat. He didn't see one. Not in the parked cars scattered throughout the grocery store lot, or among the shoppers going about their errands.

Through his windshield, he could see the other businesses neighbouring the grocery store. He didn't see anything out of the ordinary there either. While his eyes never gave up their surveillance, he prayed under his breath, "All is in your hands . . . all is in your hands."

He checked his mirrors again.

Exactly 27 minutes after he hung up the phone in the pub, Charlie watched Mike pull into the parking spot beside him. Mike, still in his RCMP uniform, exited his patrol vehicle, opened the passenger door of Charlie's truck and got in. He slammed the door shut, causing the truck to shudder in response. Charlie heard the leather creak on Mike's duty belt as he turned towards him.

"I tried making inquiries on the side, but it didn't take long for things to hit the fan somewhere. In addition to my captain, I've got various municipal departments giving my superior grief. My captain told me to back off. Talk to me, Chuck."

"Sounds like you stepped on a few investigative toes."

"You can't just give me names of prominent members of the business community and accuse them of human trafficking. What evidence do you have?"

"Just rumors I've heard here and there."

"This is me you're talking to. Do I have to remind you about the time I saved your life in Kosovo?"

Charlie didn't speak. Anger rose like heartburn; he ignored this attempt at guilting him into talking. "Considering you're getting heat, there's something to the information, don't you think?"

"Help me out here. If I can go back to my superiors with something, I have a shot at getting in on the investigation."

"I really don't have anything I can give you."

"But you have something, don't you?"

Charlie didn't answer. His friend had not changed. He was still the do-anything-to-get-ahead-even-exploit-a-friend guy. Charlie knew Mike's ambition would possibly put him in a position to be a source of information, but not to the point of really trusting him.

Mike got out of Charlie's truck. In the process of opening the patrol car door, he paused and turned to tap on Charlie's passenger window. Charlie lowered it, and Mike leaned in.

"Listen. Be careful. I hope you figure out you can trust me and share what you know."

Mike didn't wait for an answer, but got into his car and drove off. In his rearview mirror, Charlie watched him exit the parking lot and enter traffic.

Then he saw the dark SUV. It wasn't there before Mike had arrived.

Charlie waited before starting his engine to leave. Neither of the two male occupants moved from their positions in the front seat. The passenger was talking on a cellphone. He let 15 minutes elapse before turning on the ignition. He drove around to the far exit of the parking lot, one that led to rural roads back to the boat rather than the highway. He was about to make another right turn, when he saw the SUV turn out of the lot and follow him at a distance.

He made a series of turns, winding his way through the peninsula's agricultural region, taking his time. The SUV stayed with him. He lowered his visor and unhooked the walkie-talkie.

"Hey, Julia?" He released the button and waited.

No response.

"Julia, respond."

Still nothing.

Charlie swore. He continued to drive in circles, buying himself time. He decided to try to lose them as he clicked on the walkie-talkie again. "Julia, respond."

The walkie-talkie crackled.

"Hey Charlie, sorry, I had my hands full of laundry. What's up?"

"I can't explain yet, but I need you to pack up your stuff and get in the kayak. Now. I'll contact you again in about 10 minutes."

"Roger."

Charlie released the button and, checking his rear-view mirror, pulled into the long driveway of one of the local berry farms. The SUV didn't follow him, but pulled off to the side of the road to wait. Charlie drove around the back of one of the larger outbuildings. Francesca Hamilton was coming out of its rear door when Charlie stopped. He didn't leave the truck, but rolled down his window. The woman set down her pile of empty berry flats and walked up.

"Hey, Charlie. Wanna come in for coffee? Art is inside working on the books. He'd appreciate the interruption, I'm sure."

"I wish I could stop, but I have a favour to ask. Could I use the back road out of your property? I can't explain, I'm in a bit of a hurry."

Charlie saw the puzzled look on his friend's face. She didn't hesitate long and nodded.

"Sure thing, as long as you stop in for a visit soon."

"Will do. Thanks."

"I'll get the gate."

He watched Francesca walk to the gate and unwind the chain that secured it.

He waved as he passed and steered his truck into the small, two-track lane that ran through the back of their property and would eventually bring him out near the landfill site.

When he passed the landfill entrance, he relaxed. No sign of the SUV for five minutes. He got back onto the main road and sped towards Deep Cove. Ten minutes later, he parked his truck in his spot and turned off the engine. He waited. He checked his rear-view mirror, then the dock for movement.

All was quiet. Not a soul was around. For a brief moment, Charlie regretted the marina's solitude. The harbour master was only on site in the mornings. Jack and Teresa were offshore for three weeks. Being a local, residential harbour, the rest of the residents were at work this time of day. He picked up the walkie-talkie.

"Julia, respond."

"Go ahead."

"Where are you?"

"Already paddling, almost to the point."

"Good. Go around the point and wait."

"Will do." Charlie watched the second hand on his watch tick three times around the face, then heard, "OK, I'm around the point. Can you tell me what's up?"

"I met with Mike. The information I passed on seems to have stirred a hornet's nest. He must have had someone following him, because I picked up a tail. I managed to . . . " Charlie didn't finish the sentence. The black Suburban pulled into the marina parking lot, in a space between him and the exit.

"Julia, stay out of sight. I have company." Charlie slipped the walkie-talkie into his coat pocket.

Two men jumped out of the Suburban. The man on the passenger side closest to Charlie looked in his direction. It was the gunman he had spoken to on the night Julia had fled to him. Charlie got out of his truck. He stood with his back against the door, hands in his coat pockets, pressing the button on the walkie-talkie so Julia could hear.

He waited. They walked towards him.

"Charles Sebastian?" the same gunman asked.

"Who wants to know?" Charlie saw recognition dawn in the man's eyes.

"So. We meet again."

The man stepped forward and Charlie could smell coffee on his breath. For a moment, he remembered another time someone had got into his face and the smell of death that clung to him. Coffee didn't scare him. He returned look for look. Then he saw the confused hesitancy. Whatever happened in the next few minutes, Charlie knew he had done all he could to safeguard Julia. He smiled.

The look of confusion in the man's eyes turned to anger. "Let's have a chat."

The two men, now on either side of Charlie, each took an arm and marched him to the locked gate. Charlie didn't unlock it.

"Still trying to catch a rabbit?"

Charlie was looking at the leader and didn't see the fist coming from the other direction. The next thing he felt was the gate's cold metal pressed into his cheek. His skull hurt where the man had punched him.

"Unlock. The. Gate."

Charlie reached up and typed in the five-digit code, and the gate released.

They shoved him through it and onto the dock. There was no further discussion. Charlie kept his eyes on the open water. Watching. Listening. His lowered head and stooped shoulders gave the appearance of submission. He put his hands in his pockets and waited for another blow.

It didn't come.

Sloppy, Charlie thought to himself. He could have been reaching for a gun for all they knew. Instead, he took the walkie-talkie in his hand. When they reached his boat, the two men stopped him.

The leader stepped onto it.

"It's customary to ask permission to board."

Charlie looked over his shoulder at the other man, smiled, then yelled, "DUGOUT!"

The man reacted with his fist and Charlie fell to the dock. He was expecting it this time. He fell in a matter which allowed him to drop the walkie-talkie into the water.

"Get up."

Charlie did. His jaw throbbed and his neck hurt from the blows. As he stepped down onto his deck, he prayed Julia had heard the code message and was paddling hard.

Like a movie, the scene in the parking lot and dock played out before Julia as she floated in the kayak. The soundtrack came from the walkie-talkie clipped to her PFD. The violence drowned out the water quietly lapping against the kayak's hull.

Julia had lied to Charlie. She wasn't around the point. But she was still hidden. She floated behind the dock of the house on the point, watching through field glasses.

When she saw the two men arrive in the parking lot and approach Charlie, she took out her camera and caught it all on film.

Julia dropped her walkie-talkie into the cold Pacific waters. Tears of loss streamed down her face as she watched her connection to Charlie drift towards shore. It got caught up in the branches of a fallen limb of an arbutus tree growing close to shore.

She secured her camera. She could do nothing more here, and if she stayed she knew there was a chance she would get caught. The plan she and Charlie had devised needed to succeed, no matter what.

She was afraid what that "no matter what" might entail.

Julia put her paddle in the water and pulled her bow around. She started the slow ploughing motion that would propel her to safety.

Thirty minutes later, as she was rounding Warrior Point, it began to rain. Gentle at first, it washed the dried tears from her cheeks. When it increased, she stopped paddling to pull up her hood and made sure her skirt maintained its seal. She wiggled her toes and flexed her hands and fingers around the double-bladed paddle.

She watched the rain plopping on the water, making bubbles across the surface. There was no wind and she was warm and dry inside her rain gear. Grateful for small mercies, she dipped her paddle once again. Her mind numb, she regained her rhythm, propelling herself forward one stroke at a time.

At Patricia Bay, she cut across the open water as she and Charlie had on that first paddle. The road came too close to the shoreline for her sense of safety. Her rain gear acted like a sauna and she was grateful when she rounded Yarrow Point. As she approached the beach where she and Charlie had shared lunch that day, she was tempted to stop. Instead, she unzipped her coat halfway and put the small rocky shore behind her. She didn't need a break as she once had; a couple of months of daily paddling had prepared her for this. Charlie had prepared her for this.

The rain had stopped by the time Julia reached up under the edge of the dock and pulled out the waterproof key holder, slipping it into her jacket pocket. She secured her kayak, disengaged the skirt from the opening and pulled herself onto the wooden surface. The calm of paddling was replaced by apprehension. What if someone was here? As quietly as possible, she walked up the dock and looked in the windows. It was empty. She walked around the building and saw no sign of recent visitors.

Back on the dock, she scanned the water beyond to make sure she wasn't being followed or watched. There were no boats to be seen. Hidden among Arbutus trees lining the shore, the boathouse and dock were invisible to neighbours. Satisfied, she walked back down to the kayak. Reaching into its interior, she pulled out her pack, double-checking it was still dry and then put it next to the cleat at her hip. She pulled the kayak from the water and placed it upside down on the dock.

She stripped off the skirting and carried it and her pack up to the boathouse door. Looking over her shoulder towards the water one last time, the tension in her body released. Satisfied, she unlocked the door to the cosy boathouse and stepped in.

She dropped her pack on the floor near the only table in the cabin, no bigger than a card table, adorned with a small vase of dusty pussy willows.

According to their plan, this B&B would be her home for the next week. When Charlie was able, he would call his friends in Arizona and they would then call Julia at the boathouse. She got to work getting moved in. She turned on the water. When she flicked on the power switch, she heard the fridge come on and the quiet hum filled the silence of the small space. The face of the microwave flashed, indicating that the clock needed to be set.

She checked the cupboards and found only basics: coffee, tea, cooking oil and some spices. She opened her backpack and lifted out the dry sack. She sat on the bed, unfolded the top and pulled out the laptop followed by some clothes. In the bottom of the sack were a few canned goods she had stashed there weeks ago. She put the cans in the cupboard. Next she rinsed the saltwater from the kayak skirt in the bathtub. She hung it up on a coat peg inside the back door.

She filled the kettle and took down the tea and a mug. She stood at the window, looking out beyond the dock. The sky had cleared and the last of the afternoon sun sparkled on the inlet's water.

The mental list of tasks now complete, she couldn't avoid the solitude anymore. For the first time since Hal's death, Julia faced being alone. The heartbreak resurfaced and she gasped for air. She didn't hear the keening agony that flowed out on an exhaled breath.

Julia woke with a start as a vibration shivered through the cabin. At first, she wondered if it was an earthquake. Then she heard the hollow sound of a boat bumping against the dock.

Someone coming to the cabin was more of a concern than an earthquake. Julia lay for a few minutes, frozen in fear. Her heart was racing, and she began to break out in a sweat as she listened for footsteps.

She could hear muffled conversation and wood striking wood, so she sat up and looked out the window. A couple in a tandem kayak were clinging to the end of the dock. The woman in front was tying their line to one of the dock's cleats, while the man in the back assisted by holding the kayak firm.

Julia looked around her in panic, not sure what to do. She grabbed her clothes and dressed in anticipation of fleeing the cabin. She kept her eye on the couple as she zipped her jeans, using the table against the window as a shield for her movements.

The woman was pulling their dry sacks out of the hull and dropping them onto the end of the dock. Puddles of water formed around them. When she had retrieved the last sack, he loosened the line and lifted the kayak onto the dock.

Julia started stuffing everything she couldn't leave behind into her backpack. Her heart was racing; her sense of panic grew.

"One, two, three," the man said. They tipped the kayak upside down and rocked it side to side. Water poured out.

Julia stopped stuffing her backpack.

They lowered the kayak back into the water and reloaded. Julia relaxed. They weren't here for her.

Only when they pushed away from the dock and dipped their paddles back into the water did Julia sit. The pack sat on the floor at her feet, stuffed haphazardly with her belongings. Her heart rate eased to a normal rhythm.

It had taken two days for Julia's fear of capture to subside. Now it was back.

The fear for Charlie's life, however, had not subsided. Silence from him only caused it to grow.

Julia pulled the camera from the backpack and lay down on the bed. She turned the rear display around so she could watch the video she had taken of Charlie and the gunmen, as she had done repeatedly for the last couple of days. She recognized one of them from the night Hal was murdered. He was the one with the gun who had stood over Hal's body.

Every time she watched it, she was taken back to that night. But she couldn't stop.

Their treatment of Charlie was brutal. But she held out hope that when they didn't find her on the boat, they would have left him alive. And dare she believe, unharmed?

She hit rewind and then play.

CHAPTER 13

AYDEN SAWYER WALKED DOWN the stone steps of the Businessmens' Club looking for Allenby. Seeing him across the street, Sawyer advanced towards him. The two kept moving, making their way to the inner harbour where their conversation could not be overheard. It was a typical February day, overcast with the threat of rain. Very few people were around.

"Did you get it?"

"No."

"Not good."

"That's the way it goes with a court-ordered sale. It's in the hands of the judge in a closed bid. We were outbid. Simple as that."

"I told you to offer more than asking."

"I did, but we were outbid by $25,000."

Allenby was one of the top men in the collection of local entrepreneurs Hayden Sawyer had carefully accumulated. Those businesses made up a network that ensured the legitimate diversion required in the clandestine human trafficking enterprise that had taken Sawyer years to build. Sawyer had a reputation for ruthlessness, and the look on Allenby's face revealed his nervousness in passing on the disappointing news of not getting the house that had belonged to Harold Bowen. Allenby's expression pleased Sawyer. Keeping the other members of the human trafficking ring in fear was a prime directive in keeping tight control of the business enterprise.

"Why did you even want that house?"

"Spoils of war."

CHAPTER 14

J ULIA WATCHED THE TOURISTS flowing out of the bus and walking through the entrance to Butchart Gardens. The payphone receiver felt cold against her palm as she listened to the line ringing on the other end.

When the call was picked up, she turned her back to the tourists.

"Hey Stan, Hallie here. I'm looking for Charlie."

Raindrops meandered down the side of the phone booth while she listened.

"No, thanks. No message."

She hung up the receiver. It had been eight days.

CHAPTER 15

STILL IN THE PAJAMA BOTTOMS and T-shirt he slept in, Lincoln Warren stood looking out the floor-to-ceiling windows in the dining room of his newly acquired house. He admired the back garden; the rhododendrons that lined the fence on either side of the yard were just starting to bloom. There were three other bushes he couldn't identify against the back fence separating the garden from the forest. Until they blossomed, he wouldn't know what they were. *It's going to be a year of seasonal surprises,* he thought to himself. He drained his cup, turning to pour another before entering the library to attend to the boxes of books still waiting to be unpacked.

Passing the front door, a shadow appeared in the side light.

The dog was back.

Lincoln opened the door and stood aside, letting it enter. The grey Irish Wolfhound walked right in and made its way to the dining area, lying down in an empty space between boxes. He let out a deep sigh, then raised an eyebrow at Lincoln.

Lincoln followed and put his cup on top of a box, before crouching down to scratch behind the dog's ears. The tail lying on the floor gave a weak thump, but no more.

"Well, that's a good sign. Are you starting to warm up to me, fella?"

Lincoln stood, pulled out a bowl from one of the cupboards on the island and filled it with water. He placed it on the floor.

The dog did not move.

Lincoln picked up his cellphone and typed in a number from a sticky note he had on the fridge.

"Hey, Nick. Lincoln Warren here . . . He sure is." Lincoln looked at the giant dog dominating the available free space on the floor. "3:00 P.M. works for me. I'd really appreciate that. See you then."

He put down the cellphone, then moved to crouch next to the dog. "Well, Aengus. It looks like you'll be staying from now on. Would you like that?" He petted the wiry fur on the dog's neck and let his hand rest on his side for a moment.

At three that afternoon, the doorbell rang. Lincoln came out of the library and noticed that Aengus was still in the same spot, but was now sitting up, watching.

Lincoln opened the door and saw that Nick had already placed a large bag of food on the front porch and was now pulling out a wooden structure from the back of his SUV. Lincoln lifted the hefty bag and carried it to the kitchen. When he turned back, Nick was stepping inside.

"Come in, come in."

Nick removed his boots, then carried what Lincoln now recognized as a raised dog feeder towards him.

"I had this collecting dust in my garage, so I'm passing it on. Have you had a large-breed dog before?"

"No, medium breeds."

"I've made a copy of the instruction sheet from my breeder." Nick withdrew it from his coat pocket, unfolded it and handed it to Lincoln. "Things to be aware of, food and health issues related to the breed mainly."

"I appreciate it."

"I also added some notes pertaining to Aengus in particular." Nick crouched down and rubbed behind Aengus' ears. He lifted the big head and touched his nose to the dog's. "I'll miss you, boy." Nick stood. "I can't stay. I have to pick up my kids from school."

"We'll be OK. Thanks for everything."

"It's the least I could do. Hal and Julia would have done the same for my Fergus. I hope he is happy with you. It's one thing to be in familiar surroundings, but this breed makes strong attachments with their humans. You'll have to give him time. If you have any questions or issues, don't hesitate to call."

Lincoln picked up the cash he had put on the kitchen island and handed it to Nick. "Thanks for picking up the chow and bowls."

"You bet." The two men shook hands.

Closing the door behind Nick, Lincoln turned and looked at Aengus. The big dog got up and walked into the library. Lincoln followed and watched as Aengus crawled up onto his large sofa, rested his chin on the arm and looked at him. Lincoln thought, *I'm going to need a bigger couch*, then started breaking down empty cardboard boxes, happy for the company.

CHAPTER 16

A S JULIA ENTERED THE SECOND-HAND BOOKSTORE, the bell above the door startled her. She hesitated for a moment, wondering if she should keep walking, fearful of being recognized by someone. A tall, lanky man in his 20s looked up, offering a friendly welcome before turning his eyes back to the book he held. A coil of red curls fell forward as he bent his head, obscuring his view of the room. His limited vision and cursory interest in her eased her fear, and her hesitation lasted only a few moments more as the smell of old books pulled at her senses.

The bookstore, tucked away in a small courtyard in Brentwood Bay, was a happy discovery. She and Hal had not really explored the village, despite their proximity. After all she had gone through in the past months, this place was familiar, and her immediate fear dissipated for the time being. She wandered through the book-lined aisles. Among other things, she lamented the loss of her home library. Living the life of a fugitive, she didn't have the luxury of accumulating anything that didn't serve her current mode of basic survival. She was enjoying the one-room bed and breakfast lodgings, but knew she couldn't look at it as a long-term option. The owners would return in a couple of months to once again open the house in May for a new season of holiday travelers to the West Coast. Julia wondered if they would rent it to her. Yes, she had a good amount of cash, but if she had to pay the equivalent of what they could get for short-term rentals, she would go through it quickly. She put that idea aside as a display table near the front window of the store caught her eye. On it lay a selection of blank books, journals and a range of pens and writing instruments. A sign on the display table read,

"We sell no unread books. Only those books previously read, loved, traveled and dog-eared inhabit our shelves. The only exception to this rule lies before you. A selection of books in their unwritten form. In a state of want, they aspire to contain hope, adventure and all manner of possibility. They beckon all those who would dare to take up the pen."

The selection of covers gracing the aspiring tomes was chosen to appeal to a broad audience. Mugs printed with literary quotes held ballpoint pens. Wooden boxes housed roller- and felt-tips. In a separate grouping, fountain pens graced blown-glass vases next to ink bottles and blotters.

Hal had used a fountain pen for as long as she had known him. Inspired by a happy memory of him, Julia picked up a demonstration fountain pen and felt the weight of it in her hand. She rolled it between her fingers for a few minutes. On the corner of the table sat a pad of linen paper for customers to test the pens.

The tip engaged with the paper in a way that made the user more aware of the act of writing. Julia wondered if the monks in medieval scriptoria felt this way. The pen needed very little pressure to deposit the free-flowing ink onto the page. It acted as if it could pull the ideas and thoughts out of her with its momentum. The same feeling of creativity she had when painting with her watercolours came alive in her. She and Hal had always shared a working space, content in each other's quiet company. Julia remembered the hours spent painting while Hal worked at his computer.

Putting the lid back on the pen, Julia turned to select a journal. Running her hands over the various covers, she picked up a soft, limp, leather-bound volume. A small attached leather string tied the book closed.

With the absence of any word from Charlie, Julia had no way of knowing what was going to happen in the months to come. With no one to talk to, she needed a means to record and express everything she was going through. She never guessed she would tire of reading, but she was. Journaling would be a good alternative. She needed a distraction from her unceasing thoughts and dreams in the wake of losing Hal then Charlie and becoming a fugitive. She wondered if a fountain pen might aid in the cathartic nature of the writing process and, in turn, bring her a bit closer to her husband.

The shopkeeper stepped up and asked if she had any questions.

"I'll take these two items, please," Julia said, handing them to the redhead. She noticed his freckles for the first time; they reminded her of Charlie. Had his freckles been as pronounced and his hair as red in his youth?

"Is this your first fountain pen?" At Julia's nod, the man continued, "You might want a couple of extra ink cartridges. They don't last as long as a regular ballpoint. You'll need to refill much sooner than you are used to."

"Sure, thanks."

With her new purchases in her backpack, Julia left the shop. Her wariness returned. She pulled the toque down a bit further and donned her sunglasses once again, despite the cloud cover obscuring the sun.

As she passed the old Anglican church on the corner, Julia looked around to see if anyone was watching before turning down the cedar-lined lane. Feeling safe among the heavy hanging boughs, she made her way to the water's edge where the little cabin sat, its dock stretching out into the bay.

Julia was paddling for her life. She looked over her shoulder; two kayaks with dark figures were gaining on her. She focused forward and prayed aloud, "All is in your hands, all is in your hands."

With a start, she awoke to sunlight reflecting off the water onto the ceiling of the small boathouse. The gentle lapping on the dock calmed her nerves. The nightmares of fleeing from the gunmen had followed her to the boathouse's safety. A sense of violation overwhelmed her. Julia buried her face in the pillow and cried.

Rolling over, as the tears subsided, she looked at the laptop hiding under the small table. It had sat unopened since her arrival at the B&B. She couldn't bear to contemplate all it would take for her to deal with it alone. She sat up, reaching for the camera. Julia needed to see images of Charlie alive. One more time.

Was he still alive? Stan hadn't heard from him either.

Near the camera, the leather-bound journal and fountain pen sat on the table. The journal was unopened, as it had been every day for two weeks. She wasn't sure she had the guts to begin. But she had to. Until she was ready to delve into the laptop again, she needed to stop watching the video. The journal would be her new focus.

She dragged herself out of bed, showered and ate a small breakfast of fruit and yogurt. After washing her dishes, she left them in the rack to air dry. With all possible excuses out of the way, she picked up the journal and pen and sat on the easy chair by the door.

"Dear Hal,

Well, my love, you have managed to land us in a pickle. I wish you could have confided in me. You carried this alone. For how long, I wonder? Now I am carrying it alone. Who knows how things would have turned out if we could have worked on this together? Would you still be dead? I don't know. Maybe we both would have been killed."

Julia lifted the pen from the paper. Tears came unbidden once again and she brushed them away in frustration. She looked out at the water, blinking to clear her vision before writing again.

"I. AM. SO. ANGRY. WITH YOU."

A blot of ink marred the clean page.

"It was selfish of you to keep this to yourself. We lost everything. The house. Aengus. Everything I now own fits into a backpack. But those are all just things, material possessions. I could have managed the loss of them if I still had you. We came through so much. We were in this life adventure together, for better or worse. Those are the vows we made. No secrets.

You broke your vow.

I am so mad.

I could throw something. But wait, I no longer own anything that I could throw. I am sitting in a one-room boathouse with the bare essentials. I am . . . Safe. Warm. Alone."

Julia put down the journal and stood up to make herself a cup of tea. While she was waiting for the kettle to boil, she looked out over the dock to the inlet. She wasn't sure if writing her thoughts down was actually good, as she was feeling all stirred up inside.

The whistle of the kettle interrupted her mental struggle. She poured the steaming water over the loose tea in the pot. She took down what had become her favourite mug. The palm trees etched into the mug's clear glass reminded her of the Hawaiian holiday with Hal just before he was murdered. She closed her eyes for a moment, trying to recapture the vacation's warmth into her lonely soul. Too much had happened since: loss rushed in instead.

While the tea steeped, she turned to face the small but cosy room. She really was safe and secure here. She remembered Charlie's words to her about faith and God.

"Julia, if you are open and let him, God will provide for you. He will keep you safe. But if something were to happen, He will be there with you. You will have a home and food. Along the path that is before you, He will bring people to help you. Unexpected people. Strangers. But God will place them there. He can be quite strategic. I have learned that from the life of David. God is the commander of a great army, on earth and in heaven. Be open."

She poured herself a cup. She sat once again and blew a cooling breath across the surface before taking a tentative sip. She picked up the fountain pen and opened the journal to continue where she had left off. The ink blot on the page revealed the anger she had felt.

"Sorry honey, I kinda blew my top for a minute.

I have to say thank you for how you provided for me in the go-bags.

Were you afraid something like this would happen? That gunmen would come in the night? They did and took you away from me. It shattered my world.

You must have had some idea that we would be on the run. Where did you think we could go? Did you have a plan? I wish you could have written it down and put it with the money. It would have helped. Now I am figuring it all out without you.

Oh, I haven't been alone. Do you remember Charlie? The homeless guy in the forest? Well, I went to him that night. He hid me and saved me from the gunmen who killed you. After we left the woods, he took me to his boat. He actually owns and lives on a boat. Not homeless after all.

But now he's gone too. I don't know what has happened to him, but I can only think the worst, as he didn't contact me as planned. That was nearly two months ago now. He did give me a safe place to stay. But I'm isolated and have no one to confide in.

Yes, I found the laptop and papers. I'm still sorting through it all. And Charlie tried to contact a friend in the police to see if he could help. That was a week before we parted ways. I am afraid to pursue it further, especially on my own.

Charlie had God, but I have you. I am not willing to let go of you yet. Part of me still feels you are with me, looking after me. I will wait for a sign, or something, to know what to do next. In the meantime, I am here, my love. I miss you. I love you.

Julia"

Julia put the cap back on the pen and placed the journal aside. She picked up her lukewarm tea and drank it down in one long gulp. Lifting the pen again, she tapped it against her chin and looked around the room. She needed something else to occupy her time. She decided to get out of the cabin. It was time to get out on the water.

She paddled around the small island in the centre of Brentwood Bay. With each dip of the blade, she considered all that she had been doing these last several weeks in the tiny boathouse. Before fleeing from Charlie's boat, she had been at a standstill, not knowing what to do with the information on Hal's laptop. It was time to take action. But what?

CHAPTER 17

J ULIA SAT ON THE END OF THE DOCK, watching the sun sprinkle diamonds on the inlet. She swallowed a piece of the banana bread she had picked up at the market. Her inability to focus on the information on Hal's laptop since arriving at the boathouse was dissipating. She was still afraid when she considered the circumstances that had brought her to her new life of solitude. Up until now, she had tried not to face reality, but she couldn't avoid it any longer. She had come to the conclusion that Charlie was gone; what else could his lack of communication mean? Writing in a journal had helped, as did kayaking. Letter writing brought her closer to Hal; the kayaking to Charlie.

She made her way back up the dock to the boathouse. She placed the cold mug in the sink and picked up the dry sack sitting under the table. She pulled out the laptop. A few coloured pens and a coil-bound notebook she had picked up in the village the day before sat waiting on the window ledge. The flowering plum and cherry trees in the village had helped her turn an emotional corner. Those harbingers of spring and warmer days to come were a sign to her that she needed to leave behind the slump she'd been in since coming to the boathouse.

It was time.

Time to get to work. She was alone and would just have to figure it out. Her resolve gave her strength, and she felt ready to return to the information Hal had left her, despite how frustrating it might prove to be. She and Charlie had discussed the list of names on the laptop before contacting Mike, Charlie's cop friend, but she could start gathering more information on the people involved. She signed in and opened the file containing the document in which Hal explained his theory on how the local human trafficking network operated.

When she read the section on money laundering, it was somewhat confusing to her, so she added that to the research she needed to do at the library. She didn't see the big picture that Hal alluded to. Something was missing. Maybe Hal hadn't had a chance to document more.

She needed more information to understand what Hal had collected before he died. Who were the people named, and how did they all fit into the human trafficking ring? She wrote down some of the names from the folder titled Commercial Businesses into the notebook and left for the library to use the public computers to access the internet.

In the library while reading news articles, one in particular jumped out at her. It outlined how drug traffickers used casinos to launder their money. A few clicks later, she found herself on a Canadian government website that answered the question: what is money laundering? Hal's note started to make more sense.

Once her decision was made, her focus was unshakable for the remainder of the afternoon. Which was good. And bad. She got lost to her surroundings. When the library staff started to make motions to lock up, she looked at the clock on the computer screen and realized she had been here for hours. She had finished collecting data on five of the businesses, then spent time reading news updates for the last hour or so. She was so out of the loop as far as what was happening in the world, she felt lost sometimes. *Isolation does that*, she thought. *I need to visit the library more.*

When she realized she was the only person left and the staff were watching her, her nerves jumped. She didn't want to draw attention to herself. She had to be more careful about being in public. It had been months since her face was in the news, but she couldn't take any chances. She pulled her toque back on, then loaded everything back in her daypack. Standing, Julia wrapped her scarf around the lower part of her face and zipped her jacket, pulling the collar up around her neck. On her way out the main entrance, she kept her face turned away from the librarian behind the check-out desk and stepped out into the darkening sky.

Julia sat in the chair by the door, swallowing the last mouthful of coffee in her mug. She looked out at the dock and the water beyond. She had been reading through her notebook and all the information on businesses she had gathered the day before. Her next task was to do more research on the individuals in each business. That would be the job for her next visit to the library. Should she visit different libraries? How often should she go out in public?

She missed Charlie and wished he was there. He was good at safety planning; he knew what contingencies to consider. She was good at disappearing, name change, different town, but disappearing and staying put was a whole other matter.

When she gathered all this information, then what. Who could she trust?

Her eyes drifted over the small collection of books on the shelf under the window. Amongst the well-read paperback novels was a book titled *The Message*. She set aside her notebook, then bent to take hold of it. It was a Bible. She opened Charlie's book from which he had read a psalm aloud every morning. She found the section captioned "Psalms" and randomly flipped the pages. She stopped at Psalm 91.

> *"You who sit down in the High God's presence,*
> > *spend the night in Shaddai's shadow,*
> *Say this: 'God, you're my refuge.*
> > *I trust in you and I'm safe!'*
> *That's right — he rescues you from hidden traps,*
> > *shields you from deadly hazards.*
> *His huge outstretched arms protect you —*
> > *under them you're perfectly safe;*
> > *his arms fend off all harm.*
> *Fear nothing — not wild wolves in the night,*
> > *not flying arrows in the day,*
> *Not disease that prowls through the darkness,*
> > *not disaster that erupts at high noon.*
> *Even though others succumb all around,*
> > *drop like flies right and left,*
> > *no harm will even graze you.*
> *You'll stand untouched, watch it all from a distance,*
> > *watch the wicked turn into corpses.*
> *Yes, because God's your refuge,*
> > *the High God your very own home,*
> *Evil can't get close to you,*
> > *harm can't get through the door.*

He ordered his angels
to guard you wherever you go.
If you stumble, they'll catch you;
their job is to keep you from falling.
You'll walk unharmed among lions and snakes,
and kick young lions and serpents from the path.
'If you'll hold on to me for dear life,' says God,
'I'll get you out of any trouble.
I'll give you the best of care
if you'll only get to know and trust me.
Call me and I'll answer, be at your side in bad times;
I'll rescue you, then throw you a party.
I'll give you a long life,
give you a long drink of salvation!'"

Julia closed the book. Dare she? She opened it again to the passage she had just read. At the beginning it said, "say this," so she did.

"God, you're my refuge. I trust in you and I'm safe."

She didn't know if she had the right, so she added, "God, I know we've never talked before, and maybe I don't have the right to ask you for help, but I need help. I don't know what to do, where to go, who to turn to with this. Please, help me." Tears streamed down her cheeks and she couldn't think of what else to say. Then she remembered Charlie's closing prayer every morning and added, "All is in your hands and I leave it there."

Julia laid her head against the chair back, covered her eyes with the crook of her arm and continued to cry the first real anguished cry since the morning after watching Charlie being escorted into his boat by two men. It was a flood of anguish that broke her from the depressed stupor she had been in since arriving at the B&B.

CHAPTER 18

JULIA DONNED HER GEAR FOR KAYAKING and got herself on the water. She didn't think about where she was going. She just paddled and found herself back at the small bay where she and Charlie had lunch the first time they kayaked. Pulling into shore, she dragged the kayak up on the beach. She stretched her hips and legs, looking out at the bay. A raven cawed behind her. Bending, she lifted the kayak and walked up the trail to hide it in the dense brush. Before covering the it with boughs, she tucked the paddle, skirt and PFD inside the hull. She walked up the hill to the parking lot for Cole's Bay. She kept walking and followed the road towards Mount Newton.

Julia didn't meet anyone on the trails in the small park that bordered the forest behind the house she and Hal has shared. She left it and walked in the direction of the old access road in the forest. Weeds were growing up through cracks in the pavement. A newly painted sign, showing the boundary of the public park and the forest, marked the end of public access.

She kept walking. She was entering the forest from the opposite side of the mountain to where her house was. She didn't feel she could walk down her street. Even though it had been several months since Hal was murdered, there were a couple of neighbours who were home during the day, and they might recognize her. From this direction she could come in from the back and look at the house from the vantage point Charlie had shown her the night they entered the house. Most likely this was a mistake, but she was missing Hal and longing for home. All she wanted was one glimpse of the place where they had built a life.

When she came to the point in the trail that led her up to Charlie's camp, she stopped for a few minutes. Deciding she didn't need to add that additional grief to her outing today, she kept walking. She was now on the trail that bordered the forest and her house.

The same trail on which she had fled from the gunmen months ago.

She hadn't gone very far when she heard a man's voice followed by a crash in the underbrush and the pounding of feet. She stopped. Coming at her, full gallop, was a giant, grey blur of fur.

She knew what was coming, and she had no means to stop it. But she didn't want to.

She welcomed the nearly 200 pounds of fur in her arms, grateful for the forest trail's soft ground breaking her fall. The wind was knocked out of her, and she was unable to speak. She was flat on her back, a gasping recipient of a fierce series of dog kisses. She heard the man's voice closer, now commanding the dog to stand back.

The dog ignored him.

She put her arms around Aengus as he continued to lick her face, holding her down with one paw on her shoulder. Finally able to breathe, she both laughed and cried at the familiar furry affection of her dog.

"Hello!" a man said in a rich, baritone voice full of surprise. "Until this moment, that dog was the most depressed creature I have ever known."

A shiver of fear ran up her spine as she realized the helpless situation she was in. She knew she wouldn't be able to run. Aengus would prevent her from getting very far. She looked over his shoulder at the man. He stood tall, and broad shoulders filled out his plaid shirt. He looked fit and she doubted she could outrun him either.

Aengus finally allowed her to stand, encouraged by the man pulling on his collar.

Julia put her hand down to push herself up, before pulling it back in pain. She had a cut on her wrist. She ignored the dull throb.

"Are you alright?" The man held out his hand to help her up. "I'm so sorry."

Julia looked from the hand he offered to his face. His eyes showed concern and his brilliant white smile was like a ray of sunshine in the shade of the forest. She noticed for the first time his empty left sleeve. She put her hands into his and allowed him to pull her up to her feet.

"Yes, thanks. I had the wind knocked out of me. But I'm OK now."

He released her right hand, but kept a grip on her left. "Your wrist is bleeding."

"It's a light scratch. I'll be fine. I should get going."

Keeping a firm grip, he turned her wrist over to get a better look. "It's a good jagged cut, most likely from a root. It should be looked after. I don't live far. Please, let me give you some first aid. It's the least I can do as my dog was the cause."

Her body trembled in apprehension. Meeting people could lead to someone recognizing her. As much as she wanted to know how this man had Aengus, she knew she had to leave. Julia tugged on her hand again, this time he released it. "I'll be fine, no need to worry."

She bent to look Aengus in the eyes, touching her forehead to his. "It was nice meeting you, boy," Julia said, her heart breaking all over again. She turned her back on her beloved dog, but he wouldn't leave her side as she tried to back away. "You'd better take his collar."

The man didn't.

"Aengus seems to have made an instant bond with you." As if on cue, Aengus licked her bleeding wrist.

"What can I say? Dogs like me."

"I think he feels bad for hurting you and wants to help."

Julia studied the man more closely; their encounter oddly reminiscent of her first meeting with Charlie on these same trails. There was something familiar about him. And he was still not taking Aengus' collar. Instead he extended his hand towards her.

"I guess I should introduce myself. I'm Lincoln, Lincoln Warren."

"The author?"

"Yes."

"I thought you looked familiar. It must be from your book jackets. I recently read all your books," she said, returning the firm handshake. Knowing he was an old friend of Charlie's, the grip of fear in her chest eased. Only slightly.

"Not all in one sitting I hope?"

"Pretty much," she laughed, feeling more at ease.

"So, you enjoyed them?"

"I did. Very much."

"I'm glad to meet a new fan." He released her hand. "Nice to meet you . . . ?"

"Hallie." This man was Charlie's friend, but could she reveal who she was to him? She couldn't give her real name and couldn't use Charlie's last name either on the spot she decided. "Charles. Hallie Charles."

"Nice to meet you, Hallie. Follow me, and I'll get that wrist fixed up."

"Um . . . You just met me. I could be some crazy stalker fan."

"You see how big my dog is, right?"

Julia laughed.

"It's the least I can do after the tackling he gave you."

"I'm fine, really. No need."

"Well, how about for Aengus' sake. I'd like to keep him this happy for a bit longer."

Julia looked down at Aengus and back into the face of a man that revealed only kindness and concern. "OK." Her acceptance was also due to wanting to get off the trail. If someone from the neighborhood came this way for a walk and spotted her standing with Aengus, they might recognize her, and she couldn't risk it. "Lead the way."

She stepped in behind the man with Aengus at her side. The Irish Wolfhound had a joyous bound in his step and continuously looked to her as they walked. Lincoln started whistling, occasionally looking back to make sure she was still following. Until they left the trail, Julia was content to just follow along, focusing her attention on Aengus.

At the point in the trail where it ran parallel with her house, the tension came back full force when Lincoln turned down to her gate. When he lifted the latch and turned to guide her through, she stood rooted to the spot.

"Is this your house?"

"Yep. The garden backs on to the forest. Very convenient for accessing the park trail system."

Julia felt she would pass out. The trees swirled above her, and the trail fell away. Aengus brought her back to her senses by putting his head under her arm and nudging her. Her world righted, and she hugged him. "Oh Aengus." Julia put her hand on his shoulder, allowing him to lead her home.

CHAPTER 19

Stepping through the french doors leading from the patio to the kitchen, Lincoln held them open for Julia to enter. Closing the door behind her, he kicked off his boots.

Julia whispered her thanks as she removed her shoes and coat. Lincoln took it and laid it on top of some unopened boxes against the windows of the dining area.

"Have a seat and I'll get my first-aid kit."

He returned to find her perched on one of the bar stools at the kitchen island. Aengus was lying on the floor at her feet in such a position she would have difficulty getting off the stool without stepping on him.

"Aengus sure is taken by you. He is practically blocking your escape."

He noticed her face pale, and instead of responding to his statement, she changed the subject. "When did you move in?"

"A little over two months ago." He deposited an assortment of Band-Aids and a tub of salve on the island, then noticed her glance at the disarray of boxes, and he chuckled. "It takes me a while to unpack. Work has been busy. I still need to buy new furniture for the house, and this," he pointed to his empty sleeve, "slows me down somewhat."

"I can't even imagine the challenges."

Lincoln ripped off a couple of sheets of paper towel and laid them on the island. "Not insurmountable with time, ingenuity and the right support tools. That said, we're going to work as a team to get this cut fixed up."

Lincoln reached over to the island sink and turned on the tap. "Here. Rinse the cut off." While she held her wrist under the water, he tore a couple more squares from the paper towel roll and held them out to her. She patted away the congealing blood, gently drying the wound. When the cut showed no signs of continuing to bleed, Lincoln handed her an antiseptic swab. "Looks good. This'll kill any germs."

She took it from him and started dabbing at the cut. Her body tensed and she winced in reaction to the sting. Aengus lifted his head to look at her and Lincoln wondered at the dog's heightened concern, who until now had shown very little interest in anything.

"Interesting."

"What?"

"Aengus is very tuned into your emotions. It's like there's an instant connection."

"Maybe he was stressed from the move and I'm a distraction."

"I'm the one who moved, not him."

Her eyebrows raised. "I don't understand."

"He belonged to the previous owners of the house. I don't know all the details beyond it being a tragic situation and he, unfortunately, was left behind."

Lincoln saw tears well in Julia's eyes. "Hey, it's OK. I was thrilled, actually. I wanted a dog when I bought the house."

Lincoln watched Julia wipe her tears and smile. "I'm glad you found each other," she said, reaching down to pet Aengus. The big dog stood and put his head in her lap.

"Well, he hasn't done that to me yet. To be honest, sometimes I feel like he owns the house instead of me and I'm a squatter he tolerates." She laughed, and Lincoln was glad to see the tears go.

"I'm sure he'll come around."

Lincoln pushed the tub of salve towards her. While she dabbed it on her cut, he picked up a large Band-Aid from the pile. "This should cover that."

"Thanks."

"So, do you live around here?"

"What?"

"Well, he seems to know you." Lincoln was surprised to see fear in Julia's eyes. A "No!" burst out of her. She lowered her gaze. "I'm . . . um . . . I work a couple of days a month cleaning a house nearby, but I would remember meeting him."

"He is kind of hard to forget once you've met him, I'll agree." Lincoln watched Julia as she applied the Band-Aid and added the wrappings to the pile of waste on the square of paper towel. He saw a possible solution to a dilemma that had been developing for him. "Do you have many cleaning clients?"

He watched her squirm in her seat and hesitate before answering. "Um . . . no . . . Just enough to pay the bills at present." She slid off the stool and stepped around Aengus, moving to the French doors to put on her shoes.

"Are you taking on more clients?" Lincoln followed her.

"Um, sure, I guess so. Why, do you know someone?"

"Yes. Me!"

"Seriously?" She stopped tying her shoelaces and stood facing him.

"As a heart attack. I moved from a one-bedroom condo to this," he waved around him indicating the house. "And, I gained him." They both looked at the giant dog standing next to her. "I bought the house because my book collection had outgrown my condo, and I am making a pretty good income from my writing career at long last, so I can afford it. I'm feeling overwhelmed with all the day-to-day tasks of life in a house with a dog on top of my work. I've had cleaning services in the past, but since moving in I've been thinking about hiring someone to help on a daily basis."

Julia bent down to finish tying her laces and Lincoln noticed her hands were shaking. Then her hand was on the doorknob. Something urged him not to let her walk out the door. "Look, don't go. Let me make you a cup of coffee or tea and plead my case."

He could see an inward struggle as she looked at him, outside, then at Aengus. Aengus nudged under her hand on the doorknob. "Even Aengus wants you to stay for a bit longer." Aengus added his two bits with a muffled woof and moved between her and the door, pushing her away from the escape route. "Now, even if you could refuse me, how can you refuse him?"

Lincoln saw Julia visibly relax as she laughed out loud. "True. Who could refuse that face?" She touched her nose to Aengus'.

"Excellent. Coffee or tea?" Lincoln walked back to the island and filled the kettle.

"Tea, please." She kicked off her shoes and walked back over to the island, once again sitting on the bar stool.

"OK, here's my pitch." He plugged in the kettle. "I need a housekeeper and when I travel for work, a dog sitter. I'm a 65-year-old retired soldier. Lost this serving my country." He pointed to where his left arm used to be. "I need help."

"Shouldn't you go through an agency of some sort where they can give you references? I mean you literally just met me in the woods."

"He is the best reference you can get. I trust a dog's instincts without question." He waited for her answer. "Look, with everything I have on my plate, trying to find someone and going through all the interviews, etc . . . Well, it's daunting." The kettle whistled and he turned to make the tea and collect a couple of mugs from the cupboard. "Milk or sugar?"

"No, just black."

"And it would be a live-in position. So, are you interested?"

"It's weird. I don't know you, and to live in . . . " She looked down at Aengus.

"I'm harmless."

"Said the serial killer to his next victim."

"Considering how much that dog seems to like you, I think he'd protect you from anyone, even me. Not that he needs to." Aengus whined and shoved his head under her arm again, almost as if he knew what they were discussing. "I can pay well. And you would have your own private suite, just down the hall from the kitchen. It would seriously be an answer to prayer."

"Yes."

"What?"

"I think I just said yes. I can't really believe that I'm accepting with so little . . . . This would be like an answer to a prayer for me too."

"Yes." Lincoln threw his arm into the air then bent to rough up Aengus' wiry coat. "Did you hear that, boy? She said yes." The dog gave a howl in reply and wagged his tail. Lincoln stood, stretching his hand to Julia. "Thanks. You've made my life so much easier."

"Mine too. You have no idea," she said, putting her hand in his and returning the firm handshake.

"When can you move in?"

"Um, I need to sort some things out where I'm currently staying. I don't have any furniture to speak of so it wouldn't take me long to pack up."

"Well, I'm sure I can help with that. This house came with some furniture and I had my own stuff, so there will be plenty to furnish your quarters. And I have a truck, so whatever you have, I can help you move unless you have a vehicle."

"No, no vehicle. I can carry everything I own. I like to live simply."

"Let me show you the suite. I only gave it a cursory glance when I bought the house, as I was only going to use it for storage if I needed it." They both stood and Aengus picked himself up from the floor to follow. He led Julia back through the kitchen and down the hall towards the entrance to the side suite. "It's roomy," he said as he opened the door. "To the left is the kitchenette and sliding doors that lead to the garden." Lincoln turned to the right. "Through here is the bedroom and en suite." Pointing to the gas fireplace that occupied the wall between the bedroom and the living area, he said, "I'm pretty sure this works, but I'll make sure before you move in."

Their footsteps echoed on the wood floors in the empty space. "That's pretty much it." He watched Julia as she walked into the bedroom and en suite, then came out.

"So, what do you think? You will be separate and have your privacy. Will it work for you?" She didn't answer him and seemed to be lost in thought. "Hallie?"

"Sorry, yes. I think this could work. It's very nice."

"When can you start?" Julia laughed out loud, and he responded with his own chuckle, "Yes, I am desperate."

"Today is Tuesday, so maybe on Thursday or Friday?"

"Excellent."

CHAPTER 20

J ULIA SAT WITH HER BARE FEET dangling over the end of the dock. She shivered as her toes skimmed the water's chilly surface.

Yesterday she had returned the little boathouse to its state before she arrived. As she packed up her bags, grief had come in waves. She had cried herself to sleep.

It was time to move on, do as Charlie asked and figure out how to use the information Hal had gathered. Charlie said to find someone she could trust. She wondered what Charlie would think of her meeting Lincoln and her new living situation.

This morning, after folding the freshly laundered linens, she came to the end of the dock one last time.

The grief of yesterday left with the sunrise and she found herself giddy with a sense of anticipation.

On Tuesday, when Lincoln had said she was an answer to prayer, she was startled. She had prayed that morning, and by the end of the day had found a home and employment. Her first attempt at praying and, bam! An answer beyond imagining.

Tears of joy began to flow, and laughter bubbled out of her as she kicked at the surface of the water, splashing and laughing.

"God, you answered me, you really answered me. Thank you. I want to know you like Charlie knew you. Help me to know you more. I felt you nudge me to say yes to Lincoln yesterday. I trust you in whatever happens next. All is in your hands and I gladly leave it there."

She stood up and returned to the cabin. Her bags waited, but she wanted to go out in the kayak one last time.

Propelled by excitement, she launched into a steady rhythm and headed into the inlet. She would miss the easy access to the water. Being on the water had given her an outlet for the turmoil of emotions she had been living with since Hal's murder.

Back at shore, she rinsed off the kayak, skirt and paddle to remove the saltwater. Stowing the kayak at the side of the cabin, she locked it with a chain. She knew that leaving the kayak here was the only thing to do. The skirt and paddle she stored in the bathroom.

She looked at her pack on the floor and the two extra bags beside it. She had accumulated a few more possessions since coming to the boathouse.

Looking around, she felt Ben and Lisa would be satisfied with how she left the cabin when they returned next month. She walked to the end of the dock, lay on her stomach and returned the key to its hiding place. She would check in on the place at least once a week in Charlie's absence until Ben and Lisa returned. She looked one last time over the calm water of the Saanich Inlet. Shouldering her pack, she picked up the other two bags, then turned to begin the next leg in her journey.

"OK God, it's you and me now."

CHAPTER 21

WHEN JULIA REACHED TO UNLATCH THE GATE, she was glad Lincoln had agreed to allow her to arrive by the back way. Before she even closed it, she could hear an excited Aengus. Lincoln opened the French doors and smiled, stepping out of the wolfhound's way. Aengus spared her the previous tackle, for which she was grateful. He jumped around her as she crossed the lawn.

"Aengus has been watching out the windows every hour since you left on Tuesday. I kept telling him you were coming back, but he still kept the vigil." Lincoln reached out to take Julia's pack and bags as she removed her shoes. "Welcome to your new home."

Julia looked at Lincoln and noticed the hook attached to what remained of his left arm. "Thanks. It's good to be home."

"I've put some furniture in your suite and put some linen in there as well. I'll arrange for whatever you need as time goes on," he said, leading her back through the house. "But for now, this is a start."

Julia followed him down the hall. In the suite, she saw the chaise lounge, table and lamp that used to sit in her corner of the library. A large area rug gave warmth to the room that held little other furniture. Lincoln deposited her pack and bags on the floor inside the door.

"There was a bed in the upstairs master bedroom that I moved out, as I had my own. I won't be filling the guest rooms right away, so I figured it would serve best down here. I moved the rest of the furniture down here too, there are the dressers and side tables. It all fit pretty well. Do you like it?"

Julia looked at him, a bit dumbfounded. "Yes, it's perfect. Thanks. Did you do this by yourself?"

"Nah. I have buddies who work for pizza and beer. I know my limitations."

She was fighting back emotion and her voice had a rough, husky quality. Aengus licked her hand, hanging at her side. She bent to put her arm around his neck and nuzzled his head.

"Well, I'll leave you to make yourself at home. If you'd like to join me for supper, I'm going to order in. We could discuss details of our working arrangement. Chinese, Indian or pizza?"

"Oh, Indian would be wonderful. Please and thanks," Julia said, straightening and giving him a smile. "I haven't had Indian in ages."

"Indian it is then. Meet in the kitchen in about half an hour?"

"Thanks."

"Coming, boy?" Aengus didn't move. "OK, then."

Lincoln left her, closing the door between her suite and the rest of what used to be her house. Aengus was still sitting beside her and she patted his head, happy at the devotion he showed.

"Well, boy, look at us. Back together again." The big hound gave a low woof and turned to occupy the chaise lounge, his great paws hanging over all sides. "Well, you've made yourself at home. Don't you think you should be with your other master? Help me keep up this charade?" Aengus just looked at her.

Julia picked up her backpack, walked into the bedroom and emptied its contents onto the unmade bed. In less than five minutes, she had everything put away. She moved her hand along the top of the dresser and wondered what happened to the framed pictures of her and Hal that used to be there.

She put the backpack on the closet's top shelf. Next, she emptied the two shopping bags and put them with her pack.

"Right, that's me unpacked."

A set of brand-new sheets, still in the packaging, sat on the bed. She looked at the bed she had shared with Hal. As she made it, she realized that her first night here was going to be overwhelmingly bittersweet.

Grabbing the laptop and notes, she turned from the bedroom into the suite's sitting area. The exposure to the outdoors through the sliding glass doors drew her. She put her things down on the counter next to the sink, then she rested her forehead against the glass. She looked down at her stockinged feet. Feeling vulnerable and exposed, she wondered if Lincoln would be open to getting curtains. She and Hal had decided not to have window coverings on the back of the house, not wanting to block out nature. She had discovered over the last months how easily someone could look in.

Surprised by a new onslaught of tears, Julia pushed away from the glass and turned to see Aengus, tail swinging, leaning against her. She put her arms around his shoulders, giving him an affectionate hug before turning to inspect the kitchen.

She opened the cupboards and found a small collection of mismatched dishes. In the drawers, she found an equal amount of cutlery to dishes. On the counter was a tray with a kettle, coffee press, a tin of coffee and tea bags. She bent down and opened the small half fridge and saw a loaf of bread, a litre of milk and some fruit. She closed the door and turned to Aengus.

"Your new master is very considerate, isn't he, fella?"

She looked at her watch and turned to see the wolfhound standing at the door, waiting.

"Hey, boy. Is it supper time?"

Aengus barked and wagged his tail.

Stepping through the archway from the back hall, she rapped on the wall and said, "Knock, knock."

Lincoln placed a paper bag on the island and smiled. "Perfect timing. The food's arrived. I'll feed Aengus if you don't mind laying the table. Plates are in the cupboard right by your head, and the cutlery at your hip."

Julia did as bid and put everything on the table in the breakfast nook. Out of the delivery bag she pulled the containers of Indian food, their delicious aromas causing her to salivate as she placed a serving spoon on each one.

"Would you like a glass of wine?" he asked.

"Yes, please."

"I have a nice crisp Pinot Grigio."

"Sounds great," Julia said. "Wine glasses?"

"In the cupboard next to the fridge. I imagine you'll get used to where things are, as you'll be spending a lot of time in this kitchen. More than me, considering my work and travel schedule. Feel free to rearrange as it suits you. I'm adaptable."

Lincoln bent to scoop from a big bag of dog food and dropped it into Aengus' bowl. The raised feeding station stood next to the door leading to the back yard.

Julia placed the wine glasses on the table. Lincoln poured and they both sat down.

"Thank you for making my suite so comfortable. The dishes and food were very thoughtful."

"You're welcome. You have the basics to make a snack. I expect you to use this kitchen as much as possible. Feel free to make your meals here and eat with me when I'm not nose deep in work or on the road. Consider it your kitchen more than mine. If there's anything else, you just need to let me know."

"Actually, would it be possible to have curtains?"

"Absolutely. I have an online account with anythinghome.com. I'll give you access."

"Thanks."

"Over the next few months, I'll be away frequently for weekends, sometimes for a couple of week-long stretches. I don't expect you to clean the entire house every week. Keep the main parts of the house used on a daily basis clean. Guest rooms only when needed. I don't have a lot of guests, so they will remain unfurnished for now."

After Lincoln cleared the dishes away and poured them another glass of wine, Julia said, "May I ask a question?"

"Shoot."

"Why did you buy such a big house when it's only you?"

"Well, let me show you. Follow me." They walked from the kitchen and into the library. "I own a lot of books, and when I saw this," Lincoln stood in the middle of the library, "I couldn't resist. It holds all my books and I have room to expand my collection."

Julia walked along the built-in bookcases lining the walls and ran her hands along the spines. When she came to the rolling ladder, she stopped and turned to Lincoln. "Wow, there aren't a lot of fiction titles on your shelves."

"Most of my books are history- and military-related, which I have as reference materials for my writing. I do read fiction, but only certain authors."

Julia took note of the room's new layout. Lincoln had a large desk in the bay window at one end which looked out onto the back lawn and up into the forest. The bay window at the other end held a large leather sofa and ottoman, a perfect place to read on a sunny day. In the centre of the room sat another long sofa facing the fireplace and a large library table was behind it, a great spot for laying out books during hours of research. Julia noticed a wingback chair, lamp and round side table right in front of the hidden door. This made her think that Lincoln hadn't discovered it yet. "Compared to the rest of the house, it looks like you've occupied this space for years," Julia said, turning back to him.

"Yes, I couldn't wait to unpack all my books. This is the first time they've been all together in one room. Having them all in one place makes it very easy to grab something when I'm researching. I wasn't a good book organizer. Searching throughout the house on various shelves often proved frustrating." Lincoln grinned, looking at the filled shelves. "Buying this house with this library was more exciting than when I bought my first truck. And I loved that truck."

Julia laughed.

"When I said earlier to not worry about keeping the unused sections of the house clean until needed? It's because I knew keeping this room dusted was going to occupy a large part of your time. That and keeping me fed. When I'm writing, I'm pretty focused and in the past have survived on steak, eggs, fruit and coffee. Easy to make and eat when I'm working on a deadline."

Julia nodded in understanding. "Are you working on a deadline at present?"

"I'm between books. I finished a book tour a couple of months ago, and have been focusing on finding and buying a new home," Lincoln explained. "But my agent is starting to pester me about the next one in the series. Now that this room is operational, I can get started. Can I consider you on the job starting tomorrow?"

"Well, I'm all moved in, so I see no reason not to," Julia answered, smiling, then returned to the kitchen to help Lincoln clean up their supper mess.

The next morning, Julia woke up early. She was not sweating, and her heart was beating at a resting rate. It had been a nightmare-free night. She felt rested and at peace. It was the first dreamless night since Hal was murdered. Relief brought a welling of tears and she threw the covers off and put her feet on the floor. She was expecting the exact opposite.

"God, is this a sign I made the right decision? Thank you."

She found Aengus lying on the hall floor outside her room. "Good morning, boy." She bent and petted him. "I hope you didn't sleep out here all night."

"No, he came down with me this morning. He sleeps on a big cushion in my room. I've already taken him for a walk," Lincoln said, standing just inside the archway to the kitchen. His empty sleeve was folded up under and pinned to the side of his shirt just above his waistband.

Julia rose and walked towards Lincoln; Aengus stood up to follow her. "I'm sorry, I should have been up earlier to put the kettle on and get breakfast started."

"No need to worry about breakfast too much. I usually make a smoothie and have some toast." Lincoln reached to pet Aengus, who had come to stand next to him. "I'm a pretty early riser, a hangover from my military days. I've already fed

Aengus and had my coffee. I usually make it first thing and drink it while he and I walk the neighbourhood. We sometimes go up into the forest."

Julia began making them both something to eat and then started a list of Lincoln's favourite foods while they sat at the table. "You have a pretty good stock of food which should get us through the next couple of days. I'm not someone who overstocks, as I find things don't stay fresh long enough. How would you feel if I arrange an account in your name with one of the grocery stores? I can order online and have it delivered. That way, you don't have to worry about reimbursing me, or me asking for money. It will just save time and make it easier for both of us. I'll do an order twice a week and menu plan accordingly."

"Sounds good to me."

"I'll have an envelope where I'll put all the receipts for anything I purchase for the house."

Thus began the routine they fell into. Lincoln and Aengus would be up at the crack of dawn and out before Julia awoke; she would have a light breakfast made when they got back. Lincoln would then retreat to the library. Julia would occupy her time with housekeeping and meal prep duties.

Two mornings a week, Lincoln would go into town for meetings or other personal errands. It was then that Julia would clean the library. She didn't dare venture into the hidden room yet. The possibility of discovery by an early-returning Lincoln stopped her. Aengus would spend his days either sprawled out on one of the sofas in the library or on the big cushion in the dining room close to Julia, depending on whose company he desired that day, or rather who was worthy of his presence.

Lincoln worked hard on his latest literary endeavour, and Julia kept him well fed and the house in order. It seemed to be working well.

In the evenings, Julia worked on the data on Hal's laptop in the privacy of her suite. Having access to Wi-Fi enabled her to fill out some of the information Hal had gathered. But it wasn't enough. She knew she had reached a dead end as far as making sense of the lists went. Based on her experience working in a law firm, she knew it was time to start gathering evidence. She just had to figure out the best way to go about it.

CHAPTER 22

L INCOLN WALKED INTO THE KITCHEN and lifted the tin foil off the roasted chicken Julia had pulled from the oven.

"My goodness, that smells good. I am going to miss your cooking when I'm away."

"What time do you leave again?" Julia asked, pulling a salad from the fridge and putting it on the table.

"Before light. My flight leaves at 6:00 A.M. The UNAMIR reunion is in Ottawa on the weekend. I'm going to spend some time with old army buddies while I'm there. Then I have a series of meetings for my book in Toronto. I should be back in a couple of weeks."

"What is UNAMIR?"

"United Nations Assistance Mission in Rwanda."

"You were in Rwanda during the genocide?"

"Yes."

Julia realized that Lincoln and Charlie had served together in Rwanda, and the few stories she had heard from Charlie she now attached to Lincoln's military experience.

"I don't know what to say. I've heard stories. I'm sorry you experienced that."

"It is what it is." Lincoln topped up his coffee cup from the press, then popped it into the microwave to reheat.

She realized the books he wrote were more than likely birthed out of that experience. She wanted to ask him more, but knew from her experience with

Charlie that it wasn't something those who survived the mission in Rwanda could easily talk about.

"Will you tell me about your writing?" she asked, as she started to plate their supper.

"What do you want to know?"

Making sure to stay out of Julia's way, Lincoln filled Aengus' dish then sat at the table and stretched his legs out before him.

"Why writing?"

"When I got out of the military, I had a few difficult years. More like decades, really. It was a hard transition from a strict daily schedule to retirement. The trauma of Rwanda certainly didn't help. I had issues. PTSD wasn't really on everyone's radar until more recently. I had been dealing with it for years. I finally got into counselling the last 15 years or so."

"I'm sorry your service led to that." She brought their plates and joined him at the table.

"It was rough for a long time, but I've been doing quite well for the last couple of years. I kept journals all through my service, things I did and saw. My counsellor encouraged me to write down the things I couldn't talk about. It was she who suggested I take a writing class. I used the journals as a source."

"And your protagonist, was he based on someone you served with?"

"A combination of a few."

"And the protagonist's name, Abel Cayne, where did that come from?"

"A friend. We were in Rwanda together. We saw the worst and the best of mankind there. Chuck found God after we got back, and he was the one who suggested the name, based on the two sons of Adam and Eve, one good and one not-so-good. Through our experience on that mission, we saw that man has the capacity for both good and evil. I decided to create the character with that in mind. I actually dedicated my first book to Chuck."

Julia remembered, with a mixture of joy and sadness, that first day on the boat and reading the dedication in Charlie's signed copy.

Lincoln took his empty plate to the counter. "Any chance of seconds?"

"I just so happen to have made extra tonight," she said, laughing. "Help yourself. It's an easy dish to freeze, but at the rate you're going there won't be any leftovers."

"It is part of my plan to keep your cooking skills up by eliminating leftovers."

She laughed. "I'm glad you like my cooking."

"Like? I love your cooking. I am a lucky man to have found you. You've saved me no end of stress and heartburn."

"I'm glad. I'm very lucky too. I'm happy with how it has worked out." Julia started washing her dishes and cleaning up. "I'll most likely get by on toast and soup while you're gone. No sense in going fancy for only me."

When he finished his second helping, Lincoln laid his fork on the empty plate. "Thanks for another fantastic meal. I'm going to take Aengus out for a walk. Would you like to join us?"

Julia still hadn't ventured out when she knew neighbours might be around, not wanting to risk the chance of being recognized, so she declined.

"Hallie, you never seem to go out. Why is that?" Lincoln asked, bringing his empty plate over to the sink.

"I don't know. Looking after you, this house and a giant hound does keep me somewhat busy. And I like my own company," Julia said, shrugging her shoulders. "I'll clean up the kitchen and read in my room tonight. You have a nice walk."

Aengus was waiting by the door, having heard his name and the word "walk." He barked when Lincoln lingered in the kitchen.

"Hallie, I know I pretty much occupy the library when I'm here, but I want you to feel free to use it while I'm gone. Read anything you find that strikes your fancy and sit in there if you like. But I hope you'll get out more. You won't have the same demands on your time, and it would be good for you. Feel free to use the truck anytime you like."

"Thanks. I'll have to take over walking Aengus, so we might venture further afield if I have the truck. He'll miss you when you're gone, so I'll keep him entertained."

"He seems to be more attached to you than he is to me, so I think he'll be just fine." Lincoln bent down to Aengus and gave his neck a great hug. "You won't transfer all your affection, will you boy? We'll still be buds?" Lincoln looked up at Julia. "This is the first time I'll be away for any length of time since getting him."

"I'm sure he'll be fine," Julia said.

"I've booked a taxi for early tomorrow. I'll let him out to do his business, but you'll have to take him for his morning walk."

"Well, it certainly won't be as early as you take him," Julia laughed. "I prefer daylight walks."

"Yes, the nights are still long, but they are shortening." Lincoln put his coffee cup in the top rack of the open dishwasher. In a conspiratorial whisper, he said, "As much as I love summer, I enjoy the dark, rainy months. Don't tell anyone." He laughed. "I call them the writing months. I tend to get more done when the weather is cold and rainy. No sun to pull me outdoors." Lincoln looked at her. "Well, I guess that's it. You'll be in your room when we return from our walk, so I'll say goodnight and I'll see you when I get back."

"Goodnight Lincoln, and safe travels. I hope all goes well," Julia said.

Lincoln left the kitchen and made his way to the front door, donned his jacket and grabbed Aengus' lead, the big dog on his heel. Julia put away the last of the dishes. She turned out the kitchen light and left the door to her suite ajar so Aengus could come in when Lincoln left.

The next morning, Julia woke up to a dog panting in her face as Aengus looked at her. "Ugh! Aengus." He put his nose under her hand resting on the pillow next to her face. "Do you need to go out, boy? OK."

In Lincoln's absence, Julia created a new morning routine. One thing did not change from that first morning: she still woke up to hot, smelly breath from Aengus panting in her face.

She would let him out into the back yard from the kitchen. She would then fill his dish while the coffee was brewing. Once Aengus was back in and happily eating his breakfast, she would sit down with her coffee and pick up the Bible she had brought with her from the B&B. She started from the beginning of the Psalms and, following Charlie's example, read aloud. One psalm each morning, after which she would write her thoughts down in her journal.

Later in the morning, once all the neighbours were at work for the day, she ventured out. She stayed in the forest at first, nervous to go too far. She wasn't sure if anyone in the neighbourhood would recognize her from before. The forest was safer. After the first week, she decided to take Aengus further afield. From the hidden cave of the garage, she loaded him into the truck and drove to remote beaches and fields where she hopefully wouldn't run into any familiar faces.

CHAPTER 23

THE SECOND AFTERNOON AFTER LINCOLN LEFT, Julia dared to access the hidden room in the library. She moved the chair, table and lamp allowing her to reach the cornice piece that would open the latch. She pushed the section of shelving, reached in and turned on the lights. The room smelled like old books and dust. Fresh air entered for the first time since she and Charlie had hidden there all those months ago. She reached up, took a couple of books down and put them on the chair to read.

"God, thank you. This part of my life is still intact."

Her main goal, though, was the pile of papers under which she and Charlie found the laptop. She was hoping there might be more information giving clarity to what was on the laptop. Taking the untidy pile, Julia brought them out to the table and started to sort them. Her hope was not in vain. Among them were further lists of names and dates. Julia figured Hal had not had time to enter them into the laptop.

When comparing all the lists, Julia came up with three identifiable groups of names. One included birth dates, making names of children the first pile. Ministry officials made up the second. Members of law enforcement were in the last group. With the exception of the list of children, they all had dates of service linked to their respective government agencies.

A fourth group of names was only half a page in length. She didn't recognize any of them. No dates or further notations gave Julia any indication of their connection. She didn't know the importance of those names or whether the list was complete.

Julia focused on trying to connect the information on the laptop with these new lists.

Needing a break from the hours of concentration, Julia wandered along the library shelves to further investigate Lincoln's book collection. On one section of shelving, she found a collection of books on the Rwandan conflict and genocide. She pulled down Shake Hands with the Devil, a book Charlie had mentioned she should read. In the late afternoon, she left the library to feed herself and Aengus and to let him out in the yard for a break. Once the kitchen was clean, she returned to the cosiness of the library for the rest of the evening.

She closed the book at midnight, overwhelmed with sadness for what both Charlie and Lincoln were a witness to. No wonder Charlie had lost faith in his fellow man. The atrocities she read about were beyond her comprehension. They were not the acts of men, but those of soulless monsters. She couldn't help but reflect on Hal's research. The perpetrators of human trafficking were not men with consciences either.

Julia pulled up the hood of her jacket and dashed from the stationery store to Lincoln's truck. For the past week, the rain had poured down more like winter than spring. However, Julia was grateful for the poor weather, as it created the circumstances in which she could hide in public with her hood up and head down. She tossed her bag of supplies onto the passenger seat and hopped into the truck, slamming the door.

She had a plan to create a wall collage of names and dates like they used to do in the boardroom of the law firm when they were working on a big case with lots of players involved. Creating a visual might help with understanding what she was working with. The shopping bag she put behind the seat contained paper, pens, markers and a thumb drive. The thumb drive was to ensure there was another copy, which she would hide in the library's secret room. She couldn't risk losing any of the information Hal had gathered and anything further she could add.

When she pulled the truck into the garage, she hit the remote to close the door behind her. She hung her raincoat on the hook, next to a treadmill Lincoln had installed beside a rack of weights. She stopped. She had gained some weight over the last few months. She wasn't as fit as she once was and wasn't sure she could escape like she could before. She decided to add a fitness regime to her daily routine. Time to lose the excess weight in her body and mind and focus on what she needed to do.

The next morning, Julia walked out of her bedroom and looked at the papers strewn across the floor of her private living room. It wasn't easy keeping them organized with a hairy beast sprawling out in the same space, but she dared not venture with them into the rest of the house. Aengus stood by her sliding doors, waiting to be let out into the yard.

She closed the door after him, not wanting to let the early-morning chill into the room. *At least the rain has let up*, she thought.

The doorbell rang.

Julia panicked. She saw the papers spread out and started gathering them to hide them away.

The doorbell rang again. Frantically, she shoved them into the fridge-freezer. Then, glad Aengus was sniffing the plants at the far end of the garden and unaware of the doorbell, she cautiously ventured into the main floor of the house.

A third chime of the doorbell.

She looked through the security peephole and saw the delivery man from the organic produce store. He was supposed to leave the bin and take the empty. She saw the empty sitting inside the door and cursed herself for forgetting to put it out the night before. She pressed against the door and waited, the guy didn't ring the bell again and left the full bin on the porch.

Relief allowed her to peel herself off the door. She waited until she heard the truck leave, then opened the door and brought in the lidded plastic bin.

She was getting too relaxed. Too at ease in her old house. What made her think she was safe? She wasn't before, so she had no reason to think she was now. It was time to step up her personal awareness and security.

She put the produce away and let Aengus in, wiped off his muddy paws and went in search of her discarded go-bag. Time to get back to a level of preparedness. She made a list of everything she needed to replace and counted her money to see how much she had left. Then, following Charlie's example, she decided she needed to make a plan in case she had to flee again. She was alone in the house, she thought, with only a dog for protection. She looked at Aengus, who sat nearby watching her. He must have sensed her unease. She reached out her hand and he walked to her and licked her face.

"Well, boy. I guess if I had to be here on my own with just a dog, you are the perfect one to protect me. Just your size would scare off most." She hugged his neck and then rose to take him for a ride in the truck and a long walk on a deserted beach. The fresh air would do them both good and help her devise an escape plan in case she needed it in Lincoln's absence.

CHAPTER 24

TWO DAYS BEFORE LINCOLN'S RETURN, the rain persisted. Julia came in from the garage with a towel around her neck to dry the perspiration from her workout. She walked into her suite and stood for a moment to peruse her handiwork. Hidden on the wall behind the door to her suite, Julia had a visual info-spread that would make any of her law colleagues proud. Using flip-chart paper, she had created three columns. Each represented one of the folders on the laptop: Names of Government Agencies; Names of Private Individuals; and Commercial Businesses.

Under each heading she used smaller sheets of paper to add names to each column. She wrote profiles on the companies and individuals on these pages. A separate sheet per name would allow her to shuffle them around later.

She put the names from the list unassociated to any category to the side for now. She decided a prayer was in order. "OK, God. I need you to guide me in this."

On the laptop, she opened the folder containing the document in which Hal outlined his theory. The folder also contained what appeared to be information gathered from different sources based on a bibliography-type document that Hal had included. The resources were mostly from the internet and, considering the document's page count, the web had plenty to offer. Julia had previously skimmed over the notes about what human trafficking was, but had focused mainly on the lists of names and organizations.

It was time to educate herself.

She spent the remaining hours of Lincoln's absence on the minute details of this one main folder, grateful for the ready access she now had to the internet.

She typed in the question: What is human trafficking? The internet had a lot of answers. After a few hours of reading various websites and articles, Julia came up with a working definition. There are three elements of human trafficking: an act, the means and the purpose. A trafficker commits at least one act against another person, by using at least one means, for the purpose of exploiting that other person for financial gain or material benefit.

Julia made a table on a fourth piece of flipchart paper for a visual reference when creating a human trafficking résumé of various names Hal had given her.

ACTS + MEANS + PURPOSE = HUMAN TRAFFICKING

ACTS	MEANS	PURPOSE
Recruit	Violence	Sexual exploitation
Transport	Threat of violence	Forced labour
Transfer	Coercion	Slavery/servitude
Harbour	Abduction	Organ removal
Receive	Fraud	
Give/receive benefit	Deception	
Control	Abuse of power or position of vulnerability	

Julia stood back and looked at the makeshift corkboard the wall in her suite had become.

It was a start.

CHAPTER 25

L INCOLN DOUBLE-CHECKED HIS BANK STATEMENTS; Hallie had not cashed any of the cheques he had given to her for wages. *Odd*, he thought. For the first time, he began to wonder about the woman he had hired to live in his house. He had been so happy to find a solution to the problem of house and dog when he travelled, he didn't do the normal due diligence of an employer. Not smart.

He closed out of his online bank account and opened Facebook. In the search bar, he typed in "Hallie Charles." There were three, but none of the pictures matched the woman in his house.

According to LinkedIn, there was no profile attached to the name of "Hallie Charles."

He rocked back in his chair and considered other options. He then typed her name into Google. What came up was a list of ancestry.com links to a number of obituaries for Hallie Charles. Most born over 100 years ago.

He went in search of Hallie.

Lincoln found her cleaning up the breakfast dishes. "Hallie, when you're done, can you come into the library please?"

"Sure."

Fifteen minutes later, she knocked on the door frame of the entrance to the library.

"Have I done something wrong?"

"Have a seat."

Lincoln pulled a spare chair over to his desk.

Lincoln studied Hallie. She sat, back straight and hands clutched in her lap. He noted the tension in her face.

"I've been going through my bank statements. You haven't cashed any of the cheques I've given you for your wages."

"Oh. No, I guess I haven't. I haven't had time. I put them on my dresser and forgot about them."

Lincoln wasn't convinced. "What have you been doing for money?"

"Considering room and board are part of the compensation for my work here, I haven't really needed any cash."

"You don't go out; you don't have friends that I have seen."

"Thus, I don't need much spending money."

Lincoln paused. He was interrogating her and it didn't sit right with him. Maybe there was something else he should be asking.

"Hallie, are you in trouble?"

"What makes you ask that?"

"Well, besides not going out and meeting friends, you only take Aengus for walks in the forest. You don't have a cellphone that I've seen." Lincoln softened his voice. "Hallie, is there an abusive husband or boyfriend you're running from?"

"What? Um . . . no."

"I'm sorry, I don't mean to pry. I want you to know I'll help you in any way I can. Just ask."

"I appreciate your concern. If I need anything, I will come to you," she said, as she stood to leave. "Is there anything else?"

Lincoln sat back in his chair, looking at her. He sensed something wasn't right. But she wasn't ready to trust him.

"No."

He watched her turn and leave the library.

Two mornings later, Lincoln was out for his morning walk with Aengus when Julia entered the kitchen. She found an envelope with "HALLIE" written on it sitting on the counter. It contained cash and a note from Lincoln.

"Dear Hallie,

Please accept the enclosed cash sum equating your salary for three months. I have cancelled all cheques I had given you. No questions asked. I am here if you need anything further.

L"

Julia counted out the cash then read the note again. No questions asked. She knew there would come a time that she would have to answer questions, even if they were not asked. For now, she would take Lincoln at his word. She returned to her suite. She removed the cash from the envelope and replaced it with the cheques. She wrote on the envelope, "Thanks. Hallie."

She added her wages to her hidden stash of cash. In the library, she placed the envelope on Lincoln's desk.

She felt some relief from the tension that had been between them in the two days since Lincoln had confronted her about the cheques. It affected her sense of security living there. She had feared she might have to leave.

Lincoln opened the door leading to the back garden, Aengus burst in and immediately came to Julia. She bent and hugged his neck. He was warm from his walk in the forest. Despite her reawakened fears, his furry affection reminded her of what she had here: safety and love.

Could she leave Aengus again? She looked up at Lincoln, who was removing his boots. Despite his questions, Lincoln wanted to help her no matter what. She prayed she could continue to trust him. For now, she felt secure enough to stay.

CHAPTER 26

I T TOOK A FEW WEEKS, but their easy camaraderie did return. Lincoln couldn't shake the feeling there was something wrong, but until Julia opened up to him, he wasn't going to press her. He was glad they'd returned to their regular routine. He was planning a trip, and at breakfast one morning he gave her the heads-up.

"In July I'll be going to Alberta to visit some friends for a holiday. A bit of a break before starting the next book."

"Do you have another story in mind?"

"Not yet. I'm not sure what direction I want to go next. I've been considering doing an off-shoot series from one of the characters in Abel Cayne's world."

"I can't imagine coming up with an idea and then writing it in a coherent story. I guess I'm not creative in that way. I used to draw and paint with watercolours. I haven't done it in a while."

"Similar process, but instead of paint or ink, I use words. The same components that go into creating a picture go into telling a story." Lincoln looked at her. "We use different artistic instruments, that's all."

"I suppose you're right."

"Spring blossoms will be gone before you know it. Maybe it's time to get out there and capture it."

"Maybe I will."

Looking at her, Lincoln got an idea to get Hallie out of the house. He had a plan, but first — back to the business at hand.

"Well, I'd best get back at it. I have a few more calls to make."

❖

Julia heard Lincoln leave the house. Aengus nosed his way into her suite through the door she kept ajar for him. He circled twice and then sprawled out on the area rug.

"Well, hello to you too," she said. "Did Lincoln abandon you for the afternoon, fella?" Aengus looked at her through his bushy brow without lifting his head. He thumped his tail on the floor.

Julia chuckled and went back to her work on the spreadsheet on the wall.

She refocused on the computer screen open before her on the table. She had created a phony online identity and email for research purposes. She signed into LinkedIn and created an account, which would help her search for more information on the various individuals on her list. She looked at the names she had.

Choosing one, she typed, "B-R-A-D-F-O-R-D M-E-E-K"

Over the next couple of hours, Julia added to her notebook and wrote more on the wallcharts.

❖

She was updating a page on Bradford Meek when Lincoln returned. Aengus jumped up and Julia looked at her watch.

"I guess it's time to start getting supper ready, aye fella?" Julia ruffled Aengus' wiry fur. She followed him through the door.

She entered the hallway as Lincoln was coming into the house from the garage. Closing her door behind her, "Hello," she said. "I'm going to get started on supper."

"Excellent, I'll meet you in the kitchen."

Julia, focused on the task at hand, didn't hear Lincoln come into the room, and turned to see him standing on the opposite side of the island. Between them sat a box.

"Hi, what's this?" she said, looking at him over the top.

"I decided that you have been doing such an amazing job and, in turn, you've enabled me to better focus on my work. I have implemented a bonus into our work contract," Lincoln said, putting his hand and hook on the top of the box.

"You pay me well, it isn't necessary," Julia said, feeling a bit awkward.

"Nonsense. Please accept this with my gratitude. Here . . . " he said, pushing the box towards her with an excited gleam in his eye and a grin that stretched from ear to ear.

Julia stepped forward and opened the top of the box with a knife from the butcher block. Folding the flaps back, she removed the crumpled filler paper and looked in. She lifted out a complete watercolour kit. The highest quality available. "Oh, Lincoln." Next came a palette with enough wells to mix up to six batches of paint. Julia began to get excited as she pulled out more items. Brushes, pads of paper and pencils. When she had it all spread out on the island, Lincoln took the box away and placed it on the floor.

"Wow, this is amazing. I'm speechless." She looked up at him. "Thank you so much."

"You're welcome. You've been so busy around here looking after Aengus and me, and I wanted to show my appreciation. I figured I'd get you all stocked up. You could take some time while I'm away and get back into drawing and painting." He smiled at Julia's shocked silence.

"I will," Julia said, as she started to gather the supplies to take them to her room. Lincoln retrieved the box and helped her load it again. When they had cleared everything, he closed the flaps of the box and pushed it towards her.

"Thank you again. I'll put these away and finish getting supper on," Julia said.

"I'll be working in the library."

❖

That night after supper, Julia stood in her suite, the box of art supplies open on the table. She once again pulled out the items and separated what she wanted to use that night from what she would use later. She would organize them tomorrow or the next day. Tonight, she wanted to sit with pad and pencils and see how rusty she was. For the next few hours, Julia drew and drew and drew. She drew everything she could see, a mishmash of odd collected items from around her suite. She was working old muscles of putting what she saw onto paper.

The first sketches were rough and ill-proportioned. The more she worked, the better she could deactivate the part of her brain that dictated what it knew. She struggled to ignore her mind's preconceived image. But as she continued to draw, the more it allowed her brain to translate what she saw before her to her hand.

It felt good to spend a couple of hours in sheer creativity. No spreadsheets, no puzzles and no worries. She was a creative being again and it felt good, freeing. When she finally put aside the pad and pencils for the night, she had filled a few pages. Bits and pieces of drawings, some finished, some outlines or shadows. She went to bed and slept. It was a night with fewer dreams of gunmen and fleeing through the forest.

CHAPTER 27

D URING LINCOLN'S TRIP TO ALBERTA, Julia continued to work on the puzzle of information and names, but this time she had a pleasant way to break up her task. She took her art supplies with her on walks with Aengus. Spending time drawing and painting gave her a new sense of solace.

By the time Lincoln returned at the end of July, the spreadsheet on her wall contained every scrap of information Julia could gather. She had been able to collect background data on companies and connect some of the names. She knew it wasn't complete, but it was all she could do. She had also added another chart on how organized crime used money laundering. This chart hung next to the human trafficking breakdown equation.

A package wrapped in plain blue tissue paper sat on the kitchen table as a welcome home present for Lincoln. When he came into the kitchen, he saw it immediately. Smiling, he asked, "For me?"

Julia nodded.

He tore into it, leaving the tissue paper in a heap on the table. The package contained a watercolour of Aengus she had painted.

"Hallie, this is amazing. Thank you. You are very talented."

"You're welcome."

"I have something for you."

From his luggage sitting on the floor inside the garage door, Lincoln retrieved a package wrapped in brown paper.

"I was walking one afternoon in Calgary and passed by an art supply store. This was in the window and I thought of you," he explained as Julia ripped open the package. In it was a messenger bag designed to carry enough art supplies for a day's outing.

"It's perfect," she said, opening the flap and noting the slots and notches for pencils and brushes. "Thank you."

"You're welcome. Now, I'm going to sit here at the table while you cook. I'll tell you about some of the amazing veterans I met while I open my mail."

He sat in the breakfast nook. The watercolour of Aengus was propped against a vase of flowers from the garden. He attacked the pile of mail, using his hook like a letter opener. He discarded the destroyed envelopes and junk mail into a paper bag at his feet for recycling later. Aengus rattled it with the odd swing of his tail when Lincoln got animated in his storytelling.

During the tale of a particularly enthusiastic fan, Lincoln stopped mid-sentence causing her to look up from stirring a pot.

"Is everything alright?" she asked when she saw the distressed look on his face.

"No. A friend has died."

"Oh, Lincoln, I'm so sorry." Julia came around the kitchen island with a cup of coffee for each of them and sat across from him at the table.

"I'm his executor. I haven't seen him since before Christmas."

"How did you know him?"

"He was an old army buddy. We served in Rwanda together." Lincoln focused on the papers from the large FedEx envelope. "These documents are from his solicitor." He looked at the envelope. "It was delayed getting to me because of my move. I should have had this months ago."

Julia had been lifting her mug to take a sip, but stopped with the cup halfway to her mouth. Her hand started to shake.

"He didn't own much," Lincoln summarized. "In addition to his bank account, there's only a truck and a sailing boat for me to . . . "

Julia's heart stopped. She whispered, "What was your friend's name?" He didn't look up as he replied, "Charles Sebastian. Chuck, to me."

Julia lost her grip on the coffee cup. It crashed on the floor, spilling its contents. Aengus jumped to his feet to get out of the way.

"Hallie?"

Her hands were shaking. She didn't hear Lincoln's voice, but she saw the mug and spilled coffee.

"I'm so clumsy. Let me get a cloth." She couldn't get up; her legs were jelly.

"Hallie, what's wrong? Hallie?"

Julia felt a warmth on her shoulder. Gradually, she became aware of Lincoln's presence. Aengus was trying to get her attention by putting his nose under her arm.

"How did he die?" Her words were barely audible.

Lincoln looked at the papers. "It doesn't say. It gives a date of death, no cause."

"What is the date?" Julia asked, still not explaining her reaction.

"Let's see." Lincoln flipped through the papers. "January 27."

"Oh, Charlie," Julia cried and covered her face with her hands. She began to weep.

"Hallie, please talk to me. Did you know Chuck?"

"Yes. And I'm the one who got him killed."

"What do you mean? How could you have gotten him killed?" When she didn't answer, Lincoln gave her shoulder a gentle shake. "Hallie, talk to me. How did you know Chuck?"

"He . . . was helping me."

"In what way?"

"I'm afraid if I tell you, you too might be in danger." Julia sobbed into her hands, "Charlie, I'm so sorry." She looked up at Lincoln. "When I didn't hear from him . . . " She couldn't continue.

Lincoln went into the library. He returned with a glass containing a finger of amber liquid. "Drink this. Don't sip, swallow it down all at once." Julia did as asked, coughing in reaction, then alert from the bracing shot of alcohol.

"Ew, what is that?" Julia handed him the empty glass.

"Whisky. It's usually good for a jolt to the system, and you needed one." He took the empty glass from her and put it on the kitchen island. Taking her hand, he led her around the broken pieces of mug on the floor and towards the library.

Lincoln sat next to Julia on the couch. Aengus followed them in and lay down at their feet, watching intently.

"Now, take a deep breath and start from the beginning."

Julia still hesitated, not out of fear for herself, but for Lincoln. She didn't want to be responsible for another human life.

"Look, I have money and means to keep you safe, so spill. If you were a friend of Chuck's, then you are a friend of mine. Please Hallie, trust me."

Julia looked at Lincoln. In that moment, she felt a sense of peace flood over her. Hadn't she prayed for someone to trust? Lincoln was the answer to that prayer. God had heard her.

"OK," she said, clearing her throat which was still rough from the whisky. "But

I want to ask you a couple questions first."

"Go ahead," Lincoln nodded, sitting back against the arm of the couch.

"When was the last time you saw Charlie?" Julia asked.

"Early December. I stopped in a pub in Sidney to see him and gave him a copy of my book."

"I'll be right back." Julia went to her suite and retrieved the book and her wallet. Returning to the room, she said, "He gave me this book for Christmas last year." She handed it to Lincoln. "Read the inscription."

"This is made out to Julia. I remember signing it. I guessed Charlie . . . wait. How do you have it?"

"I'm Julia."

"Chuck said it was for a friend going through a rough time. Quite the coincidence that we met." He handed the book back to her and she placed it on the side table.

"Oh, you have no idea." Julia saw the puzzled look on Lincoln's face. She opened her wallet, withdrew her driver's license and handed it to him. "To prove it is really my name."

Lincoln gave it a cursory glance, putting name to face then handed it back. Julia didn't take it. "Check out the address on the license."

Lincoln read more closely, then said, "But this is my address."

Julia could see the wheels working in his mind and waited.

"Chuck told me about this house that day in the pub. I was on my way to meet my realtor."

Lincoln sat up straight, and Julia waited for him to make the connection. "So, Chuck was helping you at that time?"

"Yes."

"What happened, and how did Chuck get involved?"

"I'll first tell you how I met Charlie, which will explain how he got involved. My husband Hal and I designed and built this house. While Hal was busy with work, I oversaw the contractors and building. I was walking in the forest one afternoon and I met Charlie on the trail. He said I surprised him. Of course, I didn't have Aengus with me that day."

"Wait, you surprised Chuck . . . in the woods. That's almost unbelievable, he was an incredible woodsman," Lincoln said.

"I know. You should have seen the look on his face." Julia smiled, remembering that day. "It became a game after that. I'd go for walks at different hours to see if I could surprise him again. I don't think I ever did. At first, we just nodded and passed each other. Eventually, because we happened to meet fairly frequently, we started walking and talking. It was nice. He even showed me his little camp up in the forest."

"Showing me his camp saved my life. At the end of August last year, Hal and I spent a week in Hawaii. The night we returned, I was up in our bedroom unpacking our suitcases, when I heard something and came out to the landing. What I saw was a man with a gun standing over Hal's body. When he was distracted by another man in the library, I managed to escape. But it didn't take long for them to start searching for me. They chased me into the forest. While I was hiding in Charlie's camp, he had an encounter with the gunmen. I couldn't hear everything, but he managed to convince them he hadn't seen me."

Julia lay back on the couch and focused on the painting over the fireplace mantel while deciding how much to tell Lincoln about that night. "To make a long story short, those men killed Hal and made it look like I did it. Maybe because I was supposed to die as well."

"The next day, my face was plastered all over the news and in the paper. The same afternoon, Charlie took me to his boat and passed me off as his niece, 'Hallie,' who was visiting from back east."

"Which is why you introduced yourself as Hallie when we met. So, you are on the run."

"Yes."

"From the police, and obviously someone else. Which explains why you didn't or couldn't cash the cheques I wrote you. There's obviously more, but right now I need a drink." Lincoln went to pour himself a whisky.

Julia watched as he stepped over Aengus. He pulled the top from the glass decanter and it chinked as he lay it on the metal tray. He splashed some into two glasses. Once again stepping over Aengus, he held them out and Julia took one. He sat with his back against the arm of the couch, facing her, lifted his glass in salute and took a big swallow.

She mirrored him.

"OK, ready," he said. "Continue. But don't make the long story short. Give me details."

Julia went on to tell Lincoln about the night she had fled into the woods. The gunmen, Charlie hiding her in the dugout and the news he brought back from observing events on her street the next morning.

"That's when we found out they suspected me." Julia felt the fear and despair she had experienced that night wash over her. "Charlie suggested we wait to find out more before coming out of hiding. Now, Charlie's dead and I'm still hiding."

"Wow."

"Several weeks after that night, I convinced Charlie to come back here. I wanted to get something from the house. Did you find the safe in the master bedroom?" Julia asked.

"Yes, I did. When I moved your bed into the spare room to allow me to move mine in." Lincoln looked at her. "At the time, I thought it was an unusual place for a safe. Later, I realized it was quite clever; no one would think to look there. I haven't used it, not knowing the combination. I've been too busy to have it replaced. Looks like I won't need to now."

Julia smiled faintly. "Yes, I'll give you the combination. That night, while still in the house, we were almost caught by the security company. They had installed a motion sensor for a silent alarm at the French doors in the dining room. Unknowingly, we triggered it."

"Good thing you got out. Getting caught would have been a shame."

Julia hesitated, but decided to come clean on everything. She had nothing to lose and she needed help. "We didn't get out."

"And the security man didn't see you? Remind me not to hire that company."

"We hid in this room, actually."

"But there's nowhere to hide." Lincoln looked around the room.

Julia smiled sadly, "There's a secret room; it was Hal's idea."

"You're kidding me." Lincoln looked at her dumbfounded. "Here, in this library?"

"Yep. I was relieved when I realized you hadn't discovered it."

"You mean to tell me you've accessed this room since you've been here, working for me?"

"Yes, but not while you've been in the house; when you were travelling," Julia answered. "I was too afraid you'd return and catch me. Now that you know about it, see if you can find it," Julia challenged, relaxing into the couch and taking another sip of her whisky.

Without a word, Lincoln stepped over a sprawled Aengus to stand in the centre of the room. He put his glass on the table and turned in a circle, first away from the wall that contained the fireplace to face the opposite wall.

"My guess is that it's on that side of the library. There's no unexplained wall space between the foyer with this room." Lincoln looked to Julia for confirmation and she nodded.

Starting at the end of the wall where Julia sat on the couch, he moved along the shelves for a closer inspection.

"I spent hours organizing my books on these shelves. I can't believe I didn't notice anything." Julia watched as he pushed and pulled some of the woodwork.

"I give up." He turned to her from the other end of the wall. He had gone over it several times.

"If I had a cruel streak, I would drag this out," Julia said, rising from the couch and placing her whisky glass on the side table. Aengus got up with her, curious at the sudden activity. She pulled the small side chair into the centre of the room. Lincoln helped by moving the table and lamp. Julia smiled. "Ready?" she asked.

"Yes." Lincoln motioned for her to get on with it.

"It's a two-part mechanism. You have to push in with your toe here."

Julia put her toe against a small panel of the baseboard next to the electrical outlet.

"Then you push on this cornice piece like this."

Doing so, a section of the library shelving popped outward.

"If you don't push on both at the same time, you won't trip the mechanism. Making it impossible to discover by accident." Julia stepped into the chamber with Lincoln on her heels. She flipped the switch that turned on the rope lighting, giving the space a warm glow. She sat in the chair in the far corner and smiled up at Lincoln. "So, what do you think?"

"I have no words."

She watched Lincoln as he investigated.

"What are these?"

"Hal and my private collection of rare and priceless books. It was a passion of ours. We'd both been collecting for years."

Julia looked up at the shelves. This secret space, once belonging to her and Hal alone, seemed steeped in a dream, a dream rapidly losing ground to reality. But, in the worn and weathered manuscripts, allies remained. Every book held an association with Hal. Even if the house were no longer hers, she would always have the books. Julia felt loss overwhelm her and she stood.

She choked out the words, "I need to start supper."

Lincoln led the way out. Julia turned off the lights and pushed the shelf closed behind them. She felt the mechanism click into its locked position. As she turned, he stood blocking her path to the kitchen.

"Julia, as long as you live in this house, I will not enter that space again."

"That's sweet of you Lincoln, but not necessary. You freely let me use your library. I want you to have the same freedom to explore mine." Julia offered, raw emotion evident in her voice.

"I appreciate your generosity in light of how much you've lost."

Julia nodded, emotion robbing her of the ability to form words. A tear escaped to run down her cheek. She left the library.

During supper, Lincoln studied Julia. She seemed to have regained her emotional stability. He wondered if she had told him everything.

He closed the door on the dishwasher and finished wiping the counter. When he hung the dishrag over the faucet, he was about to ask if there was anything else she needed to tell him, but she spoke before he voiced his question.

"The night that Charlie and I hid from the security guard, we found something."

"What was it?"

"A laptop. It took weeks before I got past the password protection. I almost wish I hadn't."

"What did you find?"

"Follow me." Julia led Lincoln down the hall towards her suite, with Aengus wandering behind them. She showed Lincoln her research wall.

"Hal had somehow got involved in, or uncovered, a human trafficking network in the city. His notes were on the computer."

"So, you think someone became suspicious of Hal and killed him?"

"Yes, this is what got Hal and Charlie killed. I've been trying to put it all together since I've been here. It has been my project in the evenings while you are away." Lincoln watched as Julia touched various pages of names and dates on the wall mosaic. "I've been trying to puzzle all the pieces Hal left behind. But I've reached a dead end."

"Julia, this is . . . horrifying and dangerous." Lincoln looked at her, rubbing his hand over his bald pate. "What are you going to do?"

"I don't know. I am terrified. There is so much missing, and it lacks connections. I'm not sure how useful it would be at this point if I went to the authorities." Julia crossed her arms, feeling a little chill. "I think it would look like a crazy conspiracy theory that I cooked up while on the run and I'd only end up in jail anyway. To make a tragic story worse, Charlie contacted a cop friend with some of this information and a few days later I was alone running for my life. This time with no one to run to."

"How did you get away?"

"Charlie, again. He devised a plan to get me away from the boat if he felt I was in danger."

Julia explained the plan Charlie had laid out, how she got out of the boat and into the kayak. "I was sitting on the water waiting, when I saw two men escort Charlie onto his boat. That's the last time I saw him. When he didn't contact me in a week's time, I feared the worst. And now the worst has been confirmed. I had been staying in a B&B he told me I could use to be safe. Two months later, I met you and Aengus in the forest."

"Wow!" Lincoln crouched down to pet Aengus as Julia sat on the chaise lounge.

"Have you clued into the weirdest connection of all?"

"What's that?"

"Aengus," Julia said.

"Aengus?"

"He was my and Hal's dog."

"Of course." He looked from Aengus up to Julia. "Nick told me Aengus belonged to the previous owners. So, he wasn't being friendly to a stranger. He found you after losing you."

"Can you tell me the long version of how you came to have him?"

"Shortly after I moved in, he showed up at the front door. I was going out for a walk and nearly tripped over him. When I opened the door, he just pushed his way in. After searching in every room of the house, he lay down in the library in front of the fireplace. The following morning, Nick Keegan came by asking if I'd seen a big Irish Wolfhound. He took him away that time, but after a couple of repeats, we formed a plan. If Aengus came back one more time, he'd let me keep him."

Julia sat down and wept. Aengus got up from the floor where Lincoln was petting him and put his head under Julia's arm. She put her arms around his neck.

"Looks like we both found our way home, aye boy?" Julia took a couple of gulps of air and wiped her cheeks.

"Sorry, not my home anymore." She looked at Lincoln as she released her grip on Aengus.

Julia let it all pour out, "Home, but not home. During the day when I'm working in the kitchen with Aengus sprawled out on the floor in the sun, it feels like home. My kitchen. My house. My dog. There's even that moment, less than a minute, when I forget my reality. My heart leaps for joy in my chest when I hear the garage door open. Aengus jumps up to go and greet you, then that moment is gone. I realize it won't be Hal coming through the door. It takes the two or three minutes before you come in to gather the pieces of my broken heart. I put on my welcome home smile, and pretend that it isn't my kitchen, my house and my dog."

"I miss Hal so much. Some days I'm so angry with him for this mess he left me with. But I know I have to follow through with what he started. If I don't, I'll be running forever. And they, whoever they are, will eventually catch me. I won't believe Hal and Charlie died for nothing. This has to be worth it. But I just don't know what to do with it."

Lincoln pulled a few tissues from a box that sat on the floor next to the chaise and handed them to Julia.

"Julia, I can't express how sorry I am for all that's happened to you. But I do know this: you are not alone anymore. Do you understand? I'm in, we'll do this together. Whatever happens."

Julia wiped her cheeks. "OK."

The next day after breakfast, Lincoln held out his cup as Julia drained what remained at the bottom of the coffee press into it.

He nodded his thanks. "I've been thinking."

"Thank you, cause I'm tired of thinking." Julia pulled the plunger from the press and rinsed it under the tap.

Lincoln chuckled. "I'd like to join you in investigating the human trafficking ring and help get you cleared in the eyes of the law. Not to mention, keep you safe from the ones who killed Hal and Charlie and, if at all possible, tear the whole organization down."

"How do you propose to do all that?"

"By helping you investigate further and eventually figuring out how it all works. First, we should create a working space that's not in your suite. I want you to continue to have your privacy."

"Thank you."

"There isn't wall space in the library for the spreadsheet. Are you OK if we move the workspace and wall display up to one of the empty bedrooms?"

"It makes sense. It's still hidden from the main part of the house, making it the safest place to have it on display."

It had felt awkward for Julia to have Lincoln in her private space. She was grateful for his consideration.

Alone in her room that night, Julia sunk to her knees beside her bed for the first time. Tears of gratitude flowed, and words poured out, "Thank you, God. Thank you, thank you, thank you."

Emotionally spent, Julia crawled into bed and slept.

CHAPTER 28

TWO DAYS LATER, THE TWO OF THEM had created a research hub in the smallest of the two spare bedrooms. Lincoln had picked up an old used library table at a thrift store and a couple of folding chairs, and situated them in the middle of the room with a vantage point of the two walls. A newly acquired printer sat on one end of the table, a full box of copy paper on the floor below.

To the largest of the walls, they taped the spreadsheet from Julia's suite. During the process of this transfer, there had been much discussion for the best way to organize it to accommodate any new information that would be added. On the smaller of the two walls, they had decided to put the background research on what human trafficking and money laundering consisted of.

Julia started unloading the box of stationery supplies and organizing it on the table while Lincoln studied their handiwork. He stood with his one hand on his hip for what seemed to Julia like forever. Was he finding flaws? Did it look valid, or more like a conspiracy theory as she feared?

"You've done an amazingly detailed job."

"It's a start." She could hear the relief in her own voice.

Lincoln turned to her. "No. It's more than a start. You've done all this." He waved at the wall. "I think Hal would be proud."

"Thank you." The warmth from his compliment faded quickly. "But where to now? Any suggestions?"

"Just a few possible next steps. Let's take the information on human trafficking and money laundering you've gathered and apply it to what you have here with the individuals and businesses. For instance, if we take the human trafficking equation — Acts, Means and Purpose — and apply it to all of these individuals and businesses separately, we can see what they have in common and how they might work together. We can do the same for money laundering. What businesses on our list can be used to launder the money coming in from the human trafficking earnings? It might be the key to unravelling the network."

"I like it."

"And one other suggestion: now that we have a printer, let's print off any pictures of individuals. It might help with the visualization aspect of the players involved. I think I purchased some photo matte paper. It should be in the box."

"OK, I'll do that first. There was one website I came across a while ago, the Ministry of Justice has an Office to Combat Trafficking in Persons. They even have a course to help service providers and others identify trafficked people. It took me a few days to complete, but it's worth it if you're interested."

"Good idea. Then, let's make a list of aid groups organized to help victims of sexual trafficking." Lincoln walked over to the table where Julia sat writing in a notebook. "I want to stay away from law enforcement agencies at the moment."

"Because of what happened to Charlie?"

"Yes, in part. Until we know who we can trust in law enforcement, it's best to stay clear of them. The focus of aid organizations are the victims coming out of their enslavement. They will have the current information. They can tell us what exploitation and trafficking look like on the street here in Victoria. Often they'll know the names of the players on the street and in other levels of society."

"Sounds logical. I seem to remember a list like that on the government website," Julia said. "But how do we get them to trust us?"

"Hallie, my dear. I mean Julia. That's going to take a few attempts."

"No problem. I don't mind Hallie. I'm rather used to it."

Lincoln nodded and continued, "I'm a very popular author. I have managed to get information from even the most tight-lipped imaginable. A little charm, a dash of maimed-in-service to our great country and fellow man and they open up like a flower to the sun."

Julia looked at Lincoln. "Makes sense." She felt a new energy and lifted the lid on the laptop. A few minutes and a few more keystrokes later, she found the list. She searched first in Victoria then on the mainland. There weren't many. Julia wondered how victims coped once rescued with so little support.

"There are resources for women in abusive relationships, but not much for victims of sexual exploitation."

"Another idea. Try looking for newspaper articles on human trafficking in British Columbia," Lincoln said.

Julia bookmarked the webpage for reference later, and after a few clicks, said, "Here's a website that has some articles mostly about government funding cutbacks to the Office to Combat Trafficking in Persons."

"Add the names of the journalists who wrote the articles to my list of people to contact. They might be a good resource."

"I think I just found the person to put at the top of your journalists lists. This gal wrote an article connecting foster care children and their susceptibility to sexual exploitation. Listen to what the article says:

'There are a variety of reasons why the child welfare system takes children into custody, but the most common are parental substance abuse, alcohol abuse, domestic violence or neglect. A childhood of abuse and neglect greatly increases the chances for children to be recruited or abducted into sexual exploitation for profit.'"

Julia paused. "OK. It looks like she interviewed a member of the RCMP and they said that foster kids and runaways have the same vulnerabilities to being trafficked. The mountie says here that a high percentage of trafficked kids are from the foster system."

Julia looked up at Lincoln. "This fits right in with Hal's folder on Ministry Sources."

"I have enough to get going tomorrow. I'm going to start reading all the articles."

"Right." Julia handed him the pages from her notebook. "Lincoln, I'm still terrified, but thank you. It feels good to not be alone with this anymore."

He took the pages from her and turned to the furry carpet on the floor between them.

"OK Aengus, shall we go for a walk in the woods before supper?"

Aengus got up and stretched. He went over to Julia and she put her arms around his broad neck and rubbed his chest then released him, saying, "Have a good walk, you two." She went to the kitchen, a lightness of being giving her the feeling of floating down the stairs. This is how it felt to share a burden. The oppressive weight was lifted from her soul.

CHAPTER 29

I T WAS A HOT AUGUST AFTERNOON and Julia wanted to get into the cool of the woods. At the garden gate leading to the forest, Julia saw Lincoln step out of the kitchen. She waited a moment as he jogged across the lawn towards her and Aengus.

"Can I join you?"

"Of course."

"I was kind of hoping you would show me Chuck's camp."

Julia hesitated. Was she ready to visit it? Every time she had gone for a walk through the forest, she'd avoided the trail that led down that emotional path. The last time she had gone there was the night Hal was murdered. She looked up into the forest, the sun was high and reaching down through the canopy. She had Aengus with her and now Lincoln was here. Time to be brave, she thought.

"Sure."

Julia led the way with Aengus at her side and Lincoln close behind. It had been nearly a year since that fateful night. The trail had grown over, but she was still able to follow it up the mountain. Aengus was happy, occasionally leaving her side to crash through the undergrowth chasing squirrels and rabbits.

When Julia stopped at a small clearing, she turned towards Lincoln.

"This is it." Lincoln looked around and Julia saw the astonishment on his face.

"Not much, is it?" Julia asked.

"No, but I think that's kind of the idea."

Aengus appeared in the clearing from a small game trail, his chest heaving, his wiry coat covered in forest debris. He sat between them and pressed against

Lincoln's leg.

"Did you have fun, boy?" Lincoln reached down and thumped on Aengus' shoulder. The wolfhound pressed harder against him almost pushing him off balance and they both laughed.

"Let me show you Charlie's genius," Julia said, as she walked over to the inconspicuous pile of branches. "This was my home for nearly 24 hours. It was a good hiding place."

Lincoln followed her and looked at the branches. "How on earth did you hide in that?" Aengus came to investigate, sniffing around the pile of brush wood.

Julia smiled then bent down and grabbed hold of the large branch that lifted the whole lid off the dugout. "Voila!"

"Wow, this is amazing! Chuck was a genius." Lincoln stepped down into the cavity in the earth. "And you spent hours in this hole? That's even more amazing."

"Yes, well, we can add that to the list of non-transferable skills on my résumé."

Lincoln climbed out and lowered the lid of branches. "I was honoured to serve with him."

"I was very grateful for our time together." Julia looked at Lincoln. "We both have a different experience with Charlie. Collectively we probably have the best idea of who he really was. It was here that Charlie said he found God."

"I knew about Chuck's faith. He shared a lot of how it got him through the darkness we brought home from Rwanda."

"Do you believe?"

"I do, but I wouldn't call myself a churchgoer or anything like that. And nowhere near Chuck's level of faith. But I do, yes."

"Me too. Until Hal was killed and I spent those months with Charlie, I had never really given religion much consideration."

They stood in the midst of the clearing, feeling the presence of the man who had brought them together.

Aengus was the first to break the moment when a squirrel ran across the edge of the clearing and he took off after it.

It was going to be another hot day. Julia opened the doors leading to the balcony in the master bedroom to let in the cool morning air. She turned to strip the bed linen. She walked into the closet, reached up for the clean sheets and proceeded to remake Lincoln's bed.

On her way out of the room, the dirty linens in her arms, she stopped and dropped to the floor still clutching the sheets. She could see a man standing over a prone body. Her heart was beating out of her chest. She closed her eyes. Leaving the pile of sheets, she crawled backwards into the master suite and searched the floor for the go-bags she and Hal had put by the windows that morning.

They were gone.

She stopped and started to weep.

"Julia."

Julia screamed. She frantically looked for somewhere to hide and started crawling towards the walk-in closet.

The man grabbed her, preventing her from getting to safety.

"Julia."

Julia didn't look at the source of the voice, but kept her eyes closed. She kicked out at the hand holding her ankle and continued to scream, clawing at the carpet in hopes of pulling herself free.

"Julia, it's me, Lincoln," the voice said. "Julia, you're safe."

Julia stopped struggling.

She opened her eyes and looked at the man who was holding her captive, then cast her gaze around the room looking for an escape route.

"You're safe," he said. "Look at me, Julia." She looked back at the man.

"That's it, look at me," he said, still gripping her ankle. "Breathe, Julia. That's it. Keep looking at me."

Julia could feel her lung function gradually return to normal. Her heart slowed. She looked at Lincoln, finally recognizing him.

"Lincoln?" she said. She put her face in her hands.

"What did you see, Julia?" Lincoln gently released her, but didn't move away.

"I saw a man standing over a body." She looked towards the door to the bedroom then back at him.

"I was standing downstairs and saw you drop to the floor and crawl away," he said. "It was just me, Julia."

"But I saw . . . "

"You were having a flashback," he said. "Is this the first time this has happened?"

"In the daytime, yes," she answered.

"You've been having nightmares then?" he asked gently.

"Yeah," she said, drawing her knees into her chest and hugging her legs.

"Well, considering you are back at the scene of the crime, I am shocked this is the first time it's happened. Tell me about your nightmares."

"I have a couple that seem to rotate."

"OK, tell me the most frequent one."

"I am running from men with guns through the woods. I keep running and running, and they keep getting closer and closer."

"But they don't catch you, do they?"

"No, never. I always wake up just before. But even though they never catch me in my dream, I still have the same feeling of terror every time. I wake up with my heart racing, and the sheets are damp from my sweat as if I had been running."

"The mind can do that. It can seem so real that our bodies react with the same heart-pounding adrenaline rush. What is the other dream?"

"I am buried in a hole in the ground and I can't find a way out. That one isn't as frequent as the chase through the woods, but it is more terrifying. I wake up with such a sense of hopelessness."

"Buried, that is beyond terrifying," he said. "That's one I've never had."

"You've had nightmares of men chasing you?" she looked at him, surprised.

"Yes, only they didn't have guns. They had machetes."

"Did you wake up before they caught you too?"

"No," he said pointing to his missing limb. "I relive this."

"Oh, Lincoln."

"I don't have that dream very often anymore, maybe a couple times a year. I can tell you it does get better."

"In the meantime, here I am."

"Yes, here you are, and I'm glad you are here. Remember you are not alone in this anymore."

"You're beginning to sound like a broken record," she smiled, "and like Charlie." She was grateful for all that Lincoln was becoming to her: employer, rescuer, friend and now fellow trauma sufferer. How could she not believe in a loving God after these two men, Charlie and Lincoln, came into her life at a point when she needed someone? For that matter, even Hal was a rescuer and hero in a previous chapter of her life against a different enemy.

"As long as you believe me," he said, returning her smile, pulling her from her thoughts.

"I'm getting there," she said.

"Good," he said and then his stomach growled.

"Saved by the stomach," she laughed as Lincoln helped her off the floor.

"See, I am handy to have around. Or at least my stomach is. When's lunch?"

"I'll start as soon as I put the laundry in," she said, picking up the abandoned linen.

Alone in the kitchen, Julia turned on the kettle and stood for a moment, looking out at the sunbathed back yard. Though her words had been cheery with Lincoln, shadows from her flashback still crowded her thinking.

It had rained overnight, but the clouds had cleared and the sun began its circumnavigation from the front of the house to the back, quickly drying any lingering moisture. She opened the French doors to let in the fresh air and bird song. The forest chorus was the healing balm that finally banished the flashback clouds. *For now, anyway,* Julia thought as she turned to start lunch.

CHAPTER 30

L INCOLN SCANNED THE LIST OF JOURNALISTS Julia had gathered. She had put the title of the articles next to the names and he decided to read them first. An hour later, and five articles under his belt, he decided on Bess Delaney. He picked up the Bluetooth attachment to his phone and fixed it in his ear. The paper's switchboard connected him to her extension.

Lincoln arrived 15 minutes early. A pint of Guinness was sitting in front of him when Bess Delaney showed up.

"I hope you don't mind the snug. I'd prefer not to be overheard."

"Works for me," Bess said, shaking his hand.

She put her messenger bag on the bench beside her. They took a few minutes to peruse the menu. The pub was busy, but the snug muffled the noise of the music and cacophony of conversation.

After preliminary small talk about writing in general, Lincoln got to the point.

"When I read your article, I couldn't help but think there was more to the story. I'm guessing the story you wanted to write concerned a direct connection between the Ministry and children in foster care ending up in situations of sexual exploitation."

Lincoln noted Bess' reaction. He had struck a chord.

She stopped chewing a piece of lamb burger. He waited for her to process what he said.

"How could you have that information?" Bess asked him, every word dripping with suspicion.

"Let's say I stumbled onto something while writing my next novel. I've decided to research, or shall I say investigate, it further."

"It would be wiser and safer to say research. I don't think you have any idea what you may be getting yourself into."

"I've done some research on you, Ms. Delaney. I like what I found. You have passion, integrity, and you don't back down easily." Lincoln looked directly into her eyes, holding her gaze. "But are you willing to take some personal risks?"

"What kind of risks are you talking about?"

"The kind of risks that, if you took them, you could end up dead," he said softly. "That kind of risk."

"It wouldn't be the first time," Bess said, tugging at an auburn curl that had slipped out from behind her ear.

Lincoln saw determination and core strength. He decided to push on.

"Will you share with me some of your research. Names of who you interviewed, for example?"

Bess narrowed her eyes. "Are you asking me to reveal my sources?"

"Yes."

"Journalists don't give their sources up, especially if they wish to remain anonymous. Everyone knows that."

"I'm not going to be publishing their names or revealing where I got the information."

"So far, I don't see how me giving you my sources is that dangerous."

"It's not your sources, but what I have that is dangerous."

"What exactly are you working on? An article? Not the usual venue for a fiction writer."

"What do you want?"

"My name on whatever you manage to get published," Bess challenged.

"That would require you to do some of the actual writing. If I use your contacts for research value, I can name you in the acknowledgments," Lincoln countered.

"Ah, yes, but I have done a considerable amount of writing. Not just the article that was published."

Bess stood her ground and Lincoln admired that.

"Our names together on whatever gets published. That's the deal or I'm out of here."

"How do I know what you have is worth publishing?"

"Because my editor was too scared to publish it. He couldn't fault my research, but wanted more and I've been hitting brick walls everywhere."

"And you've not had any threats on your life or anything?"

"Wouldn't that be a good thing?"

"It tells me what you have might not be as hot as you think." Lincoln lowered his voice to a near-whisper. "Two people have died because they had the information I now possess."

He let his words sink in before continuing.

"Have I made a mistake in coming to you, Ms. Delaney? I'm looking for information that could help cripple the trafficking of women in our city. Are you only interested in furthering your career? Those aspirations, albeit worthwhile, are small and narrow-minded in the big picture."

"Are you questioning my integrity?"

"No." Lincoln could see a shadow cross Bess Delaney's countenance. Feeling regret at misjudging how she might be willing to collaborate, he stood. Taking his wallet from his inner jacket pocket he said, "I'll pay for lunch on my way out. Good day to you."

"Wait, Mr. Warren. Wait, please?"

Lincoln sat and rested his good arm on the table.

"OK, I'll share what I have with you. I'll give you everything I have if you let me in. Work with you. No other demands."

Lincoln looked at her and saw that challenging her motives had hit a mark. "I want to see what you have first. If it fits with what I have, and helps fill in some missing information, then, and only then, will I bring you in."

Bess opened her mouth to protest, but didn't voice an objection.

Lincoln lowered his voice again. "I will bring you in. Completely. Shared credit. You have to understand, it isn't only my life on the line here. There is someone else involved. Someone who has already lost too much. I will not put my trust in you if it means putting that person in more danger."

Bess nodded.

Lincoln once again withdrew his wallet and took out a business card. "Here is my contact information. You can deliver a USB thumb drive with whatever you have to this post office box. If you do, I'll be in touch."

The following Thursday, Lincoln walked into the kitchen with a bundle of mail from the post office box. Smiling, he waved a small, padded envelope at Julia. He flipped the open end and dumped the contents onto the kitchen island. Out fell a USB stick and a business card. Lincoln left the rest of his mail and picked up the thumb drive.

"Let's see what we've got, shall we?"

Needing no further prompting, Julia followed Lincoln upstairs. She opened her laptop. Lincoln stood behind her to watch over her shoulder. When the computer rebooted, he handed her the drive.

"Here's hoping," she prayed, waiting for it to load.

The file opened.

"Two folders. One titled 'Victims', the other 'Perpetrators.'"

"The victim folder has a sub-folder called 'Business Practices.'"

"We can compare it against our human trafficking research. Let's focus on the perpetrators list. Read out the names and I'll compare it to what we have up on the wall."

Lincoln stepped from behind the table and faced the wall as Julia started reading aloud. "Only one name matches our list: Constance Dunham." Lincoln turned back towards Julia.

"Right, Dunham is a social worker. Not totally disappointing," Julia looked up at Lincoln, "but I was hoping for more." She read aloud from the list again, mainly to herself.

"Wait. I think the name Adrienne Wilder came up recently. Give me a second." She began looking through the list of aid agencies.

Lincoln stepped closer to the wall where they had profiles and pictures of various names on their lists, barring a few. "Haven't you been able to find photos for these names?"

Julia responded absently, as she was still looking through the lists on the table in front of her. "I was printing the last ones off earlier, just haven't pinned them up yet. I think I got all but one."

"Which one?"

"Hayden Sawyer."

Julia refocused on the papers in front of her. "Gotcha." She looked up at Lincoln. "Adrienne Wilder serves on the board of Dunsinane House, a shelter for victims of spousal abuse." She opened a new search tab on the laptop and typed in "Adrienne Wilder."

"OK, now we have a new person of interest to check out." Lincoln leafed through the pile of photos.

"Wait, here's another reference to Wilder, a recent press release announcing her appointment to the board of a local homeless kitchen and shelter, Haven's Door."

"So, she's on the board of two organizations that could give her access to at-risk youth and vulnerable women."

The printer hummed and spat out a picture of Wilder. Lincoln studied it for a moment before asking, "What else is in the perpetrators folder?"

"More sub-folders. Like us, she has Ministry sources which contain a list of foster families. But get this: she connects specific kids with specific families."

"She could only have gotten that kind of information from the victims."

Julia looked back down at the computer screen.

"Ready for the rest of the lists?"

Lincoln turned once again to face the wall of information. "Shoot."

"Social workers, law enforcement, gang affiliations and, lastly, corporate entities."

"We have some matching lists. Can you read from the corporate entities one?"

"Right. It looks like a list of businessmen and women and their corporate affiliations." She read them off.

"It would be a good idea at some point to sit down and look at how these corporations can be tied in with the business practices from the victims' folder."

Julia nodded her agreement, then, "Where's the half-page list of names we couldn't fit in anywhere?" She sifted through all the loose papers scattered about, then waved it triumphantly.

Lincoln took it from her. "OK, you read and I'll compare." He sat in the chair opposite Julia with the list on the table and picked up a pen.

"I'll read them off three at a time," Julia looked up and Lincoln nodded his assent.

Twelve names into the list, she stopped.

"That's 11. What's the last name?" Lincoln looked up at her.

"The next one is Harold Bowen," Julia said, her heart beating faster.

"Harold Bowen," Lincoln repeated. "Bowen — that's your last name."

Julia didn't speak, just nodded.

"Hal is short for Harold. Harold Bowen was your husband?"

Julia stared at the screen without really seeing anything. She began to lose focus.

"Julia!" Lincoln said more firmly, then reached across the table to shake her arm.

Julia came back to the present, refocusing on the list of names once again, ignoring Lincoln's reaction to the revelation that Hal was on Bess Delaney's list.

"The last name on the list is Howard Allenby. He was the realtor we dealt with when we purchased the lot to build this house. He introduced Hal to a small web design company that needed some IT help. The owner liked his work and connected him with some other local businesses in the community and his client list grew from there."

"Well, somebody call bingo." Lincoln raised his hand. "Now, we have a connection to work with. What was the name of the web design company?"

"I don't know. It was three or four years ago. About two years ago, Hal started to attend a networking group meeting once a month. He said some of his business clients invited him."

"Did the group have a name or anything?"

"No, he said it was pretty informal."

"So, most of the names on our mystery list are likely members of this business group."

"You would think Delaney would have included that little bit of information." Julia rechecked the list of businesses on the USB drive. "Considering she had these names, I can't imagine her not investigating them."

"I'm thinking Ms. Delaney held out on us, what do you reckon?" Lincoln got up from the chair and paced. "It's time to bring her in on this. How do you feel about that?" he asked.

"We might get further faster, but . . . " Julia closed the laptop.

"But?"

"The more people involved, the greater the risk of something leaking. Then there'll be gunmen in the night again. I'm terrified, considering what happened when Charlie contacted his cop friend."

"We can stop right now, if you want. You have to make this decision. I'm here to support you."

Julia watched Lincoln rub his hand over his bald head. She had come to recognize that as a sign of frustration. "Charlie asked me once if I was willing to do all that it takes." She looked at Lincoln with resolve in her heart. "I don't see us going forward without her connections. So yes, we should bring her in. But how? Right now, Julia Bowen is in the wind. There is no known connection between me and you. If we create a traceable connection between Bess Delaney, a journalist, and us, then . . . "

"Well then, we'll have to create an untraceable connection. Let me think about it overnight and see what I can come up with."

CHAPTER 31

T HE NEXT MORNING, the phone on Bess' desk rang.

"Bess Delaney."

"Bess, do you recognize my voice."

"Yes."

"Meet me in 30 minutes where we last met."

The caller disconnected and Bess put the handset back on the cradle. She grabbed her coat and stopped in her editor's office.

"I have to meet a source on something, but I'll be back in time to file my story."

Turk Badger, her editor, mumbled something without looking up.

Bess made her way to the Irish Times and had to wait in line to speak to the hostess.

"I am supposed to meet someone," she said when her turn came. "May I walk through to see if they are here."

"Are you Bess Delaney?" the hostess asked.

"Yes."

"I'm afraid your party was unable to stay, but she left a note for you." The hostess handed Bess an envelope.

"She?" Bess asked, taking it.

"Yes," the hostess said, puzzled.

"Thank you," Bess said and left the pub, ripping open the envelope.

"Dear Ms. Delaney,

Thank you for the information you recently provided. I propose a collaboration. Terms will be as previously discussed. Initially, I would request a weekend of your time. The endeavor will most likely take more than a mere 48 hours, but it will be a good start and will establish our working relationship. If this is agreeable, please meet me at Beaver Lake on Saturday morning around nine. Use the lower parking lot, start walking north around the lake on the west side. I'll find you. No cellphone, please. Arrange for someone to retrieve your car. You'll be leaving the park by alternate means.

Regards,

L

PS: Please bring the rest of your research."

Bess folded the note and put it back in the envelope. During the walk back to her office, she formulated a plan.

For the rest of the week, Bess finished off several stories and filed them with the column manager. She was grateful that it wasn't her weekend to be on call. She put her out-of-office message on her work phone and email.

Bess had been walking for about half an hour, passing joggers and dog walkers. It was a busy place; even horses used the 10km trail that bordered both Beaver Lake and Elk Lake. At one point, a woman riding a horse and leading another came along the trail towards her. The rider stopped, smiling at Bess.

"Good morning. A lovely day, isn't it?"

"Yes, it is. Especially for a ride, I imagine."

The rider leaned down, her elbow on the horse's withers. "Do you ride, by any chance?"

Bess looked at the riderless horse the woman was leading, wondering if this was the woman who had left her the note at the Irish Times.

"As a matter of fact, I do."

"Excellent." She held out a spare helmet to Bess. "Hi. Lincoln Warren sent me to fetch you."

Bess donned the helmet and tightened the straps on her backpack. Taking the reins held out to her, she put her foot in the stirrup and pulled herself into the saddle.

"Isn't this rather clandestine and just a tad unnecessary?"

"No and no." The friendly smile was gone from the stranger's face as she turned her horse to walk back in the direction she had come.

Bess applied the reins to her horse's neck, turning it and pulling up alongside the other.

"No questions until we get to our destination. It's a lovely day for a ride, as you said, so relax and enjoy it."

Joggers were coming towards them and Bess was forced to slow her mount and step in behind the other horse to form a single line, allowing them to pass. To stop herself from asking questions, Bess concentrated on the horse beneath her. It had been years since she'd ridden. The gentle cadence of the horse's stride helped calm her inner turmoil. She was apprehensive, she admitted to herself. But she hadn't been this excited about a story in a while.

Bess followed as her guide led them north until they came to the fishing pier where the trail met Bear Hill Road. They left the trail, passing the entrance to Bear Hill Regional Park. On Bear Hill Road, they rode along the lush agricultural properties of Central Saanich.

Bess was glad when they turned into the Stables by the Lakes. Her butt was starting to get sore.

They followed the drive to the second of four horse barns, where her mysterious and silent guide dismounted. A groom walked up and held the horses' bridles for them. Without looking at Bess, she thanked him and left the barn. Bess dismounted and followed.

They walked past one of two outdoor show rings towards a parking lot. Standing next to his truck was Lincoln, grinning like the Cheshire Cat when he saw Bess walking a bit stiffly towards him.

"Seriously, you made me ride a horse?" Bess said harshly. "Paranoid much?"

"Yes!" they exclaimed together.

"And the tour isn't over yet. Hop in." Lincoln walked around to the driver's side. Bess sat in the middle, her backpack on her lap, fuming at the cook's tour.

"Did you bring the information you withheld?"

"What information would that be?" Bess played her cards close to her chest.

"The information about a certain business association. You held out on me. That wasn't the deal."

Lincoln pulled out of the drive and entered traffic on Oldfield Road.

"You didn't really expect me to hand over everything. Seriously, don't take me for some naïve idiot. I had to ensure you would get back in touch. Giving you just enough of what I've dug up, with a hint of the more explosive to come, ensured that." Bess shrugged her shoulders. "And here I am."

"Yes, you are," Lincoln said, keeping his focus on the road.

"Who exactly are you?" Bess turned her attention to the woman beside her. "And how do you fit into all this?"

"You'll know soon enough."

They travelled in silence all the way to John Dean Regional Park. Halfway up the road, Lincoln stopped and put the truck into park, but didn't turn off the engine.

"Bess, here's where you hike." Lincoln pointed to the open passenger door being held by her trail guide.

"You've got to be kidding me." She turned to Lincoln. "First horseback riding, now hiking. Will it be kayaks next?" she said, not budging.

"Almost there. Now out. Or I take you into Sidney and you can find your way back into Victoria on your own." Lincoln held firm. "Your choice."

"It's just a short hike through the forest," the woman said. "It's lovely and cool, and not a difficult trail. It'll help stretch out your riding muscles. It isn't far. Honest."

Bess looked at her, then back at Lincoln. They were both waiting, so she had to decide: trust or bail.

"Fine." Bess got out and donned her pack. "Lead on."

Without any further words, the woman pushed the passenger door of the truck closed and turned, plunging into the forest without looking back to see if Bess followed.

Bess watched Lincoln drive off, then hurried to catch up to her.

Thirty-five minutes later, Bess stopped on the crest of a steep hill. She could see the trail wind down behind a house nestled in the trees.

"Please tell me that's our destination. I can't take any more of this walk on the wild side. I'm a city girl."

"It is."

Finally, they arrived at the house and the woman opened a gate before motioning for Bess to step through.

Bess' attention was captured by the French doors at the rear of the house. They opened and a giant dog bounded towards her.

Bess swore and backed up towards the gate.

"Don't worry, he's very friendly." The woman stepped forward to intercept the dog before he could knock Bess over. "Hey, fella. I have someone I'd like you to meet."

Bess stood in fascination as the woman put her hand on the dog's shoulder and turned towards her. "Aengus, this is Bess. Bess, this is Aengus."

Bess kept her hands down at her sides. Aengus stepped forward and put his head under Bess' hand. She stood still, intimidated. He sniffed and then stepped closer, encouraging her to pet him.

"I've never seen a dog this big," Bess said, lightly petting him. "It is a dog?"

"Yes, it's a dog. Aengus is an Irish Wolfhound. He's very gentle and friendly. Don't let his size frighten you."

Too late, Bess thought, watching as the woman clapped her hands and crossed the lawn to the house, the dog bounding ahead.

CHAPTER 32

THE THREE OF THEM WERE SITTING at the small table in the breakfast nook. Julia watched Bess studying Lincoln as he poured coffee into three mugs.

"Was the cook's tour necessary?"

"Yes. It's safer if you're not seen coming and going from this house. I'm the only one who uses the front entrance on a regular basis."

"When he's not here, occasionally I will take Aengus out in the truck for a change of scenery."

"You're not serious?"

"Yes, we are. When you hear the story, you'll understand why." Leaving the coffee pot on the island, Lincoln joined the two women at the table.

Julia could tell Bess was still nervous about Aengus, only visibly relaxing when he stretched out on the floor. She looked across at both of them. "I'm listening."

"Do you want to tell the story?" Julia asked Lincoln.

"Well, considering it all starts with you, you should begin. At least up until the point when we met, then I'll take over." Lincoln took a drink of his coffee.

Nodding her agreement, Julia turned to Bess.

"My name is Julia Bowen. A year ago, my husband was murdered. And the gunmen who killed him made it look like I did it."

"That name sounds familiar. I covered that story. It was on the other side of the mountain from Dean Park." Julia could see comprehension dawn in Bess' eyes. "That was near here."

"This very house, in fact. When Hal was killed, I fled for my life into the forest."

Bess watched Julia as the story poured out. At times her emotions were near the surface, her eyes filling with tears but not falling. At other parts of the story, she seemed cold and detached.

When Julia talked about Charlie, Bess interrupted.

"Can you describe Charlie?"

Julia's eyes softened and she smiled, detailing the man who had saved her life.

"I met him that morning out on the street," said Bess.

"What?" Lincoln and Julia spoke over each other.

"I was on call that weekend. I interviewed the police on the scene and the neighbours standing around. From your description, Charlie was one of the people I spoke with."

"I was hiding up in the forest when he came down to check things out."

"He stands out in my mind because he paid me a compliment on my work. That doesn't happen very often."

"Sounds like Chuck."

"I have more questions about that coincidence, but I'll wait. Please continue."

The deeper Julia got into the story, the less Bess interrupted. At the point in the tale when she met Aengus and Lincoln on the trail, as if on cue Aengus got up from the floor and came to stand beside Julia. She put her arms around the dog's neck and hugged him.

"I'm going to pass the baton to Lincoln and fix us a snack. Who wants more coffee?"

"Please."

"Me too," Lincoln raised his mug.

Glad Lincoln was now the one talking, Julia had an opportunity to better study Bess. Lincoln had met her before and, as much as she trusted his perceptions, Julia was still holding out judgment. Bess' reaction to the roundabout arrival to the house, and her seeming detachment, made Julia uneasy.

"I was an innocent bystander until Aengus dragged Julia into the house," Lincoln laughed. "I bought this house on foreclosure. A couple mornings after I moved in, Aengus showed up at my door. Nick, a friend of Julia and Hal's, had been looking after him while they were away. Julia and Hal had just returned the night Hal was murdered. So, Nick decided to keep Aengus, as Aengus and his dog were good together."

"I remember him. I interviewed him a couple of days later."

"Not long after Aengus showed up, Nick rang my doorbell. Aengus had come here on other occasions before I moved in. Nick took him home the first couple of times. When it kept happening, we agreed I would keep Aengus. A month or so later, Aengus and I were walking in the woods and we ran into Julia. Well, Aengus ran into her and knocked her down in his enthusiasm, and she cut herself when she fell."

Julia brought a platter of muffins and fruit from the fridge and poured them fresh coffee before sitting down again. Aengus lay down between her and Lincoln.

Bess looked at Lincoln. "Did you know it was Julia Bowen?"

"No. I felt terrible at Aengus' behaviour. I brought her back here for first aid and ended up offering her a job as a dog-sitter and live-in housekeeper."

Bess looked at Julia. "Still not knowing who you were?"

"Nope. Can't make this up, can you?" Julia smiled.

"No, you certainly can't."

As Lincoln continued, Julia contemplated the seemingly unbelievable coincidences. Coincidences which she now saw as God intervening. How many times in her life had she marvelled at the synchronism of events? The right social worker who showed up when her father died; the ER nurse present the night her mother fell while curling; and, of course, meeting Hal months before her stalker found her for the third time. Hal had been her salvation in so many ways.

Julia's attention came back to the conversation when Lincoln said, "Now I'll pass the baton to you, Bess. How did your investigation into human trafficking start?"

"As I was leaving a shelter one afternoon, a woman approached me. Shelly, an addict, had ended up in the hospital after an overdose. Her daughter, who was 13, had to go into foster care. It was only supposed to be until Shelly's sister could arrive from Newfoundland."

"What about the girl's father?" Julia asked.

"Not in the picture at all," Bess answered.

"If her daughter is 13, it is amazing that she had managed to keep her," commented Julia.

"They are rare, but there are high-functioning addicts out there. Shelly managed to keep a series of jobs enabling her to maintain housing. When she overdosed one night, that was it — she lost everything, even her daughter."

"That is tragic," Julia said.

"Yes, but it gets worse. Her daughter disappeared," Bess said.

"What? You said she was in foster care." Julia was shocked.

"That's what they told her. But when her sister arrived from Newfoundland, the daughter had gone," Bess explained. "It took her sister two weeks to get here.

Trying to sort things out so she could stay indefinitely delayed her. Her sister arrived when Shelly had recovered from the overdose and entered rehab. By the time the sister had checked with the Ministry, the story was that the daughter had run away from foster care."

"How is that possible?" Julia asked.

"It is more common than you think."

"Isn't the Ministry supposed to give regular reports or something?"

"In an ideal world where there is enough staff for the workload. Sadly, we don't operate in an ideal world. Government cutbacks causing low staff levels result in kids falling through the cracks," Bess explained. "In Shelly's situation, the foster parents followed protocol and contacted the social worker. The social worker had a family emergency. By the time she followed up a couple of days later, the foster parents still hadn't heard from the girl."

"What about the police?" Julia asked.

"All they can do is check the usual haunts where street kids hang out. There was no sign of her. No one had even seen her. It is as if she vanished."

"How did you make the human trafficking connection?" Julia asked.

"Well, I kept asking around and talking to the kids on the street. I learned that this wasn't unusual. Kids said that there is an odd frequency of girls going missing from foster homes. Not always the same homes, they said, that would be too easy to start investigating. Another factor is the lack of credibility street kids have with law enforcement and social workers. They don't talk because their experience is that they are not believed. So why bother?"

"That sounds like a major hurdle to overcome," Julia said.

"Yes, it is. People who live on the street have a difficult time accessing services and help. They aren't in one place on a consistent basis where the police can follow up."

Bess put the piece of muffin in her mouth and groaned.

"This is delicious." She lifted the remaining crumbs from her plate with her finger, then continued.

"I started asking questions. Social workers, Ministry lawyers and kids on the street. I put together a pretty bleak picture of kids trafficked for sex after time spent in foster homes."

"How did your investigation lead you to local businesses?" Lincoln asked.

"It was around the time I interviewed girls who had managed to leave the street. They gave me names within the local business community involved in sexual exploitation. I started digging further."

"Are the outlines in your research on how the traffickers manage the victims, fake IDs, moving them around and such based on those interviews?"

Bess nodded. "I'm still able to picture the girls as they told their stories. Some had a cold indifference to my questions, as if resigned to their fate. Others had a faint glimmer of hope that someone cared and was listening to them. I began to uncover a network of businesses with ties to victims of sexual exploitation."

"Your investigation results on the specific individuals you identified as members of the human trafficking ring are what you kept back, weren't they?" Lincoln asked.

"Yes. But for good reason. It is the nitroglycerin of my investigation. One wrong move and who knows what could happen."

"We know," Julia tapped her finger on the table for emphasis, "all too well."

Upstairs, Bess stood in the centre of the room and took in the walls and all they contained. She was getting her first look at the information Lincoln and Julia had amassed. Impressive, she thought.

"I trust you didn't bring your cellphone, as I requested?"

Bess hesitated before turning to face Lincoln who said, "I don't want to seem like a jailer, but if for some reason someone wants to track you, it puts us all at risk. Our greatest advantage right now is that no one knows who we are, what we have. You, right now, are our biggest liability."

Bess stiffened and, despite the fierce look of determination on Lincoln's face, was about to verbalize her defense.

Lincoln put up his hand when she opened her mouth. "But you are also a huge asset. The three of us working together can accomplish something, but only if we're smart and don't take any risks."

"You're asking me to cut myself off from the world." Bess crossed her arms in defense.

"Yes, I am, and I make no apologies. It is a matter of trust for us. Julia has lost enough; I don't want to put her at any further risk. Consider her life right now, cut off from the world for more than a year. I'm only asking you to give up your cellphone for the weekend."

Bess looked at Julia, then back at Lincoln. She picked up her daypack and retrieved her cell from an inside pocket.

"OK."

Bess dropped her pack back on the floor and dismantled the phone, taking the battery out and separating the SIM card from the body. She put all the components into a paper envelope Julia had retrieved from the recycle bin. She handed it to Lincoln.

"Thank you," Lincoln said, leaving the room and returning a few moments later. "Right, so give us the basics of what you brought us." He stood against the wall behind Julia, who now sat at the table.

"I have specific names and businesses I believe are involved in the human trafficking ring. I don't know the hierarchical structure or who the leader is, but I know the players. These are local businesses active in the legit business community, but unlike a lot of other businesses who broadcast who they are, this group keep a very low profile."

"We have names and businesses too, but that's all. We've been working on how they are linked," Julia said.

"Why don't you break this all down for me?" Bess indicated the walls of information.

Given the floor by Lincoln, Julia presented her with the basic outline. When she finished, she looked to Bess.

"What do you think?" Julia asked.

"Speaking from a journalist's perspective, I'm impressed. The clearer we can make the connections in this network, the better our chances in tearing it down."

"The three of us working together can create the environment to do that," Lincoln said.

"I hope so," Julia looked at the other two. "For the first time since Hal's murder, I actually have a spark of hope. Thanks to you both."

"I don't come from the same emotional starting point that you do, Julia. But believe me, sitting on this mass of moral deprivation in my back yard had caused me to lose faith in mankind," Bess said.

"Charlie said something like that to me once. He lost faith in mankind after Rwanda."

"Every one of us did," Lincoln agreed.

"I was on my way to being a hard-hearted journalist, frustrated by inability and fear." Bess looked at Julia. "Thanks to you, I don't feel bound by that inability." She smiled. "There's still fear, a lot of fear. But, like you, I'm not alone with this information anymore."

"Keep that fear," Lincoln said. "We all need to be afraid, but smart. If we are, we will hopefully accomplish our goal. So, let's look at your list."

Bess bent again to her pack on the floor and pulled out a piece of paper. "Once we make some comparisons between your list and mine, we should create a better idea of how they function." She handed the piece of paper to Julia, then turned to the wall containing the individual players and photos. "But before we just look at another list of names, I have an idea. May I move these around a bit?"

"Of course," Lincoln said.

"Julia, using some of your copy paper, would you make me four headings?" When Julia was ready, Bess spoke, "Finance, Operations, Human Resources and Marketing."

While Julia was writing, Bess moved the photos around to make room on the wall. She took the four pieces of paper and put them in a horizontal line near the top. With Lincoln and Julia looking on, she then moved the photos and profiles under one of the four headings. When she was done, she stepped aside and looked at the other two.

"This is the basic organizational chart I've come up with. I do have a few names to add to yours, but it seems we have much the same lists."

It took a while to print off the photos and profiles of the names Bess had to add to the human trafficking business organization. Once they did, they put the new additions on the wallchart.

Bess stepped closer to the table as Lincoln and Julia moved to get a better perspective.

"This is just a loose framework. To move forward we need concrete evidence linking them to trafficking," Bess said.

"And we still don't know who is at the top. The one responsible for murdering Hal."

At that moment, Aengus, who lay across the doorway, roused himself and walked over to Lincoln.

"Well, someone needs a walk," Lincoln smiled. "I think that's a good point to stop for the afternoon."

❖

Lincoln poured the last of the bottle of wine into Bess' glass. They were still sitting around the kitchen table after dinner.

"Here's to a productive afternoon." Julia raised her glass and they all followed suit. "How did you get so many victims to open up to you?"

"It just takes one to trust me. Then the word spreads. Once that first one opened up, and she saw I was on her side, she led me to others."

"Just like that?" Lincoln asked.

"It's never just like that. It took months of sitting in courtrooms listening to case after case. I also volunteer at homeless shelters and lunch carts to build relationships, so they see I'm not just in it to get a story and then abandon them. I met Amber four years ago. She was the first to open up to me. It was one whispered piece of information at a time, over months. Then she introduced me to a friend who introduced me to a friend, and so on."

"Wow, that took patience." Julia reached a foot over and rubbed Aengus' back as he stretched out at her feet.

"A journalist can go years before something can reveal the existence of a story, and then longer to crack it wide open. It paid off this time. But it doesn't always."

"If this afternoon is any indication, I think Julia and I made the right decision to bring you in. I'm amazed at how you are able to put things together from a jumble of information puzzle pieces."

"You can thank my grandfather for that. When I was little, my paternal grandfather got me started doing jigsaw puzzles. He would buy me a puzzle for Christmas every year. When I was around ten, he started giving me the puzzle in a baggie, without the picture as a guide."

"Didn't your grandfather love you?" Julia asked

Bess laughed, "Yes, very much. One year, he split a puzzle into three separate gifts. One at Christmas, one at my birthday in March and then the last one during summer break. You have no idea how frustrating it was. It is amazing what not seeing the big picture will give you. It eliminated any idea of jumping to conclusions. When you're not working on the puzzle, it's always in the back of your mind. It's surprising what you come up with without preconceived ideas dictating the outcome. That has helped me tremendously in my career."

Lincoln looked at his watch. "We should call it a night."

Julia, overwhelmed by a yawn, nodded her agreement. She looked to Bess, "I'll show you to the guest room now if you like."

"That would be great, I'm bushed. You wore me out today."

"I have a few things to do at my desk before I go up," said Lincoln. "I'll see you both in the morning."

Bess followed Julia upstairs with Aengus at their heels. She looked around the room as she laid her bag on the end of the bed. There were the basics: bed, dresser and nightstand with a lamp. She followed Julia as she moved past a walk-in closet to a bathroom. "Nice."

"Would you believe three days ago this room contained only some unpacked boxes from Lincoln's move? When we realized there was going to be a house guest, he scrambled to order the basics and have it delivered. Everything arrived yesterday," said Julia.

"This door leads to the Jack and Jill bathroom. On the other side is where we are working. There's a supply of towels and some basic toiletries. If you're going to be a regular guest, which I think might be the case, I have instructions from Lincoln to order anything you might need while you're here."

"That's very generous, thank you."

Bess nodded, turned back to the bedroom and sat on the bed. "It must be weird for you to be in your house, but have it not be your house."

"It is difficult at times, I won't deny it. But there has been some comfort in being in this house and having Aengus. Let's go, boy." Julia pet Aengus on the shoulder, turning to the door. "Sleep well."

"Thanks." Bess watched as Julia hesitated and turned towards her one last time.

"I want you to know I am very grateful for your help."

Bess nodded. Julia clicked the door softly behind her. Bess emptied her clothes and toiletry bag onto the bed. In the bathroom, she opened the door to the connecting room. She walked in and studied the wall of research illuminated by a full moon. She looked up at the moon through the window. The room overlooked the back yard and forest. In her mind's eye, she watched a terrified woman flee from the house, through the gate and into the woods. Three gunmen following.

CHAPTER 33

T HE NEXT MORNING, Julia came out of her room and was surprised to find Bess already up. She was sitting with her back to Julia at the kitchen table, looking out at the back yard. She turned when Julia walked in.

"Morning."

"Good morning. Have you been up long?"

"A good hour, I'd say. I don't need a lot of sleep. I made myself at home and helped myself to tea."

"I'm glad."

Julia saw the coffee press on the counter. Feeling its sides, she estimated that Lincoln had been out for about hour.

"Did you see Lincoln before he left?"

"Yes. I was coming down when he was leaving with Aengus. He showed me where everything was."

"He should be back any time now. He usually gives Aengus his good walk in the morning," she explained. "I'm glad Aengus isn't a problem for you. I know big dogs can be intimidating."

"'Big' is an understatement, but no. I like dogs. I admit I was a bit taken aback yesterday, mainly because it was unexpected. His size must be helpful in his guard dog duties."

"Guard dog, that's funny," Julia laughed. "No, he isn't a guard dog by any means. His breed is big, but that is the only intimidating thing with them. They are quite lazy and easygoing. He likes to be close to his people, but won't cause a problem for strangers, unless of course they threaten his peeps. The night Hal was murdered," Julia felt tears approach, "Aengus would have been killed too, because he would have done anything to protect us." Julia changed the subject. "So, no husband or kids to miss you for the weekend?"

"No. Newly divorced and no kids."

"I'm sorry."

"Thanks. I wanted kids. He didn't. I'm glad now that we didn't have any, he turned out to be an unfaithful jerk."

"I can't imagine what would have happened if Hal and I had had children," Julia shuddered. "It would have been so much worse."

"Well, you're not alone in this anymore. I'm here too, and in it for better or worse." Bess put her hand on Julia's arm. "Let's nail them."

"Yes, lets." Julia smiled, warming up to Bess. She was less reporter this morning, and more friend. Julia was grateful for the female company. She realized it had been too long absent from her life. "And thanks. I'm glad — "

One of the French doors opened, and Aengus bounded into the kitchen.

"Morning Julia," Lincoln closed the doors behind him. "We're hungry."

"One hearty breakfast for three coming up." When Aengus barked, Julia laughed, "OK, four."

"I'll feed him." Lincoln bent to lift the dishes from the feeding stand. Setting them on the island, he opened the cupboard on the side. He filled the food dish and put it down for Aengus to dig in. The water dish, he rinsed and refilled, placing it next to the food one.

"What can I do?" Bess offered, standing up from the table to help Julia at the kitchen island.

"How about chopping some veggies? I'm going to make us a frittata," Julia replied. "If you get the veggies from the fridge, I will put you at the other end of the island." Julia pulled a knife from the block and a wooden cutting board from a cupboard and placed it on top.

The three of them got on with the task of feeding themselves.

Back upstairs, they sat looking at the information they had collectively amassed and organized.

Lincoln was rocking on the back legs of his chair, then thumped down. "We need to come up with some sort of plan to investigate the people on the list."

"And have it in place before I have to return to work tomorrow."

"Why don't we start following them?" Julia offered. "We pick one or two people on the list and make up a schedule."

"Following, like in the movies?" Lincoln asked.

"Or in real-life detective work."

"And journalism."

"And journalism," Julia nodded at Bess.

"We need to be inconspicuous."

"Julia especially," Lincoln interjected. "We can't have her recognized and caught."

"I agree. She still might be the best between the three of us. I'm recognized by a majority of the local community, and Lincoln, you kind of are too."

"Well, my readers might recognize me, but other than that . . . "

"Fame aside, you have one very recognizable distinction," Bess said.

"What, this?" Lincoln waved his abbreviated arm.

"Yes," Bess said.

"I could always pull out my prosthetic arm and dust it off," he said. He hated it, though. It never felt a part of him.

"You have a prosthetic arm?" Julia asked.

"Yes, but I don't like to wear it. It's more for aesthetics than function. My hook is more practical, but it can cause an unwanted reaction."

"I still doubt you can go unnoticed."

"I'm siding with Bess on this one. You stand out, Lincoln. It's how you carry yourself as a man, a very tall, handsome, Black man."

"Well, what can I do then?"

"You can be my taxi driver," Julia said.

"From decorated soldier, to celebrated author, then cabbie." Lincoln put a little whine in his voice in an attempt to garner sympathy. The girls were having none of it, he could tell by the looks on their faces.

"Sorry my friend, but you gotta play the hand you're dealt," Bess said. Julia and Lincoln both groaned at the pun. Bess continued, undaunted.

"We are going to be following people in varying locations. It would be perfect, actually. You could drop Julia off a couple of blocks from where she would need to be and then pick her up later."

"That would work," Lincoln nodded. "Then I am also close if you need me." He felt better about Julia venturing further into public. This allowed him to keep a better watch over her.

"Who should be our first target?" Julia asked.

"Let's start with Howard Allenby, real estate agent," Bess suggested. "We can get a list of his properties and watch them. It might be good to follow him for a week or two to get a pattern. It could help us identify the properties used for trafficking purposes. Then we watch the ones that are suspect."

"I'm on board with that."

"Me too," said Julia.

CHAPTER 34

JULIA WAS SITTING AT THE KITCHEN TABLE with Hal's laptop when Lincoln and Aengus came in from their walk. "What are you up to?" he asked.

"I'm doing a web search on all of Howard Allenby's real estate listings." Julia made to get up, but Lincoln waved her back into her seat.

"I'm just going to make some toast this morning."

"Not feeling well?"

"Feeling fine, just that my clothes are a bit tight. You are too good a cook, and I have been overindulging," he laughed. "Time to make some changes or I'll have to buy new clothes soon. How are you feeling about putting yourself out there? I am concerned about how this might work against us if you are recognized."

"Well, we will have to make me unrecognizable then. If I make myself look like a homeless person, I might be overlooked a bit more. As I have a limited wardrobe, I want to go to a second-hand store and pick up some things to go with my homeless persona."

"I still don't like the risks involved with getting you out in public. But considering you're the best one for the surveillance gig, it might be good for us both to do a practice run without any of the players involved."

"I also need a haircut."

"Why?"

"Last fall, to change my appearance, Charlie cut my hair really short, but it's grown out considerably to the point that I look like my old self. Not good if I'm going out in public more."

"So, you had an encounter with Chuck the barracks barber?"

"Yes," Julia laughed.

❖

Julia caught her reflection in storefront windows. Her long hair gone, she felt more confident being out on the street. She walked into one of the downtown used clothing shops and bee-lined for the men's section. She kept an eye on whether or not she drew any attention, but most other browsers and the shop workers didn't give her more than a cursory glance. She managed to find a couple of shirts, a pair of pants and some funky glasses. She paid and left the shop. Her next stop was Value Village near Chinatown.

It was here she hit the goldmine: a couple of pairs of shoes, another pair of pants and an old, beat-up Tilley hat with some travel patches on it. She added a Vancouver Canucks windbreaker and an old, tatty backpack, and she figured she had what she needed for the charade.

She had 30 minutes or so before she was to meet Lincoln. Deciding to do homework, she stopped in a downtown park frequented by homeless people.

She found a spot against a rock formation facing the water, pulled out an apple she had bought in Chinatown and enjoyed a quiet moment to observe and listen. There was a couple who were obviously on a work break, but the people in the park were mostly a mixed age group looking to sell or score a fix. There were also a few young people sitting in the midst of their assorted belongs in various types of bags playing an array of musical instruments. There was a guitar, a mandolin and an African drum. They were quite good and very entertaining.

As she sat quietly observing, she was approached by a young guy with a tattoo of a bluebird that started on his neck and extended up to his cheek in front of his ear.

"Hey, how's it going?" he asked.

"Good," she answered. "I love your tat."

"Thanks," he smiled. "I'm Stu, but everyone calls me Bird."

Julia took the hand that was offered and shook it. "I'm Simmie. Short for Simone."

"Can I join you?" he asked.

"Certainly," she answered, moving her backpack to the ground between her legs.

"I haven't seen you here before," he said as he sat next to her. He smelled of pot, and his eyes were a little droopy and dilated. On the side of his face where the bluebird tat was, his black hair was shaved close above his ear, but the rest was long.

"No, I'm new in town," she said.

Bird absently picked at a scab on the back of his hand. "Where are you from?"

"Oh, here and there. I move around a lot."

"Well Simmie, if there is anything you need," Bird said, running his fingers through his long hair, "I'm in the know."

"In the know about what, exactly?" she asked.

"If you need a hot meal, cup of coffee and a snack, or a hot shower, I can hook you up."

"Good to know," Julia said. "Where do you suggest for all those things?"

"Well, Haven's Gate has three hot meals a day and a nutrition bar for between meals. They aren't too far from here," he said. "They are good people."

"Thanks, I'll check it out," she said.

"Are you sorted for a place to sleep tonight?" he asked.

"Someone told me about Tresle Bay," she answered.

"Yes. There is also Dunsinane House, that's women only," he said. "Just in case you would feel more secure. Gotta be safe."

Another guy approached, "Hey Bird, we're outta here."

"OK." Bird turned to Julia. "Nice meeting you."

Bird and his friends picked up their belongings and left the park in the direction of the Inner Harbour. Julia sat a bit longer and decided to go back towards Chinatown where she had arranged to meet up with Lincoln. She hoisted her backpack and walked up to the street. Making her way through Market Square, she turned onto Pandora and cut through Fan Tan Alley. Lincoln was in his car in the parking lot next to a local café that used to be an old garage. She slid in the passenger side and threw her backpack in the back seat.

"Nice backpack. I especially like the Def Leppard symbol on it," Lincoln said, turning on the ignition.

"Yeah, man. They rock," she laughed.

"Get everything you need?"

"Yes, I think so. It was fun, actually. I even met a very nice young street guy named Bird."

"Bird?"

"He had a tattoo of a bluebird on his neck," she said. "It was quite beautiful, actually. It couldn't have been cheap — it was very good quality."

"No problems?"

"No, he was quite nice. He gave me all sorts of advice about free meals, showers and housing."

"Where was this?"

"Just down in the park, by the bridge," she answered.

"That is a known park for drug dealing, so be careful if you go back there."

"I will."

CHAPTER 35

BIRD SAT ON THE STONE WALL across from the Businessmen's Club entrance, his hat on the sidewalk in front of him, hoping for handouts while he played his guitar. He was waiting for Hayden Sawyer.

The lawyer exited with a lunch companion. They shook hands and parted ways. Sawyer walked across the street in Bird's direction.

"I have a couple new girls I am grooming," Bird said. "It will be a few months before they are ready."

"Good. Time to bring in some new merchandise."

"There's something else," Bird said, pulling a piece of paper from the brim of the hat on the ground. He handed it to Sawyer. "I spotted her."

"Where?"

"Bridge Park."

"Did you follow her?"

Bird sniffed and rubbed his nose on his sleeve, afraid of the violence his answer would bring. "No."

"Not what I want to hear."

"It's been a year. She doesn't look like the photo." Sawyer's fist closed over the photo.

"But I know where to find her again."

"You'd better be right."

The crumpled photo dropped into the hat.

CHAPTER 36

J ULIA SAT ON THE SIDEWALK across the street from Howard Allenby's office, her back against the brick wall warmed by the sun. On the concrete in front of her was a cloth sack for loose change and a sign that read, "Anything Helps, God Bless." She had managed to claim this spot just as Allenby was arriving at his office. An hour later, he came out of the storefront and Julia quietly picked up her paraphernalia and stood. She followed him discreetly from the other side of the street.

He met someone for coffee at Starbucks, then returned to the office. Someone was in her spot when she returned, so she decided to sit on the same side of the street as Allenby's office, just down from its entrance. At lunch time, she saw Howard exit his office again and walk in her direction. She kept her eyes on the sidewalk and watched his shoes as he strolled past: nice leather, two-tone loafers with a tassel.

When he stopped on the corner waiting for the light to change, Julia again collected her things and got up to follow him. He walked down towards the harbour, and she saw him enter the Businessmen's Club. She made her way down to the benches on the cross street to wait for him to exit. Ninety minutes later, he appeared with who Julia presumed was his lunch appointment, but she didn't recognize them as one of the people on the human trafficking ring. She took a picture with her cellphone. They continued up the street, Julia following at a discreet distance.

When the two parted ways, Allenby didn't return to his office. Julia followed him to a public parking lot near a downtown market and drugstore, where he got into a car. Now she knew where he parked, as well as his car's make, model and license plate number.

For the remainder of that week, she continued to follow Allenby. It was predictable and by Thursday she was bored and glad the weekend was almost here.

That night over spaghetti and meatballs, she and Lincoln discussed next steps.

"Allenby is a boring subject. He works in the office in the morning. This week he met someone for lunch. Then he either returns to the office or leaves in his car. He usually has lunch at the Businessmen's Club, so I can't follow him in there."

"Well, it looks like my membership at the Club is going to pay off in more ways than I imagined. We can tag-team."

"I like that. And as the weekend is coming, Allenby could be visiting some of his properties getting ready for open houses."

"Makes sense."

"And if we follow him, we can see which of his properties he is showing and which ones he isn't."

"I doubt the ones he's showing will be used for sex trafficking purposes."

"Exactly. We can then eliminate them from our list of potential stakeout locations."

"Excellent idea."

Lincoln checked his cellphone. No new texts from Julia. Good, he thought. Hopefully he'd have no interruptions during his lunch with his editor. He dropped the cell back in his pocket just as she walked up the stairs towards him.

"Gloria," he said, holding the door for her and giving her a warm hug. "I'm so glad you could join me."

"I was thrilled to get the invitation, it's nice to get together. Do you have another book to send me?"

"No, not yet," he said, taking her arm and guiding her to the dining room. "I am in research mode at present. I thought it would be nice to just have a lunch to touch base and as a way to show you how much I appreciate all your efforts to make my drivel worthy of publication."

"How sweet of you to say that. When did you get a membership here?" she asked. "It isn't somewhere I would have imagined you would buy into."

"Well, a friend brought me here for dinner once, and it was always in the back of my mind. Becoming a member gives me the opportunity to build other professional connections. It is also a perfect place to hold a reading or literary event downtown, in a venue that isn't a bookstore."

"But you told me you loved doing the local bookstore events," Gloria said as they were seated.

"I do, don't get me wrong, but there have been times that a larger venue has been necessary," he explained. "And if I ever want to do a reading with some other authors, a larger crowd can be more easily accommodated here."

"I guess," nodded Gloria.

"Also, I would like to get involved in a local charity or two and it would be a good place to have fundraisers," he smiled. "The clientele here would garner a higher ticket price."

"Well, that makes sense then," she said. At that moment, their waiter came to take their drink orders and they took a few seconds to look at the menu.

Handing them back to the waiter, Lincoln noticed Bradford Meek come in with a female companion. Lincoln recognized his face from their wall of personalities; he was a local motel mogul with a reputation for shady business practices. Lincoln couldn't believe his luck when they were seated at the table next to him and Gloria.

"So, what kind of research are you doing? What kind of predicament is Abel Cayne getting into next?"

Lincoln laughed, focusing once again on his editor. "Well, I haven't quite decided yet, that's the purpose of my research."

"Well, I can't wait, so hurry up." Gloria smiled.

"You and my agent must be conspiring on the side. He's saying the same thing. But enough about my work, how are things going with you? Work busy? How are the grandkids?"

Lincoln took a drink of his coffee and listened to Gloria's news, while keeping one ear open to the table next to them.

The arrival of lunch put their chatting on hold, enabling Lincoln to focus on the conversation between Meek and his companion.

"I'm going to have to move the hospitality staff and clients. They will have to be distributed among a couple of my other properties," Meek said.

"It isn't exactly convenient at present."

"Well, there isn't anything I can do about that. If I don't move them around, it is harder to show consistent income and profit for any one of my properties. The logistics and personnel to do the redistribution isn't my issue. It's yours."

"I pay you . . ."

"No, you don't pay me," he whispered harshly. "I am given my share in a monthly payment from Avery's firm. We are all stakeholders in this business. We all take the risks."

"If it wasn't for me, there would not be a business. Don't forget that."

Their conversation was halted by the arrival of their waiter. Gloria, her initial hunger satisfied, now took the time between bites to once again continue her conversation with Lincoln. Unable to hear any more from the neighbouring table, he focused on his editor. The small portion of the conversation he had heard was a goldmine in terms of connecting more names on their list.

Lincoln couldn't help but wonder who Meek's lunch date was. The tone of their conversation indicated she could be higher up the chain in some way. But who was she?

After saying goodbye to Gloria, Lincoln was walking up the street towards his truck when his cellphone chirped, alerting him to a text message.

Julia kept her eye on Nigella Ford who had started packing up her camera equipment in the park across the street. Five minutes ago, Carlton O'Hara had pulled up and sat waiting in his truck while she finished her photo assignment.

Julia had texted Lincoln for an earlier pickup. That was four minutes ago.

Still no Lincoln.

She forced herself to sit calmly on the steps to the cathedral, rather than pace on the sidewalk which is what she really felt like doing. A minute later, she watched Nigella Ford walk towards O'Hara's brown SUV. Lincoln's truck pulled up to the curb and she hopped in.

"Hi," he said.

"I was beginning to get discouraged with this whole surveillance thing. But not today," she said, unwrapping the striped, tattered scarf from her neck.

"Because?"

"Look," she said, pointing to the SUV pulling away from the curb half a block up the street. "That is Nigella Ford the photographer and Carlton O'Hara, the man with the renovation company. You're here just in time to follow them."

"So that's why you texted me with the change of time and pickup location." He pulled away from the curb into traffic a couple of cars behind O'Hara's vehicle.

"Yes, I was following her from her part-time job at the photo studio on Fort Street. She was carrying the camera bag and she met up with O'Hara at the coffee shop in the YMCA. I went in and ordered a smoothie and overheard them talk about her taking some photos at one of the locations he was renovating. And that she would be getting the photos to 'Bell', whom I'm guessing is Arthura Bell, the web developer on our list."

"Hmm."

They both focused on the vehicle a few car lengths ahead, making sure they didn't lose it, while also ensuring they wouldn't be too close and get noticed. They followed the SUV out of the downtown core. When it drove into the three-car garage of a large, two-story house in a quiet cul-de-sac, Lincoln pulled over on a side street where they could observe from a distance.

The garage door closed behind the SUV.

Lincoln turned off the ignition.

"Lincoln, look at the sign on the lawn of that house." Julia pointed. It was a real estate sign listing the house for sale. It had a SOLD sticker across the top. "See who the realtor is?"

"Howard Allenby. Bingo."

They sat quietly watching the house. They were there half an hour when the garage door started to rise. They were expecting to see the brown SUV back out, but instead a white passenger van with a rental logo on the side passed them. It pulled into the now-open garage. A couple of girls in their teens were herded around the back end of the van before the garage door lowered again.

"Oh my. Did you see who was driving the van?"

"No, did you?"

"No. Do you think we should call the police?"

"And report what?" Lincoln asked. "A possible photo session? That isn't a crime."

"True."

They waited another 15 minutes before Lincoln started the engine. "I think we've seen enough from here. I don't want to draw any attention to the fact we are two people sitting in a vehicle on this residential street."

"As much as I would love to follow the van next, I agree."

"Oh, we're not going home."

Lincoln drove down half a block before making a U-turn and pulling over to the side of the road. He turned off the engine and leaned back to wait.

"Now we're pointing in the same direction the van came from. Hopefully they'll leave going that way too and we can easily follow."

Julia sat back in her seat to join the vigil.

"How was lunch with your editor?" she asked, breaking the silence a short while later.

"It was good. Guess who was having lunch at the table next to me?"

"Nope, not guessing. Out with it."

"Bradford Meek and a woman. And they mentioned someone named Avery, which is likely Colin Avery, the accountant."

"Wow, that is great. But I think I win."

"Oh, I don't think it is a competition, but I'll give you this one. Only because of this little excursion which has paid off in spades."

An hour later, the white van pulled out of the cul-de-sac. They were led back to the university where the van pulled into one of the lots adjacent to a block of residences. Lincoln pulled into a parking spot and turned off the engine. Julia took a small pair of binoculars out of her pack and aimed them in the white van's direction.

"Recognize anyone?"

"I count five girls. The woman in the front passenger seat is talking to them. I think I recognize her. It could be Pramita Joshi, but with the light fading it's hard to tell. The girls seem to be excited about something." Once the occupants of the van had entered one of the residential buildings, its driver backed out of the parking spot and left. Julia lowered the binoculars, turning to Lincoln. "There must have already been a few girls at the house when Ford and O'Hara arrived."

"Well, it could be all very innocent for them at this stage. They may not suspect what they are being pulled into."

Lincoln put his hand to the keys and turned on the ignition and lights. "I think we've had enough for today. Let's go home."

"I agree," Julia said, stuffing the binoculars into her backpack.

CHAPTER 37

Bess knocked on the sliding doors from the kitchen. She had hiked in through the forest, as per her usual routine. Lincoln let her in and took the pumpkin pie she held while she removed her coat and boots.

"Welcome, and happy Thanksgiving." Julia hugged her and took her coat.

"Smells good, and the table looks amazing."

"The turkey will be ready in a couple of hours. Everything else is prepped. That'll give us a chance to catch up. Can I get you a before-dinner drink? Wine? Whisky?"

"I'd love a glass of wine," Bess said, bending down to greet Aengus who was sprawled out on the floor on the edge of the dining area.

Lincoln poured them all a glass. "Shall we sit by the fire in the library? I was just about to light it."

"Before you do, I'd really like to see the results of your surveillance over the last few weeks. I know it's Thanksgiving, but . . . "

"Of course. Text messages aren't the same as an in-person update."

As they left the kitchen, Aengus rose from the floor and led the way upstairs.

Julia and Lincoln stood back sipping their wine, while Bess walked up to the wall with the photos, swirling her drink in the glass while taking it all in. After a sip, she turned to them.

"So, you've managed to get visual confirmation of the links between Pramita Joshi at the university, Carlton O'Hara, Nigella Ford, Howard Allenby, Arthura Bell, Bradford Meek and Colin Avery. I like how you've been taking photos during your surveillance."

"Well, Bell and Avery were just verbal confirmations from overheard conversations," Julia added.

"I see you have photos up for everyone except Hayden Sawyer."

"He's remained elusive. His charitable work is mentioned in the media, but no photos that I can find."

"Can I look through your photos?"

"Of course. Here's a pile, and I have more on the computer." Julia pushed some photos across the table and sat down to pull up her file of pictures on the computer.

Bess looked at each printed photo captured by Lincoln and Julia during surveillance.

"Here you go." Bess dropped the pile and handed Julia one photo.

Lincoln came around to look over Julia's shoulder. "No, that's Colin Avery," he said.

"I'm not talking about the man in the photo." Bess waited for the penny to drop.

"You mean Hayden Sawyer is a woman?" Julia looked up at Bess.

"You've got to be kidding me." Lincoln took the photo from Julia's hand to get a closer look.

"I thought you knew all along." Bess started sorting through the remainder of the pile and pulled out more pictures of Sawyer with other identified members of the human trafficking ring. She added the separated photos to the wall. When she was done, there were pictures up with Sawyer meeting almost all the people they had attached to the ring. Finished, Bess stood back next to Lincoln and Julia, who had come out from behind the table.

"My friends, I think we have our leader. Hayden Sawyer is the only one who has met with nearly everyone on the surveillance list so far."

"Who would fathom a woman would lead a human trafficking ring?"

"Well, there are two ways to leave the life. Get out, which is extremely hard, or move up."

"I'm just as stunned as Julia."

Bess pulled a memory stick out of her jeans pocket and handed it to Julia, who plugged it into the laptop. "I brought something to add to the research. This is a recording of an interview with an ER doctor I did recently."

They listened as the woman told her story of girls coming in beaten, sometimes raped or just sick from deprivation and neglect. The girls the doctor saw were usually accompanied by their boyfriend.

"It was during a night shift. A man brought in a teenage girl. She had been beaten and raped. When I examined her, I discovered two tattoos, one of a dollar sign on her inner thigh, another of a man's name on her vulva. All her pubic hair had been removed. I had heard stories from other ER doctors about young girls with tattoos, and that they suspected they were usually trafficked for sex. That was the first time I saw a girl with branding. I've seen other types of brands since, but that one will always stand out in my mind."

"Now I know why a tattoo artist is on the list of businesses," Julia said. "I think Nissim Varghese is going to be next on the surveillance list."

The other two nodded and all three of them took a drink from their wine glasses.

Bird walked into Hayden Sawyer's office. The angry expression on the lawyer's face was a not-so-subtle warning that this meeting wasn't going to go well.

Bird hesitated inside the door. "Close the door."

He closed the door.

"Sit."

Bird sat.

"I have not had a good Thanksgiving, Stuart. Can you guess why?"

Bird remained silent.

"What was the one thing that would have made me grateful this Thanksgiving?"

Bird looked at the holes in his high tops.

"Can you guess what that might be?"

Bird shrugged, but he knew.

"I only wanted one thing, the whereabouts of one person. And that one person was last seen by you."

"She hasn't shown up again."

"When we last met, you assured me you knew where she would be. That was almost a month ago."

Bird had nothing to say.

"Remember, I am the only one that stands between you and some serious jail time."

Bird looked up, fear now revealed in his expression.

"You'd better hope she turns up in the next week because your sentencing date is on the 15th. My submissions on your behalf could make or break you."

"I'll find her."

"Your next appointment to discuss your case is the 12th. I don't want to see you again before then, unless it is good news. If you spot her, I want you to text me immediately."

"Understood."

"Dismissed."

Bird left Sawyer's office much faster than he had entered.

CHAPTER 38

FTER TWO WEEKS OF FRUITLESS DAYS staking out the tattoo parlour, all Julia had learned were the hours that Nissim Varghese worked and where he regularly parked his car. It had been the same every day: when Varghese exited his shop, Julia followed him to his vehicle. Lincoln would pick her up and they'd return home for the night and start the whole scenario again the next day. Julia was getting tired of it. He had to be on the list for a reason, but it seemed more like a dead end.

Julia looked at her watch. She got up off the sidewalk and was about to step into the sandwich shop behind her, when she saw him exit his shop carrying a metal case, similar to those used by photographers or makeup artists.

She sent a quick text to Lincoln, then followed Varghese to the usual parking lot four blocks away. On the opposite side of the street, Julia jumped into Lincoln's idling truck as Varghese loaded his case into his trunk.

No conversation was necessary as Julia and Lincoln focused on traffic.

He led them to a house in James Bay where he pulled into the drive. A white panel van was parked in a covered carport. Lincoln managed to find parking on the street.

He retrieved his case from the trunk and made his way around the back of the house. Lincoln and Julia waited in silence. It was several hours later when they were alerted to movement, as a motion-sensor security light illuminated the side of the house. Varghese exited and, after putting his case back in the trunk, got in his vehicle and left.

Julia looked at Lincoln.

"I say we wait and follow the van."

He nodded in agreement and they once again sat in silence.

It was two in the morning, and Julia was sleeping in her seat when Lincoln gently touched her arm to wake her. The two of them slid down so as not to be seen. The light had come on again, and they saw two men leading a group of five young women from the back of the house.

They could not make out clearly what exactly the women or the men with them looked like. Once loaded, the van left the carport and backed out of the driveway. Lincoln turned on his engine.

Julia was glad for Lincoln's old truck. It meant they could follow without their lights on until they pulled into traffic.

They were able to keep track of the van as there were very few vehicles on the road. It made three stops. At each one, they deposited one or two of the girls. At the last house, the van pulled into a garage and Lincoln and Julia decided to call it a night.

Awoken by Aengus, Lincoln walked down the stairs, still in his pajamas and robe, to find Julia similarly attired, but dicing peppers.

"Well, good morning," she said.

"How long have you been up?" he asked.

"Twenty minutes. Long enough to let Aengus out, feed him and then send him to fetch you."

"What woke you?"

"Hunger," she answered and cracked eggs into a bowl. "How does a Denver scramble sound to you?"

"Like a good start."

They finished making breakfast in silence, taking turns passing a yawn back and forth. Once their brunch was plated and they were sitting at the table, Aengus sat at their feet waiting for any wayward morsels.

Julia took a sip of her coffee. "I've been thinking. It might be a good idea to stake out the four addresses from last night."

"I'm not too sure I like this idea. You are going to stand out, especially if you camp for the day."

"Well, I am not going to sit on the curb. I'm going to camp out at the end of the street and monitor the traffic that goes to the houses. It might give us an idea of who is going there and how often."

"I still don't like it, but it sounds like a plausible idea. But you're not going alone. You will set up at one end of the street and me at the other. You will monitor the traffic turning in on your end, text me descriptions of vehicles and licence plates and I will do the same on my end."

"That is a good plan," she nodded, and got up to pour herself another cup of coffee. "Let's gather lawn chairs, fluorescent vests, clipboards, sunglasses and hats so we look the part. We can pretend we're gathering traffic information for civic planning."

"Good idea."

"I say we shop tomorrow, then start the next day. I am still absolutely bushed and don't think I will be very attentive."

"Fine by me."

Julia had been sitting in her lawn chair with vest and clipboard since seven o'clock in the morning. She could just make out the two-story house with a three-car garage, four houses in from the corner. She was on the opposite side of the street for the best view. There was a straight line of sight up the street to the next intersection. She could just make out Lincoln, similarly attired. It had turned out to be a good plan, they blended in with the landscape.

For the first two hours of their vigil, most of the vehicular traffic was exiting the street or passing through. Typical for residents driving to work. There was no activity at the house. Around 9:30 A.M., a car turned onto the street. Julia kept her head down and noted the description and licence plate number. Her mirrored sunglasses allowed her to get a good look at the driver in the front seat without being seen as observing.

A single white male, mid-50s.

The car pulled into the driveway of the house. Before the driver exited, the garage door rose. Julia could see a black SUV parked in there, and the new arrival came to a stop next to it. The garage door lowered.

Julia picked up her phone to text the information to Lincoln. Ten minutes later, a message from Lincoln told her a car was coming from his end of the street. It turned into the same driveway. Like the vehicle before him, the garage door lifted, then lowered once he was inside.

Over the next several hours, two cars would arrive and leave in the same staggered fashion every half hour. The last two cars arrived around 4:30 P.M. Residents returning home from work increased traffic to and from the street. Gradually the neighbours returned and lights came on as evening darkness fell.

At 5:30 P.M., when only the black SUV remained at the house under surveillance, Lincoln drove up and Julia hopped into the passenger seat after tossing her lawn chair into the back of the truck.

"Well, what do you think?" Lincoln asked as she buckled in.

"With all the comings and goings, it appears to be a place of business, but there is no advertising signage or anything. Not even a real estate sign marking it associated with Howard Allenby."

"Not the kind of business you advertise in the usual fashion, I am thinking. And I don't think Allenby would want the visual association if anything goes wrong."

"I wonder how they do advertise?"

"Most likely managed through an internet booking program."

"Hal's note did say he started keeping records when he realized one of the businesses had an escort website in the course of his work as an IT consultant."

"I'm wondering what they do with the girls at night. I can't imagine they let them have the night off."

Lincoln turned to drive back down the street and pulled over to the side next to a house under construction. The workers had left for the day. He turned off the engine. "Are you really hungry?"

"Not yet. Why?"

"I would like to sit and watch for a while to see if there is any activity." He looked in his rear-view mirror, then back at Julia. "Keep an eye on all the houses for movement in the windows. If the neighbours get suspicious, we shouldn't stay very long."

"Will do."

An hour later, the garage door began to rise. Lincoln looked in his rear-view mirror. He touched Julia's arm, and they slipped down in their seats once more. They looked over the dash as a Lexus pulled into the drive.

The garage door opened. But didn't lower.

Two men and one woman exited the vehicle. They retrieved various bags from the trunk. The woman carried what looked like a makeup kit. The men carried camera and lighting equipment.

"Looks like they are getting organized for some kind of photoshoot, if that equipment is any indication."

The light in the garage made it easy to view all the parties involved. Two men exited the house and held the door for the woman. When she entered, the men leaving had a brief conversation with the people arriving before getting into their vehicle and backing out of the driveway. The garage door lowered.

"That looks like a shift change to me. I think we should go." Lincoln turned on the ignition and pulled away from the curb. As they passed the house, Julia looked up and saw someone putting blackout material in one of the second-story windows.

"I don't want to think about what they might be filming." Julia looked at a silent Lincoln, his face illuminated by the dashlights.

❖

After following the same routine for the other three houses with similar results, Lincoln and Julia were sitting around the fire after dinner on Friday night.

"I can't imagine what Hal saw or overheard to start him gathering information. Or investigating . . . whatever this is."

"A rabbit hole," Lincoln said, and Julia looked up at him. "This is a rabbit hole."

"And I'm Alice tumbling into the abyss."

"No, you are not. Alice was alone. You aren't."

"You sound like Charlie."

"He was a smart man."

"Yes, he was," Julia replied. "And so are you, so let's talk about the business at hand."

They could hear a tapping on the kitchen sliding door. Aengus barked and went into the kitchen.

"Hold that thought." Lincoln got up to follow. They returned with Bess in tow. The two women hugged.

"So, how did it go this week?" asked Bess.

"We were just sitting down to discuss that very thing. Have you eaten?" Julia asked, picking up their coffee mugs and leading the way to the kitchen. "There's some chili in the fridge I could warm up."

"Chili sounds fantastic."

"Well, then, let's move this party out to the kitchen and sit at the table," Lincoln suggested.

"Coffee, Bess?" Julia asked

"Please. It's been a long day and I need to have some wake-up juice."

"Lincoln?"

"Not for me, thanks." He sat next to Bess at the table. "You're welcome to spend the night. If you're tired, no need to drive back into town later."

"I think I'll take you up on that, thanks. I'm not working this weekend." Bess took the cup of coffee Julia handed her. "So, tell me about your stakeout week."

"During the day it seems each of the houses is a drop-in brothel. There was a steady stream of cars visiting the house at timed intervals. All the drivers were men," Julia said, stirring the pot of chili.

"We recorded the make, model and licence plate numbers of all the vehicles that came to the houses during the day," Lincoln added.

"What kind of time frame are we looking at?" Bess asked.

"The main flow of traffic to the house was between 9:30 A.M. and 4:30 P.M.," Lincoln answered.

"Makes sense. That way the neighbours won't be suspicious."

"I am sickened to think what those girls are going through." Julia placed a bowl in front of Bess and sat at the table beside her.

As Bess ate, Lincoln and Julia filled her in on all the details from the week's surveillance.

"So, have you decided who's the next surveillance subject?" Bess stood to rinse her bowl, then loaded it into the dishwasher.

"I was talking about that with Lincoln last night. I suggested Adrienne Wilder."

"Because?"

"She's on the board of Dunsinane House and Haven's Door."

"How did she make it onto your list, Bess?" Lincoln asked.

"Her marketing company has done some work with sex industry apologists."

"Apologists?"

"Those who are trying to rebrand the business of selling sexual services. Pimps become business agents, Johns are consumers and the women trapped in these services are now called sex workers rather than prostitutes or hookers. Similar to the attempt by pro-slavery advocates to rename slaves as assistant planters."

"A rose by any other name, as they say." Julia got up to put her coffee cup in the dishwasher.

"Exactly. Pimps and Johns, no matter what you want to call them, still view and treat women as commodities, bought and sold to serve the sexual appetites of men."

Julia looked at Lincoln. "Present company excluded."

"Thank you."

"Did you two come up with a plan to follow Wilder?"

"I'm going to stake out her office, follow her around and see where it will lead."

"And I'll play my usual role." Lincoln mimed driving a car.

"But at some point, I think I will present myself at Dunsinane House as an abuse victim to see what I can learn."

"What?" Bess looked at Lincoln then back at Julia. "When did you come up with this idea?"

"This is the first I'm hearing it too." Lincoln raised his hand in surrender at Bess' accusatory tone.

"Well, short of anyone coming forward and confessing, I don't see any other way to actually get hard evidence. Do either of you have a better idea?"

Silence.

Then Lincoln spoke, "We'll try to come up with something, but in the meantime we'll keep gathering evidence by surveillance."

CHAPTER 39

I T WAS THE EIGHTH DAY OF FOLLOWING ADRIENNE WILDER. Eight days of
watching her come and go from her offices, meeting people outside the
office in coffee shops and cafés. From what Julia observed, she never met
with anyone else from their list of potential members of the human trafficking
ring. Other than her presence on the two Board of Directors, nothing seemed a
potential link.

Finding shelter in a small coffee place across from Wilder's office, Julia sipped
from a cup of hot chocolate. It was a cold and rainy November day and she needed the hot liquid to warm her up, inside and out.

She had been texting with Lincoln to pass the time. He was bored too, albeit
more comfortable at the public library.

Julia abandoned the near-empty cup when she saw Wilder exit her office.
Out on the street, she followed at a discreet distance, sending Lincoln a text as
she walked.

Adrienne Wilder entered Haven's Gate's courtyard. Julia hesitated, watching
from the sidewalk.

"Simmie, how's it going?"

Julia nearly jumped out of her skin. She turned and looked into the face of
Bird. "Good. Bird, right?"

"Ah, you remembered me."

"That tat is hard to forget." She looked over Bird's shoulder at Wilder, who
was speaking with someone at the coffee cart in the far corner of the courtyard.

"Have you been keeping safe? It is a dangerous world out there."

"Yes, so far so good."

"Where have you been sleeping?"

"I had a nice sheltered spot along the Gorge until someone else decided they liked it too, so I had to move on." She shrugged as if it was no big deal.

"That's good," he said. "Don't forget about Dunsinane House."

"I'll keep it in mind." Julia saw Wilder go into the outreach centre and itched to follow.

"Can I get you something hot to warm you up?"

"That's sweet. Yes. I could use a cup of tea."

For the next 20 minutes, she tried to be engaged in her conversation with Bird while keeping an eye out for Wilder. She positioned herself so that she could watch over Bird's shoulder while appearing to listen to his ramblings on street life. Needing to keep him occupied and not wanting to talk too much about herself, Julia said, "Tell me about your bluebird tat. What's the story behind it?"

"When I was a kid, I tamed a bluebird that had a broken wing," he said. "I kept it in a cage for a long time until it died. I loved that bird. It was the only pet I ever had as a kid. My dad didn't like animals and wouldn't allow me to have a dog or cat."

"I had a dog as a child. What did you name the bluebird?"

"Blue," he laughed. "Unoriginal I know. I always remembered that bird, and after I got my first tat," he pushed up his sleeve to reveal a barbed wire design that ribboned around his forearm up to his elbow, "I decided to honour Blue and all he meant to me when I was a kid. It's kind of like he is still with me, sitting on my shoulder."

"Whoever did it did a fabulous job," she said.

"I bartered for it," he said. "I knew someone who worked in a tattoo parlour, and I cleaned the place for the tat."

"Smart," Julia answered, increasingly distracted. She wanted to get inside to see where Wilder had gone. "Bird, I'm sorry, but I need to find the ladies room. Will you excuse me, please?" Julia knew where it was, having checked out the facility early in the surveillance days. She'd known she'd be coming here at some point and wanted to know the lay of the land and all the possible exit points. But she wanted to get out of her conversation with Bird.

"Sure, I'll hold your tea."

"Thanks." Julia handed him her cup and walked away.

Julia looked behind her and saw Bird talking with another guy his age. She entered the building into a large dining space lined with tables. She wound her way through the tables towards the washrooms on the other side, but didn't enter. Instead, she ducked around a corner to watch the dining room.

Adrienne Wilder came out of a corner office followed by Zachary Porter, the director of Haven's Gate. Julia recognized Porter from the centre's website. Hayden Sawyer was with them.

Julia watched as the three left the central dining area and entered the courtyard. She was just about to follow when she saw Sawyer separate from Wilder and Porter, and walk up to Bird. Julia pulled out her cellphone and snapped a couple of pictures of Sawyer with Bird. Bird was animated in his conversation and pointed to the dining area. The hair on the back of Julia's neck prickled. She dropped the phone back into her pocket and looked around, saw the fire exit next to the office and decided to duck out. It led her into the delivery alley behind the centre. She ran. When she was a couple of blocks away, she pulled out her cell and called Lincoln.

"Hi. Everything OK? You usually text."

Julia was still out of breath from running. "Yes, but I'm done for the day. I just hit gold following Wilder. Pick me up at the Cathedral."

"Will do." Lincoln disconnected.

Julia turned in the direction of the Cathedral, happy to be walking, but she still looked over her shoulder to see if Bird was looking for her. She only relaxed when she climbed into Lincoln's truck.

Late the next afternoon, Julia was tired. She had been watching and following Hayden Sawyer all day. It didn't produce anything new, so she was a little disappointed. Bird had entered the office about 10 minutes ago, but since Julia wasn't a fly on the wall, it didn't give her anything actionable. She pulled out her phone to text Lincoln for a pickup when she spotted Bird coming out of Hayden Sawyer's offices. She ducked into a storefront doorway so as not to be seen. She didn't know where Bird lived, so had no way to create a surveillance plan. This was the perfect opportunity. Julia decided to follow him.

She kept a block distance between them until he turned a corner, then she hustled so as not to lose him.

He was heading towards the homeless shelter in the more seedy and industrial area of town. He stopped to talk to one of the girls working the street, and Julia stepped into a doorway to wait.

A car pulled up and another girl got out. When she turned and saw Julia, she didn't look happy and walked towards her.

"This is my block."

"I'm not working."

"Move on."

Julia looked towards Bird, but he was still talking to the girl. Not wanting to step out of the cover of the doorway, Julia didn't listen to the suggestion.

"You heard her. Move on."

Julia wondered where the man had come from. "I told the lady I'm not working." She turned to keep an eye on Bird's whereabouts and noticed he was walking away. Before Julia could step out and follow Bird, the pimp plowed her in the face. She hit the sidewalk, stunned.

"That was your warning." The guy leaned over her. "NOW. MOVE. ON."

Julia pushed herself up and walked in the direction she had come from, Bird now forgotten. A safe distance away, she pulled out her phone and texted Lincoln. When he pulled over to the curb, she hopped in.

"Julia, what happened? You're bleeding."

Julia pulled down the visor to look in the mirror. Her eye and cheek were starting to swell and there was a fine line of blood coming from a small cut on her cheek. She touched it and sucked in air.

"What were you doing down in this area?"

"I saw Bird leave Sawyer's office and decided to follow him."

"Without texting me?"

"Sorry."

Lincoln pulled away from the curb and drove them home in silence. Forty minutes later, Julia was crouching down in the front seat as Lincoln pulled into the garage. They could hear Aengus howl on the other side of the door as Lincoln pushed the remote to close the doors behind them.

Julia's face throbbed as they made their way indoors.

Lincoln let Aengus out into the back yard and then turned to Julia.

"Sit."

Julia sat at the small table in the kitchen nook while Lincoln pulled an ice pack from the freezer and wrapped it in a tea towel that was hanging on the oven door. Before applying it to Julia's face, he took a minute to do a full inspection of her injury.

"You don't need stitches. You were lucky." He pressed the pack against her cheek.

Julia flinched as she took it from him and held it herself. "Are you still mad?"
"Yes. But I'll get over it." He stepped back and rested his hip against the kitchen island. "Promise me you won't go anywhere without letting me know."
"I promise."

❖

That night Lincoln, Bess and Julia looked at the much-expanded charts on the walls of the spare bedroom. Julia was still holding an ice pack to her cheek. They had put together a loose connection between most of the businesses in the framework of a human trafficking ring. Hayden Sawyer and Adrienne Wilder were now situated at the top of its hierarchy.

"Short of adopting illegal hacking practices to gain hard evidence, I'm not sure how much more we can do." Bess sat next to Julia and looked up at Lincoln.

Julia laid the ice pack on the table beside her. "It's time for me to check into Dunsinane House."

"I don't like it."

"I agree with Lincoln."

"Look you two, there really is no other way to draw Wilder or Sawyer out," Julia said. "We know Bird is connected to them on the street level of recruitment. We've established a connection between Wilder and Sawyer, and Wilder is on the Board of Directors of two organizations that should be helping women but might instead be used to traffick them. One of those organizations being Dunsinane House. Everyone else on this list is doing the business' trench work. These two are at the top of the organization. If Bird pressuring me to go into Dunsinane House is any indication, we could find out a lot."

"You could also disappear," Lincoln pointed out.

"For the potential gain, I think it is worth the risk. We have so much information on paper, but a lot of it is circumstantial. We need to directly implicate these two to really solidify the evidence."

"Julia has a point. If it wasn't for the fact that I'm a known journalist, I would happily step in."

"You could still go in and find out under the cover of writing a story," Lincoln added. His frustration with the lack of options could be seen in his fingers drumming on the tabletop.

"But, again, they know she is a journalist and she'll only get the sanitized version for potential financial supporters. Bess, where are you at with writing all this up into articles?"

"Pretty much ready to go to print. The editor doesn't want to wait and has decided there's enough there to do an in-depth series. More articles will come about depending on what happens once the news breaks."

"Then that's decided. We have to get something on Wilder and Sawyer before too much makes it to the papers. We can't risk them getting out of town, or even the country."

Lincoln's fingers stilled and he nodded, knowing it was an argument he was losing. When Julia had brought the idea up previously, he knew this was the road they were plummeting down, but as much as he tried he couldn't come up with a better plan. "OK, I want to go over again how we're going to do this."

"Tomorrow I'm going to go in and present myself as a victim of spousal abuse looking for sanctuary. This should help," Julia pointed at her bruised cheek and black eye. "The timing is perfect."

"You're going to check in with me every hour."

"Yes, until I go into Dunsinane House, then every two hours."

"I would prefer every hour." Lincoln looked at her.

"I know, but that would look rather suspicious if I'm caught. Realistically, I most likely will be busy getting registered and interviewed in."

"Lincoln, I doubt they're going to recognize her right away. I certainly didn't when I met her the first time. Julia will be in a good position to really gather some information."

"Thank you, Bess." Julia turned to Lincoln, who still stood rigid as a plank. "If we are all in agreement?"

Lincoln remained silent, but eventually nodded his assent.

"Lincoln, I have a spare room at my condo," said Bess. "Why don't you and Aengus stay in town at my place so you are close if Julia needs you? I'll be on duty at the paper all weekend."

Lincoln nodded.

Sensing the tension in the room, Aengus got up from his sprawled-out position on the floor nearby and walked over to Julia. She put her arms around his neck and kissed his cheek. "It's OK, boy. I'll be fine."

"I'm tired, so I'm going to bed. I don't think I'll get a lot of sleep over the next couple of days. I may not sleep at all and any shut-eye I can get now would be good." Julia stood. She hugged Bess then retired to her suite. Aengus followed her.

"I'll go home and get the spare room ready for you."

"Where did you park?" Lincoln looked out at the pouring rain.

"About half a mile away."

"I'll drive you to your car."

"Thanks, I won't turn that offer down. It's miserable out."

Bess crouched down in the front until they were several blocks away. When Lincoln pulled up behind her car, Bess turned to him, her hand on the doorknob. "I'm worried too, but we have a plan in place. If we stick to the plan, Julia will be OK."

"Do you pray, Bess?"

"At times. In my line of work, when I need strength and wisdom from somewhere."

"And does it work?"

"Yes. I believe it does."

"Goodnight, Bess."

Bess nodded and closed the door behind her.

Lincoln waited until Bess drove away, then turned for home.

CHAPTER 40

A T 7:30 A.M. THE NEXT MORNING, Bess welcomed Julia, Lincoln and Aengus into her small, downtown condo. Aengus wandered around the tight quarters and managed to find a space to accommodate himself in front of the gas fireplace. He put his head on his paws and watched his humans. While Bess showed Lincoln the guest room, Julia stood at the balcony windows and looked down at the street below. If it wasn't for the office building across from Bess' apartment, Julia would be able to see Dunsinane House. She was glad Lincoln would be close.

Bess came into the open-concept living space, followed by Lincoln. She looked down at Aengus who lifted his eyebrows at her. "I never realized how small my place was until Aengus arrived." She smiled and bent down to rub behind his ears. "OK, fella?"

Lincoln walked up to Julia at the window. "How are you feeling?"

"Scared, I won't lie."

"Scared is good. It will keep you on your toes and aware. If at any time you feel a serious threat, just get out. I'll come for you."

Julia nodded.

"I have to drop in at the paper for a bit. Here's my extra set of keys." Bess handed them to Lincoln. "Make yourself at home."

"Thanks, Bess." Lincoln took the keys. Bess hugged Julia. "We got you."

"I know."

❖

An hour later, Julia picked up the receiver of one of the few remaining payphones in Victoria. She took the slip of paper with the number for Dunsinane House out of her pocket. Once dialed, she turned and watched the early library users come in from the rain as she waited for someone to answer.

"Yes, hello. I've just left my husband and I have nowhere to go."

The voice on the other end was gentle and began to ask her questions.

"Yes, I'm safe. No, I'm alone. I'm calling from a public payphone. No, I don't need medical attention. I can walk there. I don't need to be picked up."

Julia knocked on the front door of Dunsinane House. She was nervous and soaking wet from the pouring rain.

"All is in your hands, God and I leave it there." Julia whispered the prayer as she looked over her shoulder, waiting.

Both hands gripped the shoulder straps of her daypack. She released them when the door opened. A middle-aged woman with blonde dreadlocks looked at her and when she saw Julia's cheek she opened the door wider.

"Oh my, sweetheart. Come in, come in. Are you June?"

"Yes."

"We're so glad you called us."

"I'm glad you had a place for me."

Julia looked back out to the street as the woman closed the door. Sensing Julia's apprehension, the woman took her hand. "You're safe now. Do you want medical attention?"

"No." Julia jumped. "I'm OK. It looks worse than it is. Are you Mona?" She attempted to cover the bruise with her hand. "I'm sorry, I'm dripping all over your floor."

Mona nodded. "Let's just get you out of that wet coat. We can hang it right here to drip dry."

Julia slipped her daypack off her shoulders and let Mona take her coat.

"Come with me, June. We'll sit you down and get a hot drink into you."

"We?"

"Me and my co-worker. There are two of us on duty at all times for security reasons."

Julia followed Mona down a hall lined with photographic artwork. None of the other doors were open, preventing her from getting an accurate layout of the floor plan. All was quiet. In the office, a woman sat at a computer and turned when they entered.

"Hey, Rhonda. This is June."

"June, I'm sorry to meet you under these circumstances. But you are welcome here and you are safe. Have a seat. Can we get you something hot to drink?"

"I'm cold and would really appreciate a cup of coffee, please."

"I'm on it. Be right back." Mona left the office.

"When did that happen, June?" Rhonda pointed to Julia's cheek.

"Last night."

"You're sure you don't need medical attention for it?"

"Positive. I've had worse."

"Do you have any other injuries I can't see that might require medical attention?"

"No."

"I just need to ask you some basic questions as part of getting you signed in. Do you feel up to it?"

"Yes."

"What is your full name? Do you have any identification with you?"

"June Rogers. And no. My husband always locked up my wallet at night. I left when he was in the shower this morning. I . . . "

"It's OK, June. Take your time. We don't even need to continue you if you feel you need to rest or have something to eat. The necessary paperwork is tedious and can take a while. You might feel drained after all you've been through, so we're going to do the basics for now and then let you rest. How does that sound?"

"Good." Julia touched her cheek. "This has been going on for years. My husband, just, I . . . I don't know, I just had to leave. Weekends when he is home from work are the worst. I just couldn't face another alone with him."

"Do you have any family close by?"

"No. I have one sister, but she's on the East Coast in grad school."

"Are you able to contact her?"

"I emailed her from the library just before I called you."

"We'll try to call her later if you like."

"Thank you."

Mona came back into the office with a mug of coffee and handed it to Julia. With a "thank you," she gripped it with both hands to warm them. She really was cold from the wet weather.

Rhonda looked down at the form she was filling out. "Are you currently on any medication?"

"No."

"So, no birth control pills? Any chance you're pregnant?"

"No, I get the Depo shot every three months. My husband doesn't know. He thinks we're trying to get pregnant, but I couldn't bring a child into that environment."

"Have you had any drugs or alcohol in the last 24 hours?"

"No."

"Are you hungry?"

"Yes." Julia looked at Rhonda. "Is that on the form?"

"No, but that's all the information I require to start. We can continue later. We'll see about getting you some breakfast and then show you to your room. Maybe after lunch we'll fill out the remainder of the paperwork for your stay with us." She smiled. "Nothing too in-depth, we just need to put you on the record to keep track of our numbers in the house. We'll also go over the general house rules, and possibly discuss what you need and how we can help you."

"That sounds good."

"We have a nurse practitioner on call in case someone comes to us injured. I am concerned about your cheek. Can I see if she can pop in today and have a look at it?"

Julia nodded. "Thank you."

"Good. I'll give her a call once we're done here."

Julia was sitting in a small room with a single bed, night table and lamp. The lamp cast an eerie glow. It seemed depressing to Julia, but for someone on the run it would feel safe for a while, which was all that mattered. Dropping her backpack on the bed, she stepped to the small window. Looking out, she could see the garbage and compost bins below. She pushed to see if the window would open, relieved when it did, knowing she had a means of escape if need be.

Satisfied, she sat on the bed, testing the mattress' firmness. She pulled her cellphone out of the inner pocket of her backpack. She had turned off all audible alerts so as not to let the staff know she had a cell. Time to check in with Lincoln. She typed a short recap of the past hour and hit send.

His reply was one-word — "good" — and came seconds after she hit send. She thought for a moment, then typed, "In case the information comes in handy later, my room overlooks the back of the house, right above the bins. The window opens, so I have an escape route if need be. Curtains are blue and green vertical stripes."

Lincoln replied, "Good girl."

Despite her attempt to go to bed early the night before, she hadn't slept well due to anticipating today's events and imagining all that could go wrong. Weariness overwhelmed her and she lay down on her side, hugging her pack to her chest. She set the alarm on her phone to wake her in two hours so she could check in with Lincoln, as per their agreement. She tucked the cell into her bra to ensure she would feel the vibration when the alarm went off. Sleep claimed her shortly after her head touched the pillow.

CHAPTER 41

A FTER JULIA'S FIRST TEXT MESSAGE upon entry into Dunsinane House, Lincoln took Aengus out. He walked the two blocks to the street where the shelter stood two houses in. There was a small park one block further and Aengus happily found a patch of grass that suited his purposes. From this park, Lincoln could see between the houses that backed onto the same alley as Dunsinane House. He focused, then spotted the green top of the compost bin, and just above it was a window with green and blue striped curtains.

Bingo, he thought, and looked around the park. A few feet away was a bench dedicated to Florence Hughes, who had planted the maple tree in the centre of the park.

Lincoln picked up after Aengus, then sat on the bench. He still had a view of Julia's window. Perfect.

Aengus tugged on the leash.

"OK, boy. I guess a longer walk is in order as I've messed with your usual schedule."

Knowing he had a couple of hours before he'd hear from Julia again, he led Aengus towards Beacon Hill Park a few blocks away.

CHAPTER 42

JULIA SLEPT UNTIL THE VIBRATION OF HER CELLPHONE woke her up as planned. Grateful for the rest, she sent a quick text to Lincoln and then listened at her door for sounds in the house. It was still pretty quiet. She looked at her watch — nearly 11:00 A.M.

She ventured from her room and walked down the hall to the washroom she had been shown earlier. Looking in the mirror, she winced as she saw her eye and cheek. The black had crept into both eyes, but the swelling had gone down somewhat with the ice pack Mona had given her. Her cheek was still swollen, but she was grateful to be able to see out of her eye, so she figured she could live with it. Once she had cleaned up, she silently walked down the hall and listened to the voices coming from the kitchen.

"We got a new girl this morning. Mid-30s I'd guess."

Julia recognized Rhonda's voice, obviously talking to someone else in the kitchen.

"Her husband walloped her pretty good. She was developing a couple of black eyes in addition to a bruised and swollen cheek."

Julia was walking towards the kitchen, but stopped in her tracks when she heard the other voice reply, "Well, that's disappointing. She won't be usable for a while then." With her back against the wall, Julia listened closely, hoping no other residents would come out into the hall and catch her eavesdropping. "We need some new blood. Is she a young mid-30s, or does she look older? The middle-aged moms with kids that have been coming in lately aren't marketable."

"Yes, but helping them gives us legitimacy. We can't whore out every woman that comes to us. Word would get out and they'd shut us down pretty quick," Rhonda responded.

Julia heard the clunk of a mug being put down on the table.

"I'll stop by in a couple of days to meet her and see if she'd be of any value," the other woman said.

Julia decided she didn't want to be caught in the hall where it was obvious she would have heard their conversation. She turned to gain her bearings. The door to her room was between her and the kitchen. Did she risk going towards the kitchen and getting caught or run back to the bathroom, not knowing if she'd make it? She decided to try for her room. She heard footsteps in the hall just as she closed the door.

She pulled the cellphone out of her pocket and sent a quick text to Lincoln with an update. She decided to wait for five minutes after hearing the front door close. In that time, the front door opened again, and she heard footsteps go down the hall to the kitchen. She waited another five minutes in case the unknown woman had forgotten something and returned. When she heard no further footsteps, Julia decided it was safe to venture forth. She stepped out into the hallway and walked to the kitchen doorway again, the useless ice pack in her hand.

Mona was standing by the counter next to the coffee-maker.

"Hello June, how are you feeling? Were you able to rest at all?"

"Surprisingly, I actually slept for a couple of hours. I'm sore, but at least I can see out of my eye, thanks to the ice pack you gave me." She didn't step any further into the room, feeling apprehensive and wanting to appear so. A woman sat at the table, looking at her over the rim of her mug.

"This is Beatrice. She's one of the volunteer dayworkers here. Beatrice, this is June, our newest guest." Rhonda took the ice pack from Julia and returned it to the fridge's freezer compartment. "Well, I'll leave you two to get acquainted. I have work to do."

Julia stepped into the kitchen to allow Rhonda to pass. Beatrice approached Julia, offering her hand. Julia took it and felt a sense of calm from the woman. "I come in four days a week and help with lunch prep, so you'll see me around. Welcome."

"Thanks. Nice to meet you."

"Have a seat. Can I get you something to drink while I start lunch?"

"I don't want to be any trouble."

"No trouble at all. How about tea, or even hot chocolate?" Beatrice pulled out a chair for Julia.

"A glass of water would be perfect, but I can get it. Mona gave me the tour when I arrived."

"Help yourself then, and keep me company while I start. There are five women and four kids in residence in addition to you. They usually come down around noon."

"Can I help, please? I would like to be useful."

"Today I would just like your company while I work. I have a system all sorted out. Relax. Tomorrow, if you are still eager, I'll definitely put you to work. Weekends are busier with kids out of school."

"It's a deal. How did you come to volunteer here?"

"Years ago, I was a guest just like you. Only I had a two-year-old in tow. He's in high school now."

Beatrice was a storyteller, and Julia was content to listen as it was exhausting to continually weave her false tale of how she came to be there. She understood Beatrice's chatter was to put her at ease and not place any demands on her. Julia wondered how many of the women and children who sought shelter here were met with the same grace. *Too many to count*, she thought.

After lunch, Julia helped with the clean-up. She was drying the last of the dishes when Rhonda came into the kitchen.

"June, the nurse is here."

"OK, thanks." She hung the dishtowel and smiled at Beatrice as she followed Rhonda.

The nurse was waiting in a small room arranged like an exam room in a doctor's office. There was a sink below some cabinets and an exam table with a cotton sheet covering it. A blood pressure cuff hung on the wall and a lamp with an adjustable arm was pushed flush against the wall behind the table. The nurse was facing the wall where her bag sat open on a waist-high shelf.

When Rhonda and Julia entered, the nurse turned around, auburn curls framing her heart-shaped face. Her smile was warm and friendly.

"Hi, June. My name is Heather. Hop up on the table and let me have a look at that cheek for you."

"I'll leave you to it. When you're done, June, please come down to my office. If you feel up to it, maybe we can finish your intake paperwork."

"I will." Julia sat on the table.

"Now, let's see." Heather stepped towards Julia and raised her gloved hands to probe the edges of the bruising. "This might hurt a little. I just want to feel around a bit to see if there is anything broken."

Julia braced herself. There was pain on the cheek, but not too much anywhere else.

"It looks like nothing is broken. I think if you keep icing it for another day it should heal up nicely. Are you in a lot of pain?"

"It just mostly throbs, but nothing I can't handle. I have been icing it, which has helped."

"I'm going to give you a few mild pain tablets. They aren't prescription-strength, but they might help if you do feel you want something."

"Thank you."

"Let me take your blood pressure while I'm here, and just do a quick general check-up. Will that be OK? I would also like to do one more thing before we finish. Would you allow me to take a photograph of your facial injuries? You might need them for court later, and it's best to get a picture now while it is fresh and at its worst. Would that be OK?"

Julia panicked, her old fear of discovery coming to the forefront. But knowing that it might also make her story and reason for being here more believable, she consented.

"Sure, I guess that would be alright."

"I'll just get Rhonda who has the camera. Be right back."

Heather entered after a knock on the door, followed by Rhonda with her camera in hand.

"Heather tells me you checked out OK, nothing broken."

"Yes, thankfully."

"I'll get several pictures from all angles."

"Where do you want me to stand?"

"You just stay sitting on the table. It's a better height for picture angles."

Heather and Rhonda worked in tandem. Heather moved Julia's head and face into different positions while Rhonda focused on getting the best shots. The flash assaulted Julia's senses. She felt exposed and humiliated. She wondered if all victims felt this way. Most likely.

"There, all done. How are you doing?"

"OK, I guess." Julia felt a sudden onset of tears. It wasn't clear whether it was the harsh pop of the camera flash, the stress she felt over the last 24 hours, or just the gentleness Heather and Rhonda offered, but she had trouble blinking them back.

Rhonda put the camera down. "Oh, my dear. You're going to be OK. You're safe and among friends here."

Heather pulled some tissues from a box on the side of the sink and pressed them into Julia's hand.

"You just cry if you want. Let them flow. Tears are healing."

Julia nodded and blew her nose.

CHAPTER 43

ADRIENNE WILDER WALKED INTO THE STUDY where Hayden Sawyer sat reading through a file in preparation for court the next day. She looked up when Adrienne appeared.

"I just got a photo from Rhonda at Dunsinane House. Here's the latest arrival." Wilder handed her the photo.

Sawyer, focused on the upcoming case, gave it a cursory glance. "Until that face heals, she won't be much use. Maybe even too old for the houses. Let's see what she looks like in a week or so, maybe she'll be good for the special requests market. Some like them older."

"I think you need to take a closer look, sweetheart."

Sawyer looked over the top of her reading glasses at her wife. The smile on Adrienne's face was reminiscent of the expression she had when giving a gift. Curious, she picked up the photo and studied it.

"Recognize her?"

Sawyer looked beyond the bruises and swelling, focusing on the eyes and mouth. Then she saw it.

CHAPTER 44

J ULIA LOOKED AROUND THE LOUNGE. It was a bright and cosy room that had
a bookcase overflowing with paperbacks and magazines. There was a television and DVD player in one corner and an old upright piano against the
far wall near the fireplace. Julia thought it would make a lovely gathering place
at Christmas, with a fire going in the hearth, a Christmas tree in one corner and
someone playing carols on the piano.

After her official paperwork and meeting with the nurse on Friday when she
arrived, Julia had been pretty much left to herself for a couple of days. On Saturday, they had included her in house cleaning duties when Julia asked to be put
on the chores list. This morning she had sat in on a group discussion session held
every weekday.

The mild pain tablets from Heather had helped with the throbbing of her
bruised cheek. Now, her face, though still terribly discoloured, looked somewhat
normal in shape. Beatrice had given her some makeup that morning to help her
hide the black and blue bruises.

The house had been busy with children over the weekend, but now they were
back in school, Julia was starting to get bored. Outside of her check-in texts with
Lincoln, she really didn't have much to occupy her time or mind. She explored
the bookcase. It was in disarray and she decided to tidy it up and organize it as a
distraction. When the shelves looked neat, she pulled down a book and relaxed
into the overstuffed and well-worn easy chair near the piano.

The book lay unopened on her lap. Julia realized the traffickers had such an
opportune arrangement. The women, like herself, most probably gave a false

name in fear. So really there was no record of Julia's visit, just some woman in her 30s named June. She had not overheard any further conversations similar to the one she stumbled across on her first morning.

Julia was three chapters into the novel when Rhonda came into the lounge.

"How are you doing this afternoon, June?"

"I'm good. Starting to get a little bored, though. That is no reflection on my time here at all. I'm just used to being a bit more occupied."

"That's understandable, but you have needed the time to let yourself heal as well."

"Yes, and I am so grateful."

"If you are interested, there is something you might be able to be involved in. It could occupy you until you are a bit more sorted and know what steps you want to take next."

"I'm interested."

"I'd like you to meet someone who has a little project on the go and is looking for some willing hands to help. Come to my office and I'll introduce you."

In Rhonda's office, she introduced Julia to a name and face on the human trafficking ring wall. "June, this is Adrienne Wilder. She works on our fundraising board. We told her about you, and she wanted to meet you."

"I'm very pleased to meet you, and that you came to us for help," Adrienne said, continuing to hold Julia's hand between her own. "You're lovely, and I'm sorry you have suffered such a terrible injury. I trust you have been given appropriate medical treatment?"

"Yes, thank you," Julia replied. "Everyone has been very kind to me."

"Ms. Wilder is involved with a new house project they're hoping to open in the next month," Rhonda said. "It's designed for women who are over the adjustment period of their freedom from their abusers. It will give them a more home-like environment to help them get established in a new life."

"That sounds interesting," Julia said.

"Yes, June. We're looking for some helping hands to get it ready in the next couple of weeks," Adrienne said. "Would that be something you would consider? I know it can be a bit of an adjustment period when someone first leaves an abusive environment, and this might be a good distraction. It would certainly help us out if you're willing and feel up to it."

"I'm more than able and willing to give a hand. I'd be glad to."

"Excellent. I appreciate it. How about I pick you up tomorrow after breakfast?"

"Sure."

"I'll see you tomorrow then."

Text messages:

J: It's a go. Adrienne Wilder is picking me up tomorrow to help organize a
    new house for women ready to move on from emergency shelter.
L: What time?
J: After breakfast.
L: I still don't like this.
J: I know.
L: Not too late to abort.
J: Not aborting. Too important. I'll text you when we're leaving.
L: I'll be close.
J: You'd better. ;-)

CHAPTER 45

A ENGUS HUNG HIS HEAD OVER THE CAR SEAT, resting his chin on Lincoln's shoulder. Both man and dog watched out the windshield, waiting. A tap at the passenger window drew their attention. Lincoln hit the unlock button on his door, allowing Bess to join them.

"Hey, boy." She ruffled Aengus' head.

"Glad you made it."

"Wouldn't miss this. Did Julia text yet?"

As though in response to the question, Lincoln's text notification sounded. He read, "Yep. Any minute now."

They didn't have to wait long before they saw Julia leave the front door of Dunsinane House with Adrienne Wilder. The two women got into Wilder's silver Lexus ES. Leaving Victoria along the highway, Lincoln kept back a safe distance so as not to alert Wilder that she was being followed.

Wilder turned off the highway and they entered the Cordova Bay suburb. Without the safety of other vehicles between them, Lincoln dropped back a little. He tried to keep the distance of a city block between them. It would allow him to be inconspicuous, but also maintain visual contact for any direction changes Wilder would make. It was working, until a four-way stop took Lincoln's attention, waiting for his turn to proceed. When it came, a pedestrian stepped into the crosswalk in front of his vehicle. He drummed his thumb on the steering wheel, "Come on!"

"Two blocks up, she turned right," Bess pointed.

Once through the intersection, Lincoln abandoned caution and applied pressure to the gas pedal. He turned right, hugging the curb. His tires gave a squeal as he accelerated through the turn.

There was no sign of Wilder's car.

Lincoln slowed down when they came to the first cross street. Nothing in either direction.

He sped up to the next corner.

"There!" Bess shouted. Lincoln didn't turn onto the street, but pulled to the curb. The back end of Wilder's car was pulling into a garage three houses in from the corner on the left. The two of them watched as the garage door dropped.

"What now?"

"We follow the plan. We wait." Lincoln turned off the engine.

"Why is there no furniture?" Julia asked as Adrienne led her into a large living room.

Hayden Sawyer turned from looking out the floor-to-ceiling windows overlooking Cordova Bay. "Because there is no need for furniture, Mrs. Bowen. Or may I call you Julia, or do you prefer June or Simmie?"

Sawyer smiled in a charming manner, but the coldness and cruelty coming from her eyes froze the blood in Julia's veins. Instinct won over planning and she turned to run. Two men appeared behind her and blocked her escape. She recognized them from the pictures she'd taken of the men with Charlie on his boat. They were more than likely the ones who had murdered Charlie — and Hal.

With no other alternative, Julia turned to face the person ultimately responsible for everything bad in her life, starting with Hal's murder. She remembered she was not alone. Lincoln was close by. But God was with her in this room. She could feel it. Peace came over her. This was the plan all along. To expose those responsible for the death of Hal and Charlie. It was finally happening. She stayed silent, hoping Sawyer would incriminate herself. Julia prayed the small recorder sewn into the lining of her jacket would pick up everything.

"I was wondering what had happened to you. Where have you been hiding?" Julia still didn't speak.

"It was very considerate of you to come to us. When I saw your photo from the shelter, I couldn't believe my luck." Sawyer walked up to her, but Julia stood her ground and stared her in the eye defiantly. "Despite your bruised and swollen cheek, I'd recognize you anywhere. Your husband was a lucky man, too bad he was a naïve fool."

She patted Julia's bruised cheek rather sharply, causing her to wince. "He started asking too many questions."

"That's why you had him killed?"

"What exactly did your husband tell you?"

"Nothing."

"I don't believe you. My two friends here might loosen your tongue. They were rather disappointed you escaped them in the woods that night." Julia stiffened, but didn't say anything further.

"Well, whatever he did or didn't tell you, it doesn't matter now. I have a private buyer who's looking for just your type?"

"And what type is that?"

"Pretty, dark hair, your body type. Naïve. Someone he can beat and train to be a house and sex slave."

Julia's skin crawled. "You're a successful lawyer. Why would you do this? You could have gotten out."

"I was young. The man who I believed was my boyfriend turned into my pimp. When I tried to leave, he beat me nearly to death. I learned then that I couldn't escape, so I got smart. I earned his trust and became his partner."

"He let you?"

"I learned how to manipulate him like he manipulated me. There was no letting me, I just did it. Then I took his place and worked my way up. I worked hard and got an education, all the while managing the men below me."

"So, you went from a nobody on the street to Hayden Sawyer, defence counsel then onto low life?"

"That's right. So, Hal told you something after all. But it doesn't matter now. I've wasted too much time on you. I'm done. These gentlemen will be your escort to your new destination. They'll take you to the mainland on the ferry and we'll get you over the border tonight. Julia Bowen will stay lost and forgotten."

The two men grabbed Julia from behind.

"Wait! If anything happens to me, the information Hal gathered will be sent to the authorities."

The two men stopped dragging her and Sawyer approached.

"What exactly do you mean? What information and who will send it to who?" Sawyer leaned closer. "I think you're bluffing."

"Try me," Julia challenged.

"If you had something you would have gone to the authorities long before now."
Sawyer nodded to the two men. While they gagged and bound her, Julia kept
eye contact with Sawyer. She saw a satisfied gleam in her eye. Julia struggled, but
the two men were too much for her.

"Get her loaded into the van. I don't want you to miss the ferry. You have a
connection to make in Tsawwassen."

In the back of the van, Julia's hands were tied behind her, and her feet were
also bound. Movement was nearly impossible. She prayed Lincoln had figured
out what happened. They were taking her off the island; if they succeeded that
would be it for her.

The stretch in her muscles from the restrained position caused Julia to moan
through her gag. The two men in the front chuckled between themselves.

"Such a pretty moaner. Too bad we can't keep you in one of our houses here."
The driver adjusted the rear-view mirror to look at her.

Julia stayed still and quiet. Even if she could move more, making noise in the
van would be nearly impossible. There were mattresses padding the walls and
floor, so banging wouldn't help her get attention. After a few turns, she knew they
were on the highway to the ferry. It wouldn't be long now.

If she wasn't rescued before they got on, she would have to figure out some
means of escape from the ferry. Passengers aren't allowed to remain in their vehicles during the passage, so Julia knew they would have to leave her alone in the
van. They wouldn't risk taking her above deck. She had to think.

❖

Bess was looking down at her phone when Lincoln touched her arm to get her
attention. He watched as Wilder's car backed out of the garage and turned in their
direction. Lincoln and Bess slid down in their seats to avoid being seen. As the car
pulled around them, Lincoln stole a glance through his side window.

"Wilder is in the passenger seat and Hayden Sawyer is driving. Nobody in
the back seat."

"That means Julia is in the house."

"The garage door is still open. I'm going in."

Lincoln barely got his door open when Bess grabbed his shirt. "Wait." He closed the door and looked back at the garage to see a black-panel van back out.

"I bet they have Julia," said Bess.

"I agree." Lincoln started the engine and directed, "Hold up your phone for me to look at when they pass us, and see who's driving. It'll look like you're showing me directions."

Bess held up the phone and glanced behind them as the van passed. "Two men, no sign of Julia." She kept her eyes on the van while Lincoln put the vehicle in gear and turned around.

"Since Sawyer was here, I'm betting they know it's Julia. She was waiting with those two men."

Lincoln stepped on the gas, chasing after the van — and Julia.

When they turned on to the highway they were heading away from the city. He moved into the passing lane to keep the kidnappers in view, always making sure there were a few cars between him and them.

"Lots of traffic. I doubt we'll be spotted."

"Yes. Ferry traffic, I suppose." Lincoln switched lanes to pass a slower moving vehicle.

Bess looked at Lincoln. "What if they are going to the ferry? If they are taking her off the island, we may lose her completely."

"Let's see."

Minutes later, they passed the turn-off to Sidney. "Looks like they are trying to make the ferry. Time to make the call." Lincoln looked at the clock on the dash. "We have 15 minutes before the incoming ferry arrives. Then it'll be another 10 or so before they start loading. It should be enough time for the RCMP to arrive."

Lincoln hoped so, as he listened to Bess talking with the dispatcher, trying to convince them there was a kidnapping in progress. "Yes, you can call me back at this number."

"OK. Now we just watch and wait."

Lincoln approached the payment booth behind the black van. When he pulled up, he handed over his credit card. "I'm with that van ahead. Can you put me in the same row please?"

"Row 32 it is. Have a nice voyage."

CHAPTER 46

TWO VEHICLES FROM OTHER PAY BOOTHS got between them and the black van. The van's driver got out and walked over to the building where the washrooms were. Bess could see the passenger in the side-view mirror. "What should we do?"

"Wait. But that doesn't mean we have to wait in the vehicle. Let's get out and stretch our legs. Hey fella, how about you? Wanna get out?"

Aengus licked Lincoln's cheek.

"I thought so. I'll take him over to that patch of grass between the washrooms and the coffee kiosk."

"I'll keep an eye on the van. Hopefully the RCMP will arrive soon."

Lincoln clipped the lead on Aengus and walked away. Bess watched man and beast cross the empty wait lanes, then refocused on the washrooms. A few minutes later, the man exited, and walked over to the café in the ferry terminal.

Bess' phone rang.

"Hello? Yes, row 32 near the building with the washrooms by the dog area. A black van in front of a red Prius and a green Chevy pickup. I'm parked behind the Chevy in a blue SUV. I'm standing next to it," she said, sliding out of the vehicle and looking for the police.

The RCMP cruiser pulled over to the curb of the empty outer lane behind the dog area.

Two constables got out and walked towards Bess when she waved at them. Bess signalled to Lincoln and he jogged back with Aengus.

"I'm Bess Delaney, this is my friend Lincoln Warren. We're the ones who called you."

Lincoln approached and Aengus sniffed at the constables.

"He's harmless."

The constables eyed him unbelievingly.

"We think a friend of ours is in the back of that van. She was kidnapped from a house in Cordova Bay."

"How do you know this?"

"I've been investigating a piece for the paper, and a friend volunteered to go undercover for me. Lincoln and I were waiting outside a house she had been taken to with someone I believe to be part of a human trafficking ring. The person she went there with left without her. A van driven by two men a short while later left the house. That van to be exact."

"OK, we'll check it out."

"One of the men is over in the terminal building. The passenger is still in the vehicle."

The constables turned to look towards the terminal. "We'll deal with the van first. Then look for the other man. Wait here."

They split up and went to either side of the van, their hands on their holsters, but did not draw their weapons.

Everything went in slow motion after that. The man tried to run, but barely got out of the vehicle before one constable tackled him to the pavement.

The other went around to the rear and opened the van doors. They could see Julia lying on a mattress, her hands tied behind her back and her feet bound.

As soon as the van doors opened and they could see Julia, Aengus howled and pulled on the lead. There was no stopping the 170lb beast, so Lincoln let go of the leash. The officer managed to only get the gag off Julia before being pushed out of the way by Aengus.

"It's OK, boy. Down! Please Aengus, down!" Julia could do nothing to help the constable, as she was still tied up.

Lincoln and Bess followed the howling dog.

Lincoln managed to pull Aengus back, enabling the constable to free Julia. She climbed out of the van rubbing her wrists and Lincoln released his hold. Julia was enjoying Aengus' affection when the officer brought the driver around, his hands secured behind his back. Bess put her arms around Julia and pulled her to the side, while Lincoln got control of Aengus.

The constables closed the van's rear doors and pushed their prisoner against it.

"This is Bravo 72 calling for assistance. We have apprehended a kidnapper and there is still one suspect at large . . . Roger that."

"You stay with the victim while I put him in the cruiser." The constable, none too gently, yanked on the arm of his arrestee and shoved him towards their car. "You're safe now," said the other constable. "Can you give me a description of the other kidnapper?" He watched Julia as she put her arm around the giant hound. Julia was about to speak when Bess pointed. "There he is. The guy in the brown leather jacket carrying two cups of coffee."

The constable stepped from behind the van. When the man saw the RCMP uniform, he dropped the coffees and ran.

Julia stepped between the cars into the empty lane, Aengus following. "Go, Aengus, get that man."

The sight hound's instincts ignited, and his body went rigid. He lowered his neck and head, crouching his limbs slightly then exploded into action. Julia followed, trying to keep up. Behind her came the constable, then Lincoln and Bess.

The man turned to look over his shoulder and abject fear came over his face at the vision of the wolfhound closing in.

Thinking he could lose the dog by running between the cars, the man ducked into the lines of vehicles. But he didn't make it. Aengus bore down on him and knocked him over. The man tumbled onto the pavement and Aengus swung around and stood over him, his front legs on the man's torso.

The man put his hands over his head to protect himself.

The constable ran up beside Julia, as she pulled Aengus off him.

"Don't move."

"I won't! Keep that demon away from me!" The constable cuffed the man and pulled him to his feet just as the back-up cruiser arrived. They put him in the back.

Once the two kidnappers were secure, the constables focused on Julia.

"Ma'am, how are you?"

"Physically, I'm fine."

"I'm Constable Winks. Can I get your name?"

"Hallie Charles." Julia reverted to the name she first adopted with Charlie. She became aware of the commotion the arrival of the police and the arrests had caused in the ferry lineup.

"Do you need medical attention?"

"What? No. But I am feeling overwhelmed."

"That's understandable. We do have a number of questions and will need to take a statement."

"Here? Now?"

"We would like to get your statement while it is still fresh for you. So yes, now."

"Can I follow you to where you need me to go? Have my friends drive me?" He looked at the other constable, who nodded. "OK. I'm going to give you my card. You can follow us to the RCMP detachment. When you get there, ask for me. We'll be taking these two in to process them so you might have to wait for a bit."

"OK. Thanks. I'll see you shortly."

Julia turned to look at Lincoln and Bess. The tears started to fall as Bess put her arms around her.

"You're OK. We got you."

Julia couldn't speak for a few moments, just hugged Bess back. When she stepped away, Lincoln took her place, drawing Julia into a bear hug.

"I must admit, I was terrified the whole time," he whispered in her ear.

"Me too," she whispered back.

"Now, let's get you out of here." Lincoln released her as Aengus barked his agreement.

Julia sat up front and turned sideways in her seat so she could look at both Bess and Lincoln.

Lincoln started the car and made his way to the service vehicle exit ramp. When they were away from the ferry terminal, he pulled into the parking lot of a local marina.

Julia started to speak.

"I want to thank you both for having my back. I had no idea when I fled into the woods the night Hal was murdered that this is where that trail would lead."

Lincoln reached out and squeezed her arm.

"I'm glad for you both. I couldn't have exposed the trafficking ring alone," Bess added.

"It's in your hands now, Bess. When will it appear in the paper?" Julia asked.

"The first article in the series is going to print tomorrow. How many actual articles in the series will be determined by what unfolds from here on out."

"Good."

"So, are you ready to face the world as Julia Bowen?"

"Yes. I pray now that law enforcement can make the evidence I'm about to throw in their laps into a winnable criminal case. I don't like the track record in Canada for human trafficking convictions that I've been reading about. I can't wait to see the looks on their faces when I tell them that the men they have in custody are responsible for Charlie's murder and possibly Hal's."

"Are you worried about being arrested?" Lincoln asked.

"No. I actually expect it. We just need to find me a good lawyer."

"Anything you want to do before we go to the RCMP detachment?"

"Food. I have no idea what's going to happen when I turn myself in and don't want to be unfocused by hunger. Drive-through is fine. I don't think we have time for a restaurant."

Lincoln turned on the ignition and drove out of the marina towards Sidney.

Julia sat alone in the interview room at the RCMP detachment. Lincoln and Bess were waiting outside.

She looked up at Constable Winks when he opened the door. "Thank you for waiting."

"That's OK. Have the men said anything?" Julia was wondering if they might have outed her identity.

"Nope. Not a word except to ask for their lawyer. Now, let's get your statement down. Can you start from the beginning?"

"It all began the night of August 24th, 2013, when my husband was murdered in our home. His name was Harold Bowen. My name is Julia Bowen. I believe you've been looking for me."

Acknowledgments

SO MANY PEOPLE played a role in seeing this book go from a rough first draft to the published work you now hold. Julia Bowen first appeared to me in a dream, as a terrified woman fleeing into the woods. Several years later, she is alive and well thanks to so many.

My friend Sandy Smith, from the rough first draft and every draft thereafter you have read every word repeatedly. You have listened and brainstormed with me throughout this books journey. Your friendship is an immeasurable gift. No amount of thanks is enough.

To the folks on boats who welcomed me aboard. Hannah and Tony you answered all my questions, showed me every inch of your boat and let me spend a weekend alone aboard. I am grateful for your generosity. To John, Tracy and Sugar, your appearance in this story as Jack and Teresa is a small measure of my appreciation for your hospitality and openness to share your life aboard. I mourned the loss of Sugar, but she lives on in this story. To Ralph, your boat ended up being the inspiration for Charlie's home on the water. Thank you for answering my questions and giving me the penny tour. And Lynn, thanks for baking me a pie for breakfast, and answering my questions. For a brief weekend you were all excellent neighbours.

Darcy Eggleston, Warrant Officer (Ret'd), you were so generous sharing your experiences as a Peacekeeper and your journey with post-traumatic stress, I am so grateful. You are an amazing man. Thank you for your service.

Louise Dickson, you are an amazing journalist who writes from the heart, even when that heart has been broken by what you have witnessed during the course of your career. Your integrity is an example to all in your profession. You answered my questions, gave me a tour of where you work and encouraged me every step of the way.

To my editors, thank you. This book would not be fit for public consumption without any of you. Jennifer at Jennifer Kaddoura Editorial Services for your work and feed back in evaluating an early draft of the manuscript. To Chantel Hamilton and Kirstyn Smith with Afterwords Communications, you polished it and created a shiny penny from my thoughts.

To Bob McMillan for answering all my questions about Irish Wolfhounds and giving valuable insight into the wolfhound's bond with their human. Aengus became more of a character and hero as a result of your love for this breed. I hope I have done you and Irish Wolfhounds everywhere proud.

To my writing community and early readers; we are all on this journey together and I thank you for welcoming my presence among you. I want to especially thank my Sunday writing friends Deb McDonald, Dalyce Joslin, Hannah Horn and Elaine Harvey, your friendship and encouragement gives me sustenance for this journey.

Finally, to my Heavenly Father who daily makes me believe I am a precious child in his sight. To Jesus, my redeemer and the lover of my soul, I don't want to think where I would be without you. And Holy Spirit, thank you for your inspiration, guidance, and for showing up every step of the way. I know I am not alone.

~ *K.L. Ditmars*

ABOUT THE AUTHOR

One of K. L. (Kelly) Ditmars' fondest memories as a child involves reading. During winter storms, when the power would go out, she and her Mum would bake a cake. While it was in the oven, they would curl up on the couch under blankets and read books. Having lived in various regions of Canada and the world, she now lives and writes in Victoria, BC, Canada. She still bakes and curls up on the couch under a blanket with a book, no matter the weather.

Sign up for Kelly's newsletter:

Keep up to date on book releases, events, and contests by signing up to her email list at *klditmarswriter.com/contest*

Kelly loves to connect with readers.

Web	www.klditmarswriter.com
Instagram	@klditmarswriter
Facebook	KLDitmarsWriter
Twitter	@KLDitmarsWriter

Made in the USA
Las Vegas, NV
20 July 2021